YELLOW GLAD DAYS

Sam Bellotto Jr.

YELLOW GLAD DAYS

DOUBLE DRAGON

Dedication

For Xanax and Paxil

Chapter 1

DEAD? Alive! He hadn't been dead more than a little while when he realized that he was not dead after all. He wasn't sleeping, either.

He'd misplaced his name but he could still do simple sums in his head, so he couldn't be dead ... two plus two is four, one hundred eighteen plus eighty-two is two hundred ... and it was nearly like an electrical light being switched on. Why had it been off in the first place? He couldn't comprehend. Focusing his mind was difficult. Nonetheless, he tried philosophy. He quickly put an end to philosophy.

Well .... If he wasn't dead, why couldn't he wake up? Or feel anything? Or scream? He tried to scream; it didn't work. If he was dead, why was he thinking? The popular notion of an afterlife seemed a suitable conclusion at the moment, yet he could recall all sorts of odd images that didn't jibe with "judgment day": a piping hot apple pie he'd relish if he could figure out where his mouth was; baroque music; the scented body of Lowia, his off-and-on girlfriend the past two years he'd relish if he could figure out where his ....

And he determined that an afterlife of this kind of disoriented cerebration could be mighty boring. A hell. Hot as hell? No, he dismissed the inferno scenario immediately, having given up the Catholic faith of his childhood sometime during his sophomore year at the University. A man's entitled to his own beliefs. Besides, from what he remembered of those religious indoctrinations, he knew he hadn't lived the kind of a life to deserve damnation. A little healthy punishment, perhaps.... This didn't make sense! Heaven, hell, or the celestial green room before you step out on stage to meet thy heavenly host, you simply don't hang around in space after death trying to visualize classic Hord Fawks westerns. He wasn't dead. He wasn't in New Jersey, either.

What was called for was some hard corporeal tangibility, he decided. A toe wiggling, the blink of an eyelid, the glimmer of an erection, a bubble of indigestion .... He calmed himself as best he could. He emptied his head. He concentrated. Like beaming the ray of a flashlight down the stairs into a darkened cellar, he aimed a mental probe around for signs of spatial dimension. He sang to himself as he explored. He whistled inwardly as he worked. Anybody at home?

He imagined himself the way he remembered he looked. That was the first step. If he willed his physical being strongly enough where he ought to be, maybe, like congruent shapes, the whole would come together and shake off this curious vacuum he occupied. It was a theory, anyway.

Last seen, he was wearing non-designer jeans (faded blue), dirty white sneakers and a brown windbreaker over a plaid shirt. Although he was several inches shorter than six feet, his lanky frame made him seem taller than he was, so many of his friends often remarked. A bit of a nonconformist, too, he deliberately kept himself unkempt and, sometimes, sported gigantic wire-framed eyeglasses (reading only) for effect: his costume was overt advertising of the group, the political and social stratus within which he functioned.

A fact. He and his colleagues weren't exactly revolutionaries. (Truth be told, they worked for a living.) No, they were not like the beatniks or hippies or dugongs of former times - though they often wished they could be. Unless they did something of an extremely violent or reprehensible nature, the Government simply left them alone. This is because there were so few of them left. And their ranks dwindled down to a precious few, year after year.

However, there were the times. Oh, there were the good times .... He remembered.

***

He remembered being sprawled across an orange sofa in a study hall at the University, working on a paper airplane. By the window, chubby Harry was arguing with George. Harry always argued, never talked. Harry was railing on that gravity and magnetism were one and the same, that the great physicists were all missing the obvious link that tied those forces together. He wondered if Harry's store of ideas could offer a solution to how he could get his paper airplane to soar twenty meters down the hall, then make a sharp right turn into Professor Jacob's office. Although he was a journalism major, he'd always had a lifelong fascination with the sciences.

"You guys going to turn on the television set?" a singsong voice queried. A large jet-black head, nearly bald, with the most angelic ear-to-ear grin

9

you ever saw in your life, eclipsed the ceiling in front of him.

"Hey, Chekah, you bastard!" he acknowledged, offering the African foreign exchange student an outspread hand.

Chekah slipped him five before proceeding to click on the tube. Chekah returned to the orange sofa and gave him a kick on the shin. "Hey, will you let a fellow sit down?"

"Come on, Chekah," he protested, "I'm in the middle of an important project here."

"You aren't. You are fooling around again."

"So you say." He cocked up his legs to give the African barely enough room to squeeze in between his sneakers and the arm of the sofa.

"That ridiculous airplane of yours will never fly," Chekah said.

He took the declaration as an affront to his paper folding skills. He sat up, aimed the craft, gave it a couple of test jabs into the air, then let it sail. The airplane arced swiftly toward the ceiling, stalled, then looped lazily downward, curving past Erik Owens and Dora as the couple entered the room, and crashed unglamourously against the wall.

Chekah laughed loudly.

He remained undaunted. "It worked, didn't it?" he replied. "The only trouble was that it turned left instead of right."

Owens and Dora had always been going together. Owens, blonde, from somewhere in the Southwest, bent down to retrieve the fallen aircraft. Owens crumpled it up and tossed the paper wad back at him. "Litterbug!" Owens accused, then pointed to the television. "You got on the election returns?"

"Certainly we do," Chekah responded. "Some of us are interested in what is going on in the world."

He grimaced at his friend's indication of what he always concluded to be pointless social consciousness. "Don't be so naive, Chekah," he said. "We all know the Moralists are going to thunder into office on horseback. Caffaro has no more chance of winning the White House than you do. The only question is whether or not this is finally the end of intellectualism and free-thinking once and for all."

"You dramatize too much, like you always do," Chekah countered.

"Yeah? Noticed this year's crop of freshmen, have you? The University is worried about budget cuts is it? Well, all these bright, well-scrubbed youngsters will solve that problem. Eliminate the whole damn liberal arts department; the school sure doesn't need it anymore!"

"Quiet," Owens demanded, gesturing. "There's an announcement on."

The dreadfully serious face of a middle-aged news announcer filled up every raster of the 19-inch color television screen. The man seemed to be choking on the words "... biggest landslide in the nation's history. We repeat, the Reverend Angus Yaramon and the Moralist Party appear to be on their way to a near unanimous victory in what has got to be the most decisive and pronounced mandate ever given by the people. With barely 20 percent of the popular vote counted, less than 23,000,000, the

Moralist Party seems to have captured all but 193 ballots. We have also been informed that, on this basis, and as the result of network computer predictions, Dominic Caffaro has conceded the election to Yaramon in a private telephone conversation. This has now been confirmed. Only minutes ago, in a telephone conversation with Yaramon, Dominic Caffaro has conceded the election .... "

Harry actually stopped arguing and stared at the television screen in hypnotic disbelief. Everyone's attention was transfixed upon the tube, and a chill suffused the room like a dozen refrigerator doors left wide open.

"President Yaramon ... " someone uttered as though the words had a bad taste.

"Who is this Yaramon fellow, anyway?" Chekah asked.

"Angus Barlow Yaramon," he pronounced the full name and continued as if reciting from a biographical sketch, "was originally ordained as an Episcopalian minister. But Yaramon departed from the church to found his own particularly fundamentalist ministry and television station about 20 years ago. Rumor has it he wove together such a web of partnerships and sub-corporations to get his 'holy roaming empire' off the ground that a spider couldn't figure it out. His little TV station burgeoned like a fat momma, which is sort of how people flocked to the bosom of his gospel. He became a network. He made powerful allies. His ratings soared. Soon advertisers were knocking themselves silly to buy commercial time on his station; Yaramon himself was going video eyeball

12

to video eyeball with the Pope of Rome for spiritual dominance in this country. You likely heard about the World Ecumenical Forums - 'mass debates' the sophomores called them-a few years back? How Yaramon got the Pontiff to verbally joust with him during prime time is beyond my understanding. Even the Pope is human, I guess. Yaramon gave the people what they wanted: that 'old time religion,' special effects, more than a dose of patriotism, and a convincing argument that they were the 'chosen ones' - things other faiths had been claiming for centuries - all in a single package. There aren't any complexities under Yaramon's conservative umbrella; everything is either simple or sinful. Needless to say, the man walked away from that tete-à-tete with His Holiness clutching all the marbles and a fucking crown. The rest you must know, or suspect. A person with so much influence over the masses can't be ignored by government. Although, whether Yaramon was jerking off the White House or the White House was jerking off him is impossible to say. The results are the same: lobbyist to advisor and, finally, to this." He saluted the blaring television.

"Better get your plane ticket back to the jungle," he advised his friend.

"This is the jungle now, I think," Chekah countered.

Something had to break the assault of the TV voice unremittingly driving home the fact that the Moralist Party had, was given, gladly, an unshakeable grip on the reins of the country. It was Harry. It would be Harry. Of all his school chums and former cronies, Harry would be the one to react from the gut.

He remembered, vividly, the scholarly youth dashing to the window, pushing it open, leaning out to the point where it seemed the fool might be about to jump, and bellowing in mock celebration, "Yaramon's the one! Yaramon's the one!"

Very typical of Harry to do something like that in those days, he mulled. He wondered what might have happened to Harry. Chekah, good old Chekah, he learned years later had been killed in the Banana Riots. Chekah was dead. Really dead. And George ... George was committed to an institution for the criminally insane. Harry, like himself, probably vanished into society. Into memory.

Those were the ebullient times, he remembered .... and sighed.

***

He sighed: an upheaval like a wave. He was uncertain if he had merely imagined an appropriate reaction to a fond recollection, or if he had finally broken through to some sort of reality. He concluded two possibilities: either he had moved or he was reincarnated as a lake. Except, there was a definite gentle rocking, and it wasn't in his mind. It was a threshold awareness of being carried. Yes. He rationalized this new sensation as, it seemed, floating to an upper plane. Upper was correct, too, because he determined he was coming out of a deeper place into a place that was ... for now ... less deep. There was a familiar sensation about this new place. He fleetingly thought a comparison of the

14

experience with the myth of Charon rafting the departed souls across the Styx seemed eerily appropriate. Were this the case indeed, it would make a fine irony flung in the face of modern religion. But he was not departed.

A chink in the wall had been broken loose. Proof. Something to grab onto, if he could grab. He must make the attempt right now. He concentrated all thought within himself and reached out an arm that was not there, stretching as hard as he could imagine, forcing the creation of an extremity that was denied to what little consciousness he possessed, yet had to exist if he did. Grab. Struggle. Push. Reach for the sky. Tote that barge, lift that bale. It was exceedingly difficult for him to keep his mind tuned wholly to the one simple task. Flashes of diverting memories sailed by. Like speeding down a highway festooned with neon signs and billboards. He fought back, envisioning a finger at a time, four fingers, one thumb, linked, skin stretching taut, the open palm, reaching, left -

Ouch!

Pain? No, that was feeling. That. Was. Feeling. He had done it! He had a hand. His left hand had returned to him and, with that, the walls came tumbling down. No sooner had he obtained evidence of a living body part than all and everything else popped into place. The arm bone connected to the shoulder bone. The shoulder bone connected to the neck bone. The neck bone connected to the head bone. It was, in a curious manner, like he was being born again. Although this had to be impossible because, he emphatically reminded himself, he wasn't dead in the first place.

He realized where he was. Now he was asleep. He had been beyond sleeping before. Now he was simply asleep and the rest of the trip would be an easy climb out to awakening. He had long ago learned how to awaken himself from nightmares. Was this one now? If it was ... all he had to do ... was ....

... open his eyes ....

Chapter 2

DELIBERATELY, he returned. His vision cleared. With each blink, a layer of time stripped away, like old paint. It revealed that he was a newspaperman, a reporter, about 33 years old. He was on his back. He feared. He loved. He hated. He shivered. He was alive. He had a name.

Astin W. Wench stared directly into a bright photographic flood lamp that had been rather badly jury-rigged to what he could see of a dingy, latticed ceiling. The light hurt. He turned away from it. He noticed, against a cinder block wall, a steel cart containing an assortment of medical paraphernalia and some empty soda bottles, knives and tin plates. He guessed he was on a table. His left arm was tightly wrapped in a cloth bandage. He felt numerous pains throughout his body - none of them very serious - and a throbbing headache. His surprise was more discomforting than any of his physical ills. He tried to say something but his vocal chords wouldn't cooperate. Out of the right side of his peripheral vision, he noticed a large human figure coming towards him. He saw that this person was wearing a stethoscope and a full-size barbecue apron like the kind suburban homeowners wear to backyard cookouts. The apron read, in capital red letters: CHEF COCK AND BULL.

Wench smiled, tried to. Apparently he was in some kind of a field hospital. It wasn't a Government hospital, leading Wench to a specific conclusion. The doctor, who was at this moment

17

taking Wench's pulse, if the person was a doctor, had rescued Wench from some calamity. So it appeared. An accident, illness, perhaps a violent attack by person or persons unknown? Wench was unable to remember. He couldn't be sure. Actually, he couldn't even be certain that this doctor was, in fact, rescuing him. But for the moment Wench was quite satisfactorily alive and that was very reassuring.

The presumed doctor approached closer, adjusted the overhead lamp and pushed back Wench's eyelids with a hammy thumb to inspect the patient's pupillary response. The hands were large and firm. The doctor's face floated within a couple nose lengths of Wench and he could see wide, intelligent eyes, a high and shiny dark-skinned forehead. Short, curled gray hair clung to the man's head like algae to a rock. A close-cropped beard of silver laced with black streaks dressed the long chin.

Wench finally got his voice box to function.

"Doctor?" he inquired groggily.

"Yes?"

"I mean you're a doctor. A physician?" Wench asked.

The other man didn't flinch, replied, "have been all my working life, a doctor. A virologist, specifically. I hold a doctorate in biochemistry. But I've a medical diploma, too, though I'm not *licensed*." He stressed licensed, then added with a sarcastic, twisty smile that was brighter than the light above, "hope you aren't alarmed. We didn't get the wrong man, did we?"

"Wrong man?"

"Forgive me. I imagine this entire situation would be a bit ... unusual, shall we say ... to wake up to after nearly nine years?"

Wench held on while a rush of panic poured through him. The doctor said nine years. Did he?

"What?

"Nine."

"Nine?"

"Give or take a month ...."

Wench swallowed. "A coma?" he asked nervously. Nine years long?

The doctor, meanwhile, was palpitating Wench's legs. "Coma? No. Of course not." The doctor gestured, went on. "Excuse my boorishness. We haven't done too many of you people and I'm still not used to it. We encounter a great deal of disorientation from you folks when we bring you around. I must admit, though, you seem to have picked up right where you left off!"

Wench blinked away more fuzz as his memory slowly continued to reconstruct itself. "Left off?"

"Try to recall the very last thing that happened to you," the doctor suggested.

Wench grappled with images. It was almost the same as trying to catch fish with bare hands. A very large room. The fear. Accusing faces. Anger. Everything brown, like in monochrome. That was it. A trial. "The trial," he said.

"Yes. You were tried and convicted. Anything else?"

"They dragged me away." Wench sucked in air violently.

"Omigod! They were going to kill me."

"What?"

19

"Kill me. Execution. Now I have it. The sentence was death."

The doctor seemed momentarily upset. "Well, you certainly weren't dead when we got you. Are you positive they - "

"But that was only a few days - " Wench halted abruptly as his mind made additional connections, splicing back together the threads of memory which had been severed. " - ago." Yes, he recollected the trial: a kangaroo court that summarily found him guilty as if they were following a prepared text. The highly unorthodox sentence of death. Dragging him away to a cramped, insufferably hot cubicle where he was going to .... And now here. Somewhere else. In a decidedly non-Government medical facility cum mess hall cum whatever. With a doctor. A civilian doctor. That was the strangest thing.

"Are you getting the picture?" the doctor asked.

"I think so."

Wench, laboriously, sat up. It was a chore, but he was becoming irritated and bored with having to converse on his back. The doctor helped him. After his blood pressure equalized and Wench ceased swaying, he saw that the room, this makeshift clinic, was all that there was. They were inside a one-room enclosure, windows on both sides, a partly open door leading to the outside world. Outside world was correct in more than one sense. Wench now guessed where he was. Where he had to be.

"Alabama?" Wench forwarded.

"With a banjo on my knee," commented the doctor in humorous agreement. "Welcome!"

Further understanding suffused his brain like water into a sponge. Wench asked for a mirror. Nine years was a hell of a long time. All the embarrassing situations he could have gotten himself into, Wench did not want to dwell upon. Once, in college, at a party, drunk, he boisterously gushed and fawned over a girl he secretly desired. That resulted in limitless day-after apologies. Funny he should think of it now. But, nine years? Let him at least see what he looked like.

The doctor handed Wench a hefty piece of mirror glass, cautioning, "watch the top edge. It's mighty sharp."

"So they didn't execute me after all," Wench observed.

"I can't understand why they didn't tell you." The doctor wrinkled his face and scratched his beard.

The waker angled the mirror glass from one position to another, turning it up, down, side to side, almost vainly gazing at his left profile, right profile, chin, neck, farther down. Wench still had all his hair; however, it was quite gray, even white in places. No longer the raven, tousled youth he thought himself to be. Youth? His leathery face now bore the scars and crevices of age, with deep lines emanating from the corners of his eyes and mouth. He still had his moustache, though it was overgrown, resembling an untended hedge. His facial hair, not a beard, was only a few days from his last shave. His lanky, supple frame had filled out. He hadn't grown fat, but a substantial potbelly nestled in his lap. Partly out of dark humor, partly in all seriousness, Wench grabbed at his groin and remarked, "well I still have my balls."

The doctor laughed.

Wench's reflected image was wearing a fairly conservative evening suit, navy blue slacks and jacket, wrinkled, but of top quality fabric and tailoring, along with a white shirt and polished dress shoes: hardly the sort of outfit Wench himself would normally select. "Hey! Where did these duds come from?"

"You had them on. But we removed your tie." The doctor held up a length of gray fabric. "What can you expect after nine years?"

"I didn't expect to be breathing," Wench admitted matter-of-factly.

"You said that. That they didn't tell you," the doctor reiterated.

"Tell me what?"

"That they were putting you in Deep BLISS instead."

"BLISS?" The realization hit Wench like a ton of feathers. He laid the mirror down flat. "Shit!" You mean to tell me that all this time I've been BLISSed out?"

"Deep BLISS," the doctor corrected him, as if there were a difference. "It was a bitch pulling you out, too. Almost lost you."

"For nine years?"

"Which makes you about 42 years old now, by my reckoning. But they didn't tell you?"

Wench was miffed. "They said nothing! I was sweating bullets and pissing in my pants. I really thought they were going to fry my brains. Must have blacked out. That's it, that's all I remember."

"Wonder when they began pulling that crap?" the doctor muttered.

"I thought I was dead."

22

"Well, you're kicking now."

Wench eased himself off the table. He felt decidedly better. A little hungry, he noted, but his arms worked and his legs were steady. He performed a short, impromptu buck and wing that he learned how to do many years ago. He was no hoofer of which to speak. Nonetheless, all systems checked out fine.

"You approve of my doctoring?"

Wench looked up. The other man began housecleaning. "Four stars, doc," said Wench, "absolutely four stars ... what's your name, by the way?"

"Titus" - the doctor extended a hand - "Titus Archimedes. M.D. Ph.D. You can call me Archie if you want to. Everybody else does."

They shook on it, warmly.

Wench felt his old self doggedly reassembling, like a reversed slow motion film of a shattered porcelain putting itself aright. He knew that, rationally, almost a decade lopped from his life ought to have him ranting hysterically. The questions were there, pressing against his very soul. What had happened all that time? What about his friends? What about the woman he loved? Perhaps it was a side effect of - what did the doctor call it - coming out of Deep BLISS that acted like a tranquilizer. Maybe later the questions would balloon into unavoidable urgency. And later might be a better time to confront them. Right now he was awash in relief and wanted to give the doctor a grateful hug.

"Doctor, about this Deep - "

With a startling shot, the door flew aside like it was blasted from its hinges.

Two giants marched into the hospital.

"Doc?" Wench stiffened.

Two enormous men with muscles like coiled shock absorbers strode forward. They carried with them an aura of militarism and a heavy smell of machine oil. They were soldiers of a sort, or guards; that seemed evident enough. They were both black. Professionally expressionless. One of the guard/soldiers wore a football jersey with a large numeral 11 imprinted back and front, and had on brand new jeans. The second guard/soldier was all in hunting leather. They both wore ponderous boots with soles like armor plates. The guard/soldier in the football jersey had a spiked dog collar around his neck. Tasteful. The two guards held guns. They were not to be toyed with.

"Hey, doc?" Wench repeated. His tension was becoming pronounced and evident. He wondered if he had not gone from the frying pan into the fire.

The guard/soldier in leather saluted the doctor, raising a clenched fist, palm forward, thumb out, to the side of his head. The doctor returned the salute in similar fashion, remaining quite unperturbed throughout.

"Friends of yours?" Wench asked the doctor lamely.

"Don't get excited," the doctor replied, then, to one of the guard/soldiers, "you can take him now."

The leather giant approached Wench. At the same time, the other, Number 11, erected his gleaming, oily firearm as if about to shoot from the hip, aiming the muzzle directly at Wench's nose.

The ugly, sexual similarity did not escape Wench's eye.

"Put that away!" the doctor barked.

The gun-toting leviathan holstered his weapon.

Wench sighed.

"I want you to go with them," the doctor ordered Wench. "It's okay, really. You're not quite out of the woods, medically. I want you to get plenty of rest, and remain undisturbed. I'll call you in the morning. Meantime, these two gentlemen will keep a watch on you. They're good men. Trust them." The doctor hesitated, then added with a smile and a wink of an eye, "we're not exactly finished with you, yet."

"Doc, what - ?"

"In due time. In due time." The doctor motioned for the two guard/soldiers to remove his patient.

Arm in arm, Wench was carried, like a reluctant bridegroom, from the makeshift hospital. The land outside was flat, an uninterrupted carpet of overgrown bluegrass. The late autumn sun hung low on the horizon, making the occasional oak tree appear to be fashioned from bronze. It wasn't chilly; Alabama seldom got chilly. But, being autumn, it wasn't insufferably hot, either. Wench caught a glimpse, way in the distance, of a tumbledown antebellum mansion, a four-story, ivy-clothed, many-chimneyed Georgian structure around which separate servants' quarters huddled like chicks around a mother hen. He'd come out of a carriage house, he saw. It'd been converted into the doctor's make-do hospital.

The guard/soldiers threw Wench into a woodshed and chain locked the door. The shed interior was dim, earthy smelling, and empty save for a single cot, pillow and blanket that had been provided for Wench's comfort. A pitcher of water rested upon the ground, next to a plate of dry biscuits. All the comforts of home.

Wench sat on the cot and lit into the biscuits with gusto. He was hungry and, after all, the doctor had told him not to get excited. The incarceration was supposed to be for his own good. He needed rest. If anything, he'd have the opportunity to reconstruct the events that got him into this situation in the first place.

Chapter 3

TEN years earlier, ten years, two months and several days earlier, to be more precise, Astin W. Wench was approaching the end of his life as he remembered it.

Life was not bad, either. Wench, slightly past thirty, kept himself in acceptably good physical shape by running two or three kilometers each morning. His job as associate science editor of Bigapolis' major daily newspaper involved pressures and deadlines that drove many a co-worker to alcoholism, coronary disease and public education, but Wench adapted beautifully. The news gathering coterie called him a natural - the best. He liked what he was doing; he was good at it. This gave him an arsenal of clout, and a readership, both of which he used, often, to get his way; salary, flexible hours, picking and choosing his own stories, extended lunches.

He could have demanded the top editor's slot on the science desk, but that position was held by the colorful Mars Gumbo, a man after Wench's own heart and a man, in many respects, Wench's equal. Gumbo was about seven years older than Wench, seven years more adept at getting doors to open, knowing who to speak to and how to get them to speak. Wench and Gumbo were colleagues and had also developed a strong bond of friendship. They made a great team. Wench had no desire to split it up. The glue between them was too emotional, too concrete.

To Wench, it seemed he had always known Mars Gumbo; the man was charmingly chameleonic, could turn empathy on and off much in the manner of a small appliance. Gumbo was likeable, all right, and called an army of people friends. No one so much as Wench. However, Gumbo's own inimitable personality shone through whichever character he chose to display; it was at least this much of a consistency, his quirks, which gave Gumbo individuality. The man could have successfully gone into politics. He chose journalism; his career was not unenhanced by his social skills. Case in point: Wench had immediately taken to Gumbo with the very first words out of Gumbo's mouth, meeting him, both of them younger, Wench less experienced, years ago, in the very same science desk offices. Upon enthusiastically shaking hands, Gumbo inquired earnestly, "you any good, Chief?" Wench appreciated the direct approach.

Physically, Gumbo was big the way a bear is big. He walked with great authority, like Santa Claus. He presented a carriage that was beyond his years. You could always hear him coming, too, ever whistling to himself, handing out friendly words like alms. He also liked to wear work boots, which meant that you could always hear him coming even if he wasn't whistling or talking. And he savored red shirts. When he had to wear a tie, Gumbo usually selected a vivid yellow one. He was an extremely colorful man, if not stylish.

This was Gumbo. This was Wench's life, then. This was the comfortable milieu in which Astin W.

Wench lived and breathed and ate and slept and loved and hated. Comfortable? Contented? Well ....

The beginning of the end of Wench's comfortable life probably came on that slow news evening in early October. This was the evening when Vice President Thackery Eliphalet Cinder, Cinder of the straw-colored hair, silver spectacles, square jaw, and cool, cooing, calculating speech, Yaramon's hatchet man and primary spokesperson Cinder, was scheduled to deliver (like pizza) another "urgent message to the citizens of our great nation," so they announced.

They being the Reverend Angus Yaramon, Cinder, and secretary of state Toshido Kwazimoto: the triumvirate of the Moralist Party, the Trinity. To Wench's mind they were the three horsemen of an apocalyptic, bible-thumping, ultra-conservative firestorm that had swept the nation from sea to shining sea more than a decade ago. The fourth horseman fell off somewhere. No matter. The Moralists were overwhelmingly popular, which was the problem, if there was a problem. The Moralists, gave the people plain answers that could be neatly folded and tucked into one's pocket, as it were.

That was the problem.

The Moralists, with popular support, wasted no time in restructuring the Constitution. Any resemblance between the new, which began "Toward a Godfearing Society ... ", and the old, which began "We the People...", was purely coincidental. The first measure they took was to repeal Article Twenty-Two so they could stay in power as long as they liked. While at it, several other Articles were tossed out for good measure:

Seven and Fourteen, on the basis of being too boring; Fifteen, Twenty-Three, and Sixteen for being too silly, or merely inappropriate. Of course this was all accomplished democratically with national referendums. The final tally always came out 70 percent in favor, 16 percent opposed and 14 percent undecided.

The Moralists espoused that true freedom could only be won by banishment and punishment. They abolished the teaching of Darwin's theory of evolution, for example, and sorely frowned upon English literature in Public Schools. This went over very big with the Holy Capitalists who insisted the educational system was spending far too much time teaching trivial, useless curricula and not enough time preparing children for careers in finance. The Moralists banned boxing, but they did not ban football, baseball or female mud wrestling. It was also refreshing to learn that, under Moralism, people were either bad or good and all of the sociological rhetoric concerning environment and behavioral disorders was pure poppycock. Bad people got locked up.

But the Moralist Regime, curiously enough, opened debate. Freedom of speech thrived as it had never done before. In a largely nonsecular society, you see, divergent viewpoints can be more easily tolerated. Like a child whimpering in a stadium packed with rabidly vocal fans, the single voice is utterly lost. Thus, many anti-Government groups, even entire population centers such as Bigapolis or San Francisco, considered to be hotbeds of liberalism, sin and home cooking, were given free rein. One could still attend a porno flick, if one could find a porno flick.

Not to paint an entirely negative portrait, it must be said that the Moralists accomplished a number of truly remarkable deeds. They negotiated landmark trade agreements with other superpowers that put an end to the threat of atomic extinction. Of course, this didn't stop the Moralists from engaging in "Neo-Crusades," conventional skirmishes with all sorts of tiny republics in an effort to spread the Word of the Lord. As explained by President Yaramon himself: "Killing for the sake of killing is murder, but lives lost in the glorification of God inspire us all." The Zoomway, that series of controlled access highways crisscrossing the nation, permitting speeds up to 320 kph, was another Moralist success. Unemployment fell, too, largely due to significant numbers of patriotic women returning to bed and broom.

The Yaramon Administration also reduced the deficit to the point where economists could wink at each other with their hands in their pockets. The solution was so deceptively simple, it was a wonder nobody had thought of it earlier. Income taxes were eliminated. Any time the Government needed to raise money it engaged in fund-raisers taking the forms of rock concerts, lotteries and telethons. The Neo-Crusades became the most popular, and lucrative, causes celebres. Whenever the Government felt a need to maintain a "presence" in a foreign land, it would tap the Moralist constituencies' religious conscience by announcing it was going to export the Word of God once more. Contributions flooded in like a paper tidal wave.

Neo-Crusades provided so much income for the Treasury, in fact, that Legislative pay hikes became commonplace. Concomitantly, with no income tax fettering the people, consumerism thrived and a golden age of spending was launched.

About the same time Yaramon took his icy hold on the heart and mind of the country, the troposphere shifted. Nobody knew exactly why this occurred, but meteorologists theorized that it must have had something to do with past underground nuclear testing; Newton was correct even in this day and age. For the most part, however, the effects of the atmospheric twitch were minimal, but not wholly unnoticeable. Primarily, the jet stream snaked badly askew. This caused the climate in the Northeast to turn rather bland and dry. Storms of any kind became virtually non-existent (at least benign) and the temperature ranged from 10 to 27 degrees Celsius, year round, shifting erratically on a week-to-week basis. Traditional seasons vanished. The old, balmy South remained old and balmy, managing, however, to acquire a picturesque veneer of snow in the winter month, which was more than most of the country could achieve. Texas baked. A searing, persistent drought plagued much of the nation's underbelly, leaving sections of the Southwest uninhabitable. Idaho froze solid. California nearly drowned in the unending rains that waterlogged the West Coast. No real catastrophe, all in all.

This was the world that Wench remembered. This was what the world was like that day when Vice President Cinder delivered his pivotal speech, shocking hundreds, pleasing millions.

Cinder on television - how long now? It must have been close to a year and a half since Angus Yaramon stopped making his own pronouncements and turned the dirty task over to his right hand and sidekick, the sycophantic Thackery Cinder - a stalwart fellow from the heartland of this country with Pilgrims on his family tree. Baloney! Sure, rumors abounded that the reason for Cinder on TV was that he, Yaramon's protege, was being groomed to take over the Presidency, or that Yaramon was too ill, and so forth. But Wench knew that in this era of media hype, you'd want the most crowd-pleasing, soft-sell image that money could buy. Cinder was that all right.

Wench had been working late when Cinder's pivotal address was aired. He finished his coffee, crumpled the Styrofoam cup and tossed it into the already overflowing wastebasket. He got up from his desk, waved on the office TV monitor, and stood, arms folded, leaning, rump against the side of the desk, watching the wallscreen.

With little fanfare, the camera zoomed in on the Vice President's smiling visage. Cinder's powdered, rouged, delineated features took up the entire frame. Cinder was short; he had the physique of a high school wrestling champ. Those heavy tortoise-shell eyeglasses gave his tanned face and hawksbill nose an intensity that magnified the viewer's particular feelings toward him. If you liked him, you liked him more; if you disliked him, you absolutely despised him. His thick, blonde hair looked painted on, squeezed onto his head in acrylics, right from the tube. He had a youthfulness that belied his age (he was creeping in on 60), offering no signs of graying or wrinkling, except around the eyes where a few crow's-feet had landed. He spoke in a clear voice, never hiding his intentions. Give Cinder points for that - he never fooled anybody, nor did he ever attempt to.

He began: "Are you scared? Do you find life to be frightening? Crime is on the increase. Random acts of violence and terrorism are more prevalent today than they've ever been. Science has fabricated a wondrous superstructure of miracles that, despite their benefits to mankind, also offer deeply hidden dangers to our peace of mind, our children, our homes. Do you dread the future? Do you wonder, even, if there will be a future to endow to our sons and daughters?

"Do you worry? Truly we are living in a frenzied world ever complicated and confusing. For most of us, this has become the age of techno-shock, incomprehensible and incurable. We can bring, and enjoy, live British sitcoms, in color, in stereo, into our living rooms with the touch of a button. Most of us haven't the foggiest idea how this is possible. We go to the moon, but the scientific explanation is way above our heads. We are awash in an ocean of marvels and don't know how to swim.

"Are you angry? Life itself is running away from us and we have no hope of catching it. Further, we are out of breath. Even planning a single day is as challenging as climbing a mountain. We send our children off to school to prepare for tomorrow having about as much an idea about the kind of education they are receiving as a raindrop knows where it is going to fall.

"Do you yearn for yesterday? Yesterday will never return. There is, nonetheless, absolutely nothing wrong with wanting a slower pace, a less complicated path to trod, a greater control over the destiny of ourselves and our loved ones. What is, after all, so reprehensible about being happy? Self-satisfaction, comfort, peace of mind, security, enjoyment - these are inalienable rights, too! We don't elect governments to burden us with uncertainty, bewilderment and dread. Let those who would lay the onus of responsibility upon the shoulders of an unprepared public, while they pursue an ivory tower existence, go elsewhere with their elitist notions. We want, and deserve, our share of Arcadia now!

"Will you join us? This Administration has the solutions at hand. We do not seek to abridge personal freedoms, your own will to lead your own life. We merely want to remove the barricades that stand in your way. You can have your cake and eat it, too. With crime, terrorism and other forms of anarchic behavior under control; with science and technology structured and channeled by a central agency solely dedicated to the good of our citizens; with foolish anxieties banished like so many bad dreams: yes, living once again can be bucolic, a never-ending golden era combining the pleasures of a simpler age with the treasures of a truly futuristic society.

"How is this possible? Dedicated Government researchers (geniuses all of them) have discovered that deep within all of us are two personalities - a kind of genetic schizophrenia. Don't be alarmed. The twin souls, if you will, have been peacefully coexisting within mankind since the beginning of time. In fact, theology has taught us that it is nature's grand design for only one these souls to ultimately emerge dominant. We see this process occurring constantly. One soul - the primitive, the animal - reigned supreme throughout prehistory, when man was required to struggle tooth and nail for sustenance, reproduction and security. Only very infrequently did the true human destiny, that other soul, have a chance to manifest itself. This we see in the formation of the family, cave paintings, Biblical inventions which brought our race out of the mud. Across the millennia, this second self took greater prominence in human development. Maybe, after several more millennia, this second self will be all there is. We can't wait that long. We have invented the means by which this process can be accelerated.

"What exactly does this imply? It is our determination that peoples' unpleasant aspects such as hatred, depression, confusion, anxiety and the like are festering remnants of the base, primitive mind within us. These emotions and mental states, to put it simply, get in the way. Individuals, functionally, are blocked from reaching their full potentials because the two souls are ever warring with each other. Obviously, you can't see where you're going if storms are perpetually obfuscating your vision. Of course you will be afraid and tense if you don't know what lies ahead. Perfection requires clear horizons.

"Will you walk into our better world? Beginning within the next week, our Government will unveil its revolutionary new process that breaks those prehistoric chains that still tether the mind to the muck and mire of barbarism. This is the process for which you have been waiting. Wait no longer! It is the Will of God! It does not hurt! It takes only minutes out of your day. It is here! Watch for the special yellow panel trucks that will be appearing in your neighborhood, soon. They are the bearers of true glory.

"Have you been scared? Have you been worried? Have you been angry? Be scared no more. Be worried no more. Be angry no more. The fruits of a blissful life, an accomplished life, a satisfying life, are ripening on the trees for all of us to harvest - in the name of the Reverend Yaramon, the sun will shine from coast to coast!"

Of course it was a barge load of unmitigated bullshit! What did that matter? All the scientists who, by now, weren't firmly aligned with the Yaramon Administration had their funding pared back to the bones. They couldn't say or do anything. They could hardly afford to eat.

Wench waved at the power eye of the jumbo megachrome TV monitor. The picture flattened into a line and winked out.

"Hey, Chief!" a gravelly voice cracked. "Ain't you going to watch *Spin For Singles*? It's on next."

"What, no cartoons?" Wench responded.

Brawny, red-bearded Mars Gumbo had entered the room and managed to fire off one of his usual sarcastic quips before sinking behind his own desk and virtually vanishing into the stacks of manuscripts, research materials, and rival newspapers that covered it. Gumbo favored printed matter. Wench and Gumbo shared the office, the science desk of the *Daily Parade*.

"Nice ladies, though," added Gumbo, referring to the prime time dating program hostesses.

"Come out of there where I can see you!"

Gumbo poked a smiling face out from behind a pile of magazines. "In the name of the Reverend Yaramon, the sun will shine from coast to coast," he gleefully recited the popular slogan.

"Don't kid yourself. The bastards are actually doing it."

"BLISS?"

Wench reached back to his own desk, shuffled through some dog-eared manila file folders, and lifted up one thick press release in particular. "Biopsychic Lavation for Intensified Stimulation of Superego." He read out what the acronym, BLISS, on the first page, meant.

"They must have stayed up late to work out that one," Gumbo jibed, shaking his head.

Wench flipped through the pages. "It's crap," he said. "It's all crap and it's dangerous, besides. People aren't possibly going to swallow this."

"Swallow it?" Gumbo turned serious. "They'll wolf it down without even chewing!" He gestured toward the window and the street below. "You're talking about the masses who changed the constitution to keep the Moralists in power for three terms now! You got people out there daffy with wonderment that their wristwatches can chime *The Yellow Rose of Texas* every hour on the hour. Mothers go into a panic every time their precious infants hiccup. Not to mention all the religious and jingoistic hype enveloping the country like fog .... Believe me, in no time we'll be up to our necks in grinning zombies!"

"Everybody won't get BLISS," argued Wench.

"No," Gumbo agreed, then, with a knowing chuckle, added, "half of them are that way of their own accord already."

It was Gumbo's contention that BLISS, like the name inferred, was no more than a super tranquilizer - a Government endorsed happy pill. What the Yaramon Administration boasted to be a glorious awakening of the mind and spirit for everyone was, in actuality, the key to universal mindless euphoria. With BLISS, the whole country could enjoy, revel in, a humdrum existence, watching television, reading novelizations of pop movies. This didn't bother Gumbo so much. What really irritated him, wormed its way right into his soul, drove him to the heights of cynicism, was that most people fiercely desired BLISS, or bliss, no matter what terms the Government used to advertise it, or how it was spelled.

Still, Wench wasn't even sure the damn process would work at all.

Wench sat down. He sensed that Gumbo was about to launch into another bout of editor-baiting, an avocation that the man positively doted upon, and Wench wanted to at least get into a position of defense.

"I mean more enlightened people like you, me, Jury, Lez ... no way we're going to sit for that stuff," Wench said. He knew the choice of the word enlightened was not the best, but too late now.

Gumbo leaned far forward, his scraggly chin whiskers mopping the desktop like a huge rusted steel wool pad. His eyebrows, ruddy caterpillars, bowed. "Enlightened are we?" he pounced. "The man says we're enlightened. What are we going to do about it?" He looked to the left and to the right, pretending to check if the coast was clear. "We going to throw gasoline bombs at those yellow trucks? Blockade the streets and not let 'em in maybe? Hey, Chief, I got it...." He lowered his voice to a semi-whisper. "Let's organize another revolution! You can be a general!"

Wench bristled. "Well, all right, then! We just throw up our hands and go marching off to BLISS like obedient children! If they want us to drop our drawers, we'll ask which cheek."

"Ours is not to question why, ours is but to spread and sigh," Gumbo punned in rapid order, adding devilishly, "don't you know, Chief? The writing's on the wall. You can't stop the earth from spinning."

"Well, you'll see. It is voluntary. More people than you think will refuse BLISS."

"The Freeyares might," Gumbo quipped.

He was referring to that quasi-religious cult of street people. Harmless and, as far as anybody else was concerned, useless. They didn't vote; they avoided any association with society except to be "punished"; they didn't wear designer jeans; they begged for pittance and that is how they lived. Freeyares would refuse BLISS. They maintained that all science, even bad science, was heresy. So what?

"There'll still be enough meaningful opposition around," Wench convinced himself.

Gumbo stared squarely at Wench, eyeball to eyeball, and asked in a monotone, "will it make any bit of difference?"

40

Will it?

Astin W. Wench pondered his colleague's ominous conclusion during the entire bus ride to Lowia's home. He figured if ten percent, one-quarter, even a full third of the population refused to undergo BLISS (wasn't it voluntary?), the ultimate outcome would not be significantly altered. With even half the country, like so many marionette puppets, dancing to a single manipulation, all one need do is let good old-fashioned pluralism neutralize the other half. The "perfect" society - for some. That is, assuming BLISS wasn't the boondoggle of the century. Even Wench with his not altogether meager scientific education knew there was no way the Administration's claims about BLISS could possibly be genuine. Hell, even if, what would be worse? A nation full of geniuses bickering and postulating from here to eternity, or wall-to-wall woodenheads doping up on soap operas and bubblegum music? The Government had been promising its so-called "dawn of a new age" since the dusk of its first term. The BLISS promise was largely responsible for the electorate gobbling up that constitutional amendment, hook, line and sinker, which enabled Yaramon and the Moralists to sweep into a second term, and then a third. It was now payday, and the Administration had to come up with something. Wench only hoped that something was not a last-ditch pasted together lobotomy. Ridiculous! People may be gullible but they're not downright jellyfish. What matter how passionate a Moralist supporter you are, if Dad, Uncle or the girl next door climbs out of one of those yellow trucks with the personality of a cabbage - you're not going to break your neck to be next in line! No, Yaramon's up to something. He's stalling for time. BLISS ... what bull!

Waiting for a stoplight to change (it must have malfunctioned; it wasn't changing), Wench, on the bus, watched with marginal concern what had become an everyday occurrence. Outside, a plump little Freeyare with more hair on his chin than his head, wearing a brown dashiki and sandals, was quietly begging. From nowhere, three muscular, teenaged males wearing their own hair stretched and *glooed* in the back as was the current fad, leapt upon the Freeyare. The boys whacked viciously at the beggar with wooden sticks and a baseball bat. The Freeyare fell to his knees, bowing his head forward, not so much as if protecting himself from the onslaught, but more as if communing with his god. The Freeyare chanted something that Wench couldn't hear above the revving bus. But every once in a while the Freeyare would cry out loudly, clearly, "Praise be to God!" or "The Lord is Good!" As suddenly as it had begun, the attack ceased. The three boys ran off in search of another Freeyare, probably: this one had had enough. They didn't want to kill him, only beat up the little fellow, which they'd done most effectively. Bruised and bleeding, the Freeyare toppled onto his side against the pavement, still chanting, with a satisfied and beatific expression across his face. Nobody rushed to help the fallen man, of course, since that would be taboo, according to Freeyare doctrine. Nobody wanted to help, anyway; if any attempt was made to succor, the Freeyare would only be insulted. This was the way of Freeyares. The light finally changed; the bus grunted and struggled on.

Chapter 4

THE reliable Bigapolis Transit System bus broke down, this night, only two short blocks from where Lowia lived. Wench was pleased that he'd have an easy walk to his girlfriend's place and not have to trudge across the seedier, adjoining neighborhood, or, worse, wait up to an hour for another bus. A good sign.

Astin and Lowia had been having problems.

Lowia Lilli rented a two-bedroom garden apartment in a very working-class section of town for herself and her eighteen-month-old daughter from a previous marriage. Slender, but far from skinny, with close-cropped black hair, olive complexion, and strong features that were ideally photogenic - Lowia often blamed her looks for some of their plight. Years ago she had been persuaded, lured would be even more appropriate, into dropping out of nursing school in favor of what others led her to believe would turn out to be a highly lucrative modeling career. And it was, for a few years. But fashions change like the weather. Latin beauties are "hot" one year, cold the next. Lowia's rocket rise to success became a plummet into unemployment.

Wench always connected Lowia's washout in the modeling biz to the rising dominance of the Moralists who were predominantly Midwestern blue-eyed blondes.

Lowia got married, got pregnant, got divorced. Now she worked from three in the afternoon to eight at night at a local quick food restaurant to supplement the meager assistance she received from the Government and her ex-husband.

The hours were fine with Wench who seldom left work himself before nine p.m. But some of their other problems were almost insurmountable.

Wench and Lowia had grown very close together, engendering a love that was comfortable, natural and, most importantly, forgiving of virtually anything. They'd often discussed marriage. Lowia, mainly, was unwilling to take the obvious step. Her lack of an education, failed career, lousy former marriage, all ganged up on her psyche to no good end. She smoked and frequently depended upon tranquilizers to keep her from flipping out. Every Thursday she met with a therapist. Wench also tried to help as best he could; his efforts weren't always enough. When the traumas of life inexorably came to a head, Wench and Lowia got into raging quarrels. Wench would storm away and drink, or pig out on Italian food. Lowia reacted with deep depressions (once bouncing into the arms of the first "pretty" male face to come along; that practically drove a permanent wedge between her and Wench), and fits of pill popping. In every instance, however, after a few emotionally turbid days passed, they managed to patch things and get back together.

Sex was disappointing. Wench maintained to himself that their Great Moments in Bed could be counted on the toes of one foot. But this was an unabashedly macho complaint he was ashamed to voice, so he never did. Wench understood Lowia. He accepted it, if she couldn't always respond to him the way he desired. The difference between them, which she had succinctly pointed out, was that he was always free to walk out the door. Besides, Wench realized sometimes it was his fault. Their relationship, therefore, while not strained, wasn't absolutely satisfying.

Wench at one time suspected that the trouble had a lot to do with the fact that Lowia had been sterilized following the birth of her child. But this was not the trouble. Many women, today, got sterilized. It was the only available means of birth control and it, too, was under fire from the Moralists. Even before the Yaramon Administration was voted in, broad ranging Fetal Protection and Childrens' Rights legislation had not only outlawed abortion and many forms of birth control (including prophylactics, by a feat of arcane thinking), but dictated how and along what lines pregnant women must bear and then raise their children. Children, too, were empowered by Congress to sue their parents for anything from failing to purchase them a birthday present to balking at their requests to enroll them in the most expensive, prestigious business school in the country. Clearly, having a family was no easy matter anymore, and certainly not an individual pursuit, even if the Government did allot a stipend to single parents. Nobody dared take a chance on an unwanted pregnancy. Better to get sterilized.

Lowia got sterilized, before she met Wench. The two of them often discussed abstaining from the physical, when lovemaking wasn't gangbusters, even to the point of not sleeping together. Lowia confessed that she'd grown to depend on Wench's presence and the security of him beside her. She wanted him in her bed - sex or no sex. For Wench, the proposition wasn't quite as simple. He felt terrible about it. He blamed his libido. She did the best she could with it but, half the time, Wench was left with a morning-after uneasiness and guilt over what he called "borrowing the use of her body." She mocked him, insisting it certainly was not the case; except his confused feelings never truly went away.

"It looks as though Yaramon's going ahead with that BLISS thing he's been threatening us with," Wench announced later as he washed the dishes. Lowia was tucking in her daughter for the night. Dinner had been a simple broiled bird, with broccoli, potatoes and an exceptional cherry cobbler Lowia had prepared for dessert.

"Why threatening?" Lowia rang back.

"You can't mean that."

"What's terrible about making people happy? Maybe they have come up with a new pill, a vaccine or something. You don't know for sure."

"It wouldn't be administered like medicine," Wench insisted. "You can't stick happiness, 'an accomplished life,' to quote our beloved vice president, into pipes and feed the stuff into everybody's kitchen like hot water. Turn on the tap and chase the blues away."

"Why not?" She danced lightly into the room, wearing one of her frilliest, most revealing negligees. "They can do a lot of things nowadays."

Slinking up against Wench, she tenderly nibbled his earlobe with her lips. Wench was suddenly glad there weren't many dishes. She whispered, "as for hap-*piness*," accenting the last two syllables. Lowia had a way with an erotic phrase.

Anticipating at least a nine on a scale of ten, Wench dashed through his remaining chores. As it turned out, he settled for a moderate six.

Lowia did, several times in fact, purr with satisfaction. Her neck flushed, her small, pleasing nipples stood firm and rosy in response to Wench's ministrations. He delicately stroked his lips along the outline of her breasts, down to her stomach and into her thighs. Her body hair prickled. For quite some time he feasted on the core of her womanhood, and she, in total enjoyment, floated, eyes closed, on a cloud of pleasure. The great leonine passion, the acrobatic sensuality that he full well knew dwelt insider her, however, did not erupt this time. Though he played her lovingly, skillfully, like the most perfect sexual instrument, and she took every chord, she would not be brought to climax. Wench, too, held back.

Fighting off primitive male anger, masculine lust, knowing not what else to do, he turned to rise out of bed.

"Honey?" Lowia put one arm around his neck to keep him from leaving her side. "Don't be annoyed."

"I'm sorry."

"I love you." Her eyes twinkled. With her other hand, she lightly teased his tensive genitals. Then, with a touch of an imp, a touch of a whore, beckoned, "we can't leave you in this condition. It wouldn't be fair."

"It's not fair to you," he added.

48

"But I want to feel your love pour into me," she countered.

Lowia had a way with an erotic phrase.

Wench gave in. He took her body completely against his own, merging her warm moist smell with his. He kissed her, drawing her tongue full into his mouth. She simultaneously drew him deeply into her femininity. With little extra effort, he yielded, pulled the ripcord, climaxed. The flesh was served. She yoked him tighter to her, reassuringly, but he couldn't shake the uneasiness of being both cheated and cheater. Again he fell asleep, dozed fitfully, and awoke in the morning unrefreshed.

Chapter 5

ANASTASIA "Boots" Motherley was affectionately dubbed "Boots" because her parents had made a fortune in the footwear business. The family name was on everyone's feet, the company liked to brag. "Boots" was in politics, however. She was an enormous woman, a real presence, domineering, dynamic, having all the qualities of a born leader. Her strong, crisp voice cut through crowded hallways as effectively as an announcement that free lunch was served. She liked to wear solid colors and ostentatious hats with plumes, which made her as recognizable as her speech was rousing (and how the TV press adored her). She was the First Consul of the United Separatist Action.

Motherley had wasted no time attacking the Government's latest endeavor. " ... Do not let them buffalo you!" she exhorted in a televised rebuttal to Cinder's address. "They seek only enhancement of the White Anglo-Saxon Moralist establishment, not enhancement of humanity as a whole! BLISS won't give you a share of their power. BLISS won't give you any of their money. BLISS won't even give you bliss. It'll only give you a swift kick in the pants ... !"

The United Separatist Action was on the boil, and getting restless. Almost four months had passed since the last round of fist-shaking from this politically boisterous coalition. The U.S.A., an ad hoc assortment of white, black, red, yellow and other minority fringe groups under the flamboyant command of "Boots" Motherley, advocated the constitution of Alabama as an independent anti-Moralist nation. Now they were as angry as a subway car full of delayed commuters - with reasonable cause. BLISS, the Separatists unanimously insisted, was racist.

Wench had predicted correctly. Not everybody was going to swallow, whole hog, Biopsychic Lavation for Intensified Stimulation of Superego.

Continued Motherley: " ... Thackery Cinder? His offering a golden future is like the scorpion wagging an inviting tail. Are we so simpleminded as to be taken in by these gangsters and their evil machinations of a decadent regime time and time again? I say stop them in their tracks. Stop this blatant attempt to coerce us into subservience and ignorance."

Wench hit the off button on the small video recorder. In a second, the magnetic disc poked halfway out of the machine's mouth like a plastic tongue. He'd reviewed all he needed of Motherley's declamation, recorded several days ago. Her rejection of Cinder's bombshell BLISS announcement sounded straightforward enough. It echoed the U.S.A. party line. But there was actually nothing fresh to be found in the woman's words, although the address did elicit much cheering from certain circles.

The battle engaged, the sides drawn, all anyone really expected was an exciting war of words which would produce a bounty of news copy and photo opportunities. The Yaramon Administration gleefully counterattacked Motherley, labeling her an egomaniac with a Messiah complex and alleged that she opposed BLISS' "offering persons of all races, creeds, religions and political persuasions a solid grasp of their own destinies with no need of petty autocrats telling them what to do" because it would knock her off her throne. Motherley responded, accusing the Administration of "genetic tampering" and "another holocaust."

Nobody expected this morning's head to head confrontation between Motherley and Cinder. The incident would later become known as the bloody Haddon Heights Uprising.

Wench handed the videocard he'd been viewing back to the file clerk, a bony woman with teased pink hair who was cordoned off from the rest of the spacious research library by a u-shaped, chest high desk. There were only windows on one far wall, and the place was quiet as a dentist's lounge. Widely spaced out in front of the file clerk's desk stood the dozen video machines reserved for use by the newspaper staff. Behind the clerk, decades of recordings, reporters' notes, films, cards, occupied tower after tower of open shelves: the morgue.

"You got the Jersey material from earlier?" Wench asked.

"On chips. Three-cm videocard, some, but mostly microcapsule audio."

"I'm not critiquing the stuff," Wench kidded, "I need to look at it."

The clerk shot back a quick "so there" expression, grabbed the disc that Wench was returning from his hand, disappeared behind the mountainous stacks of mixed media that she was employed to watch and ward, and returned momentarily with a stuffed, brown file envelope. She handed the package to Wench, informing him: "it's not all been digitized yet."

"I'm sure I can figure it out."

The clerk added, as if in defense: "what's all this got to do with the science desk, anyway?"

"Thanatology," quipped Wench, assuming the clerk wouldn't know the meaning of the word. He mused to himself that she'd probably be first in line to get BLISS. He returned to the video apparatus he was using, slithered into the chair, at the same time reached into the file envelope. He pulled out the videocard. The clerk was right. There wasn't much of it.

The news photographer who shot the material had been late arriving at the scene. Haddon Heights was served by the paper's South Bigapolis field office and, typically, their equipment had been down. A crew had to be dispatched from North Bigapolis, a good hour's drive at top speed even taking the Zoomway with emergency blinkers going and highway patrol escorts. But that's what always happens when these radical groups don't let you know ahead of time what they're up to.

Wench fed the card into the machine's gray metal maw, and hit the playback button.

He saw a fine, clear blue-sky morning with birds chirping and clouds gently curtsying to each other in the heavens. The yellow trucks had not yet begun to roll. There they were, neatly parked inside the staging hangar, in a rank and file formation that, on the tiny view screen, appeared to Wench to resemble a battalion of canaries. Nearly thirty trucks must have been housed in the hangar-like garage. Well, twenty-nine.

One of the trucks had been driven onto the wide gravel-topped field in front of the hangar and was stopped midway between the garage and the access road. The truck was smashed and burning. About ten feet to the right of the truck lay a body, face down, in a pool of blood. Farther over, a paramedic, dressed in white, was bandaging a second riot victim who was badly wounded but alive. Wench saw other bodies scattered about the scene like sticks. One of the bodies had been bludgeoned to death so ferociously it was hardly recognizable as human except for the conspicuous policeman's uniform. Several patrol cars, an ambulance, a Government limo, and the *Daily Parade* company van, lights blinking, doors hanging open, made a neat line-up along the access road. Other people, cops, paramedics, were milling around.

Wench heard the photographer's voice over: "Christ, this place looks like Disaster Beach after the first wave."

There couldn't have been more than one-half minute of videocard remaining. Wench noticed a burly, dark-suited figure, muscles aching to break out of their wrappings, crew cut, skin like pale vinyl, probably a Government agent, come into the picture from the left side and completely obscure the camera's point of view. He heard: "okay, fella, this is a restricted area. Let's kill the picture taking." The familiar voice of the news photographer responded: "hey, we've got a right. What are you doing - " The picture bounced abruptly, then steadied on a scene of the clear blue sky. The

54

Government agent stuck his beefy, out-of-focus face right up to the lens, growling, "buddy, you got no rights. Now shut that off or I'll shut it permanently down your throat." And static. That's all the video there was. The photographer was no foolish hero.

Wench jabbed at the rewind button. The machine purred smoothly then spat out the card. Wench didn't need additional video, anyway. The reporter on the scene, his friend, Lez Underhand, had gotten an exclusive interview with one of the surviving Separatists.

The group was informally referred to as the DropOut Party, with no disparagement intended or taken. In fact, the Separatists often used the moniker themselves because its connotations were less confusing and required less explanation than "anti-Moralist" (which made the only currently active Government opposition movement sound like a gang of sheep pumpers). Wench popped the microcapsule into the other machine, donned the headphones and fiddled with the volume slider. He hated sliding pots.

A throaty voice filled with wheezing and tension came through the phones. " ... We're not a violent group, really. We don't want to hurt anybody. Why'd they have to do this? All we want is to get back what was taken from us originally. It doesn't make any sense. You guys ... your paper's always given us a fair shake. Tell them we don't want to hurt anybody. Tell them .... "

"We know what your aims are. Relax." This was the smooth, tenor voice of veteran newsman Underhand, Pulitzer Prize winner and holder of the coveted Sunday Cross. "Tell me what happened this morning. Start from the beginning."

"We were only demonstrating ... a few picket signs."

"Before that. Start from even before you got here."

They took a short pause. Wench heard the sound of a nose blowing, a light cough, then the request, "something to drink?"

"Want a soda?" the reply. "Got some in the car. Mario, go grab a couple of pops. Now. You ready? Tell me what happened."

"We got here while it was still dark, me, Michaeljohn and the Bear. The three of us drove practically half the night from Binghamton. When we got here, only a few other cars had arrived; the rest weren't far behind, pulling up in a steady procession. 'Boots' hadn't got here yet, either. We couldn't see her red and white limo, but she's always late. Folks were gathering and we waited around, drinking coffee, chatting with the brothers and sisters whom we hadn't seen in weeks. You know. That sort of stuff.

"About thirty minutes later, 'Boots' finally shows, that glitzy road hog of hers tooling along like a float in the Mardi Gras. The sun was getting up, too. I mean, 'Boots' must have timed it perfectly. The whole entrance was kind of religious, you know?"

"Everybody was still on the access road? Nobody had gone down to the staging hangar, even onto Government property yet?" Underhand inquired.

"No. Nobody. We weren't going to say boo until the entire troop was gathered and we got our orders. We were coordinated good as a military operation. Some folks had picket signs - "

"What'd they say, the signs?"

"You know - BLISS IS SLAVERY - ALABAMA NOW - that sort of thing. Next thing is 'Boots' gets out her bullhorn and tells us to, quietly and orderly, march down the grassy slope from the access road to the gravel covered yard in front of the garage. With the sun rising now we could see those sparkling clean, yellow trucks lined up pretty as you please. All that brand new, white grillwork looked like sets of fake choppers. I swear, I figured those trucks were actually smiling at us ... smiling! Can you beat that?"

Colorful, Wench bemused. If this Separatist ever tires of chest-thumping for a southern homeland he'd have a promising career as a writer.

Underhand's voice again interrupted: "there was no sign of anybody in the garage itself? No guards? Maintenance crew?"

"Empty. Not a soul. Only us and those trucks. Pretty strange, if you ask me."

"Well, the Government's been getting awfully cocky lately. I'm not too surprised," Underhand commented. "Did anybody touch anything?"

"No sir! This was textbook civil disobedience, non-violence to the letter. We didn't come within ten feet of that garage. 'Boots' tells us to make a big circle, you know, a picket line. But this was in the yard, nowhere near the trucks. Sure, we were on Government property, I guess. I couldn't see anything posted, or fences, or guards. So what could

57

we get? A couple days in the slammer for trespassing? Hell, we've all done that before.

"Anyway, we begin marching around. Of course, nobody else was on hand to see us yet. But we're getting into the groove. Some of the brothers and sisters hoisted their picket signs into the air. Some chanted. 'Boots' was keeping pace with us, flanking the line from the outside. She looked like a real general in her fancy suit and feathery hat, holding that bullhorn. She barks out, 'if they want to move those trucks, let them barrel the things right over our backs!' You should have heard the roar of solidarity that went up after that. It was terrific.

"Short time later we started to see some other cars arriving. I guess these belonged to the garage staff. They weren't expecting us to be there, and didn't know what to do, I guess. They parked by the access road, got out, milled around, looked at us, didn't do anything. They talked among themselves, smoked.

We could see a number of blacks among the workers. I mention this 'cause that's when the Bear, one of the guys I came down with, shouts 'hey bros, you gonna be the white man's flunky all your life? Come down and join us!' One or two of the black workers waved back in acknowledgment. One of them even shows us a thumbs up sign. But they stayed where they were. I think they were enjoying the whole thing.

"We picked up steam and really put on a demonstration. Then the cops arrived. We could hear the sirens wailing for a full five minutes before the squad cars squealed up. Christ! What the hell did they think was going on to require sirens? A war? You wouldn't believe it: must have been one dozen cop cars converged on the place. Some of them charged right across the grass, down the hill to the edge of the gravel yard. One cop, a captain, I think, walks over to us and orders us to depart. S.O.P. Right? We refuse, of course. Right? I mean, it was like we didn't even hear the man. We just keep on marching, back and forth, chanting, waving our pickets.

"'You are on restricted territory and are required to clear the premises immediately or face forcible eviction and arrest.' The guy talked like he was reading. Nothing new. We continued marching.

"We're pros at this game. Nobody even looked cross-eyed at the cop. We were doing our thing like we were in another world, oblivious. Like I said, nothing new. We've done this lots of times. It always proceeds like a movie script: the cops move in, drag some limp protesters away in paddy wagons, to jail, they get sprung within hours from our defense fund. We only hope we can keep the festivities going long enough until you press guys show up we can get some media coverage. Don't want to waste valuable demonstration time, right?

"This captain returns to his car. He gets on the radio. He chats. Nothing happens. Nothing. Somebody must have handed us a different script. But we went on marching and chanting and jerking our signs up and down, anyway. The cops and the workers were forming little huddles on their side of the field, pointing, watching, smoking. Stalemate.

"That's when the air busts wide open by the sound of a helicopter. Not any old whirlybird. One of those sleek, jet-propelled jobs that look more like

UFOs than copters. The thing was enormous, got more lights on it than a bar and grill. It circled overhead, once, then came in real close. It whipped up dust, knocked some of the picket signs out of our hands, nearly knocked some of us over. I think it did this on purpose. Even 'Boots' hat goes sailing off her head.

"Boy, that pissed her off!

"The helicopter lands about fifty feet to the right of the gravel yard and sits there. I could see the markings on it real plain. From the Government. It was a Government helicopter.

"We'd stopped marching. We were still in place, sort of holding our ground, making a lopsided circle, but all eyes were steadfastly glued to that whining steel bird. Bear says to me: 'shit, they sending the goddam army after us now?' It wasn't the army.

"The side of the copter opens up and you could have kicked me squarely between the eyes and I wouldn't have blinked. You know who steps out? Thackery Cinder! The Vice President. Thackery Cinder in the flesh."

"Why Cinder at a thing like this?" Underhand wondered aloud.

Why, indeed, Wench also questioned inwardly.

"Ya got me, bub," the Separatist on the mCap recording responded.

The mCap played on. "Everybody's humming like a beehive. The brothers and sisters, the folks up on the hill. This sure wasn't in the script. What in Alabama was Cinder doing at a freaking demonstration? He brushed back his buttery hair, fixed his tie, primped himself like a damned

60

pussycat, then walked right up to the edge of the gravel yard like he was about to chair a meeting of the Yaramon Youth Boosters. What the heck; he's safe enough; none of us were about to lob a rock off the bastard's skull, though we sure would have liked to.

"'Ladies. Gentlemen.' He greets us with that honey smooth voice of his. Apparently, he was remotely hooked into the copter's PA system, so we could hear him. Could we ever. His amped voice could've been heard in the next county, too. 'Nice to see all of you. Is Miss Motherley with you?'

"'Boots' goes trotting right over to Cinder, always one to take the stag by the antlers, so to speak, and certainly never a woman to avoid a confrontation.

"'Ah! Anastasia,' Cinder says brightly, extending a polished hand. The balls that guy had using 'Boots' first name like they were old friends. She shook hands with him, anyway.

"'Thack,' she calls him in return, 'did you get lost or are you here to personally surrender?'

"Cinder broke into the approving laugh of a used-car salesman prior to turning over title of the biggest lemon in the lot. Then he added, 'why, I'm here on Government business. This is a Government facility, you might have noticed.'

"'We noticed,' said Motherley.

"'Good, good. Glad to have your people visit, unannounced as it might be. But I'll overlook that little trespass.' He addresses himself to all the brothers and sisters. 'You folks needn't demonstrate here. BLISS is for everybody. And it is for everybody to choose. If you'd rather not participate, why, you can simply go on with your daily lives. If you wish to join us, the trucks will be rolling very soon and we'd be more than happy to put your names on the top of the list. The trucks will be on their way very soon.'

"'They will be over our collective asses first!' Motherley vowed. A cheer burst from the crowd. Cinder held up his hands, fingers splayed out, until the crowd quieted. 'Miss Motherley, please' he oozed, 'can't we keep this dignified?'

"Motherley puffed. 'Dignified? The man is using the word dignified? Well, you go and tell everyone how dignified it's going to be when you and your machines start tampering with our brains and turn us into shuffling vegetables! How dignified is a program of virtual lobotomy for an entire people? How dignified is - ?'

"'I keep trying to tell you,' Cinder cut her off. 'BLISS is voluntary. If you believe there is any truth to your ridiculous suspicions, you don't have - '

"'Sure,' she charged, 'screw the poor suckers who fall for your BLISS codswallop. And screw them in other ways if they don't want it. It's an old, old story, Mister Cinder. How long do you think you can keep pulling something over on us? What really happens inside those yellow trucks of yours? What happens?'

"She had Cinder that time, all right. I could see in the man's eyes, fire, from where I was standing. He was burning under that tanned, pampered corpse of his. Hot. But he floored us with a real one-two punch. He offered: 'care to try it out, Miss Motherley? Here? Be the first? Now? We'll prep a BLISS truck exclusively for you. We wouldn't dare

62

turn you into a vegetable in front of your own people.'

"'That doesn't mean you haven't got two BLISSes.'

"'It'll prove we've got one - the one we claim. A very tiny risk, Miss Motherley. Care to accept?' We were thunderstruck. I mean our boots were stuck to the dirt. Bear says to me: 'She ain't gonna let that sucker diddle inside her head, is she?' He got his answer. 'Boots' snaps back, 'You and me, Thack. Same BLISS. Double blind. Your tech boys can wire that up, can't they? Both of us together. Almost like sex. Maybe better than sex, eh? Connubial mind-bending? What do you say to that, Thack? Well?'"

Wench heard a static pause. He hoped the mCap had not malfunctioned.

Underhand's voice returned. "And then what?"

"You should have been there," the Separatist said. "Cinder started steaming. Okay, maybe it was the dew, the sun, the chill of dawn, or all three. But this guy's got vapor billowing out of his ears. Anyway, Cinder simply turns and walks back to the copter. Man, we pounced on him then with boos and catcalls; but only words, just words, I swear. Nobody lifted a pinky. Then, I don't know, maybe Cinder snapped. I don't know. He made a military about face and returned to the edge of the gravel yard. His tune changed quick as a trumpeter's at a dance hall. 'People, people,' his voice implored. 'This isn't your fight. This has nothing to do with your national homeland. This isn't about Alabama. Go on home before you get duped into very serious trouble. We've got Government cars - pulling in right now - for any of you who'd like a free ride. The rest of you can be my guests onto the Zoomway. In the name of the Reverend Yaramon, let's please break this up - '"

Wench heard the man on the mCap take one deep breath, then another. "So why in hell did they want to go and do that? Why? Why did they run her down? Sure, everybody talks big. That's life. You know. But to actually, deliberately hit - "

"Is that what they did?" Underhand asked. "Did the Feds start the riot? Did they hit her?" "We heard thunder," the Separatist continued, "like a diesel motor starting up, then a roar. I didn't know what it was at first - the helicopter revving, squad cars closing in, perhaps. We were all caught by surprise. We didn't think there was anybody in the garage. So who figured to check them yellow trucks? Until one was already charging out like hell on wheels!

"This all happened a lot faster than I can tell it." "Do the best you can," Underhand said. "I was watching Cinder. The bastard. The damn bastard lopes off for the copter without a word, signaling with his right hand. Next thing I know, the Bear grabs my arm below the shoulder, bellows, 'it's going after her! It's going to hit her!' I saw 'Boots' sidestep to attempt to get out of the way, but she wasn't fast enough and that yellow dinosaur plows right into her like she was a tree or something. She went down."

More crisp static was followed by a long, ethereal pause.

"Can you talk about what happened next?" Underhand asked sympathetically.

"Yeah. It was war, man, that's what. A war. The Bear screams and runs toward the truck, his bare knuckles flaying at air. I yell back at him 'Bear, you can't do anything, man. You're going to get yourself killed!' Hell, he didn't hear me. He was already on the truck. With one yank, he rips off the damn door - the door, bang, gone. He pulls the driver out of the truck, bodily, and smashes the guy's skull, like it was a battering ram, against the front fender, again and again and again."

"Was the driver a Fed, a worker, a cop?" Underhand wanted to know the facts. That was his job.

"Christ, man, I don't know. It was getting real heavy. But the driver was dead sure by the second blow. I can tell you that much." The Separatist inhaled. "A gunshot rang out. Bear turns to look at me, a look I'll never forget. Then he fell."

"I'm sorry," said Underhand.

"Bear was a good man," reflected the Separatist.

"Then what?"

"Don't really remember too clearly. Some of us ran like hell to get out of there. Others were going hand-to-hand with the cops and Feds. I saw some of our people trashing the truck. But I high-tailed it to safety quick as a monkey. Look, I got a wife and kids. I didn't come for a battle...."

"No problem, buddy," Underhand said. "I understand. Thanks for sticking around. Thanks for talking to me."

"Like I said, you guys always give us a fair shake. Tell the truth, okay?"

Wench shut off the mCap machine. He sat quietly for a long time, not even removing the headphones, thinking, meditating. That blackout Party member on the mCap expressed it best: Why? With a capital W. What he'd listened to didn't make that much sense, indeed. First of all, what was Thackery Cinder doing at a routine demonstration? Had it been a coincidence, the Vice President on a business trip at the same place and time the Separatists had chosen? What business would Cinder have at a desolate staging zone for BLISS trucks? How did the Government find out about the demonstration so quickly? Well, the walls have ears and all that; big deal. Was it a set-up? For what reason? Was Cinder really as reckless as rumors made him out to be? Nonsense. And Cinder's bizarre suggestion that Motherley take the BLISS treatment there and then: proof positive that BLISS (as Wench suspected) was the biggest hoax since the artificial cheese scandals; instant revelation that it was dangerous; everything the Government said it was? In the latter case, they'd have been handing the Separatists the key to the store. As for the blatant instigation of what ensued - it didn't make soup. Wench worked in the kitchen long enough to know, however, that something was cooking.

"What do you think?"

Wench put the brakes on his train of thought. He took the headphones off. Lez Underhand had come into the research library and was standing next to Wench, straight as a stork, expectantly, his mustachioed face blush.

"Those are my mCaps you're reviewing. What do you think?" Underhand pressed.

"Oh. Good interview. Exceptional."

"But curious, no?"

"Yaramon's gang going to let you print anything about this? They must know. Word's leaked out by now. And with you on the beat .... ?"

"They haven't squawked yet. Not a blasted 'Whoa, Nellie' from the lot of them. And the presses are rolling."

Wench shook his head. "You'd think they were deliberately trying to infuriate every Government opponent from here to Timbuktu."

"My sentiments - "

A bronze-headed copyboy leaned halfway through the doorway into the room, drawled "Lez Underhand?"

"Over here."

"Motherley's dead," the boy said simply.

Wench and Underhand went slightly cold. "What?"

"A few minutes ago," the boy reported. "They texted it in. She was in the operating room, but apparently didn't make it. Died of her injuries. The boss thought you'd want to know."

"Dammit! Those blockheads just bought themselves a full-blown, whopping insurrection." Underhand smacked Wench on the shoulder and galloped out of the room like a bird dog after prey.

Anastasia "Boots" Motherley was a martyr. Any sense at all to the entire incident was quite beyond comprehension. At the same time, an uncomfortable goose pimply sensation seemed to confirm Wench's growing surmise that Reverend Yaramon, pulling the strings, was getting precisely what had been intended.

And on the next day, the BLISS trucks began to roll.

Chapter 6

NOT long after the infamous Haddon Heights Uprising, the Yaramon Administration put up for referendum the question of whether or not the United Separatist Action should be allowed to have their independent homeland in Alabama. It was, as were so many of the things that the Moralists did, a startling proposition. In the news, the evening before the election, all that Administrative spokesmen were quoted regarding the issue was, "in a truly free society, we cannot enjoin individuals to be a part of society."

Any further debate was lopsided.

All that was left was the vote.

Voting, even before Angus Yaramon took the Capitol, was a simple, painless and hugely democratic procedure. One voted right from one's living room - no lines, anytime: this is what made frequent referendums practical. Modern television not only offered subscription movies, cable libraries, shopping at home, game channels, university credit classes and the highly desirable video telephone service (VTP), but one entire row of buttons on TV remotes was exclusively dedicated to elections. Voting was a right, after all. The feature was included in the price of every TV monitor, by law. To cast a ballot, after the choices or candidates' names were printed across the screen, voters logged in their "askie" numbers, then made their selections or punched in a simple yes/no. Everybody with an "askie" and a TV monitor could, therefore, vote. And that meant pretty much everybody. Those who didn't own TVs were treated like Freeyares, or worse. Besides, without a tube, if a person wished to vote, he or she would have to arrange a special trip to a public voting station; these were always inconveniently out of the way. Public voting stations were cramped, overheated, and full of vermin.

Astin Wench maintained a negative stand on the issue. His conviction that Alabama should remain a part of the country derived less from any altruistic belief in unity or nationalism and more from a mischievous glee in keeping Government opposition forces like the United Separatists under the Administration's skin. This would provide "unending misery for the Moralists and their adherents," he calculated.

"If nothing else, we have to keep the pressure on."

Gumbo disagreed. "Look at it this way, Chief," he said, pointing his fork, "if we give up Alabama now, then we've got someplace to go tomorrow if the political situation turns staticky."

"Toss out the opposition now and we'll soon have no choice except to go to Alabama," Wench insisted. He jabbed at his own plate of lasagne.

The two shared their favorite checkered-cloth covered corner table, under the mural of Venice, in their favorite restaurant. They often went here for long lunches, brainstorming sessions, or merely to get away from the wracking office pace. Gumbo feasted on a tray-sized plate of spaghetti with meatballs, and plenty of bread.

He waved a sauce soaked crust. "Opposition? The DropOuts aren't opposition. If there were twice as many of them, they couldn't influence a vote on what color socks to wear."

"Three times? Four times as many?"

"Yeah, okay," Gumbo ceded. "You think the Government opposition vote has any chance of quadrupling soon, you got to be smoking some pretty funny stuff."

Wench scoffed. "What the hell would you do in Alabama, anyway? Run a movement to secede Birmingham from the Separatists? I'm telling you - "

The waitress, a short, bubbly, ashen-haired woman appropriately named Sandi, whom the two journalists had long ago come to regard as "their" waitress (at least their regular waitress), waltzed toward the table with a pitcher of ice water and a basket of bread. She refilled their glasses. She winked at Gumbo, asking, "how's your lunch?" She proffered him bread.

"Delicious, kid," Gumbo answered, accepting the basket. "How're you doing?"

"Anytime you want to find out ... " the waitress invited. She bounced away.

Wench took a bite, continuing: "we can't allow Yaramon to scatter the opposition, no matter how insignificant it might be."

Gumbo vigorously shook his head in disagreement.

"These are Separatists. They don't give a damn about who's running the country. They want out, that's all! And you want to know something? They're going to get out. Alabama. You bet on it."

Gumbo hungrily dug into the tangle of pasta laying beneath him.

Mars Gumbo was absolutely correct, of course. Wench hadn't doubted for a moment that the referendum would produce a favorable result for the United Separatists and, obliquely, an equally fortunate outcome for the Moralists. Still, he resolutely held on to an inkling of hope that Yaramon would be handed an upset on a silver platter. What the hell, Wench also always hoped someday it would be discovered that dinosaurs weren't really extinct. He wasn't surprised when the vote count was tallied: 70 percent in favor of an independent Separatist Alabama, 16 percent opposed, 14 percent undecided. He hadn't seen any dinosaurs lately, either.

Day followed day like a monotony of television commercials. The logistics of preparing the State of Alabama for Separatist occupancy, not dissimilar to sweeping out, repainting and attending a vacated apartment for new tenants took time. There was always the distinct possibility that the United Separatists, true to their nature, demanding instant gratification, would rally against what they presumed to be unwarranted delays. They'd fire barrage after barrage of accusations at the Yaramon Administration. There was always this possibility. After all, government, even a Moralist dominated government, rarely functioned quite as smoothly as a well-oiled machine. If past history of the central body politic could be compared to a wagon having its wheels set in four different directions, then the current administration might be said to have gotten three wheels to jibe. This still left one wheel out of whack.

The misalignment, it must be noted, manifested itself in a futile attempt to contest the Secession Referendum by a small lobby of Civil War enthusiasts from the Midwest. Somehow they were able to convince a couple of Senators to take up the gauntlet of their cause in New Washington.

On the other hand, the actual residents of Alabama were delighted to be able to move to a more fashionable part of the country, all expenses paid.

There was, too, a tentative motion raised by displaced Texans (victims of choking drought and heat) to give Alabama to them, but this consideration faded quickly; although Alabama was close, it wasn't Texas.

The fruitless bickering in Congress, as Wench had hoped, did in fact lead to postponements of moving day for the Drop-Out Party; these postponements got the Separatists hopping mad; the fury directed against the Yaramon Administration warmed the cockles of Wench's heart.

Certain that the unstable chemistry between the Separatists and the Moralists would once again reach the exploding point, Wench was not surprised when, Monday around 5 p.m., a potentially violent demonstration, posing real danger to life, limb and public property, broke out. He was amazed to discover that the Separatists were not at the root.

" ... an ordinary crazy man," Gumbo remarked after logging off the telephone feed.

"Not Separatists?"

"Not unless they're among the spectators."

73

"Where?" Wench wanted to know.

"Some loony has himself chained to the box office of the Valhalla Theatre," Gumbo reported. "He's threatening to blow the place to bits if - and get this big if, doesn't even have anything to do with Alabama - if the movie house doesn't stop running its current feature!"

"The guy doesn't like films or something?"

"I don't know," Gumbo mumbled, shrugging his shoulders. Then, as if getting a sudden revelation, Gumbo snapped his fingers and suggested to Wench: "hey, Chief, why don't you trot down there and see what you can find out?"

Wench had the distinct impression Gumbo wasn't handing him all the details. "This lunatic make a scientific breakthrough in terrorism? I mean, isn't this more of a job for the City Desk?"

"Touche, Chief! Forgot to mention. Seems the cops ain't going after the guy with dogs and rubber bullets. They're bringing in a BLISS truck: going to turn it into a public spectacle. Going to try it out on the poor fellow, I guess. That ought to whet your appetite. What do you say?"

A chance to get a first-hand, close-up look at the Government's BLISS brainchild in action and in living color? Wench virtually drooled at the prospect. He snatched up his jacket and micro cassette recorder as he rocketed out.

"See you later!"

"Don't get arrested!" Gumbo shouted after him.

Wench could never stand the laid back pace of the elevators in the building, particularly now. For a few flights (the Science Desk was on the fifth floor), he'd use the stairs, taking them three, four steps at a time. He reached the ground floor quickly enough. He was by no means unique in his haste, however, and nearly collided into Lez Underhand who was fast on the way up. This halted Wench.

"Going to the Valhalla, too, thin man?" Wench asked, tagging on his usual reference to Underhand's lanky physique. Certainly this was the kind of story that would demand the presence and talents of the paper's best newsman. The two of them could share a taxi.

"Fingerberg's got it," replied Underhand, dropping the name of his associate. "Haven't you heard? They cut through the Alabama tangle in Congress. It's official. We've lost a state and the first batch of Separatists are on their way to set up housekeeping. I'm grabbing a bite and then off to the bus depot for some interviews - might even drop down to 'Bama for a few days myself."

"But what about BLISS?"

"BLISS? No news value in that anymore. BLISS is your baby!" Underhand was up the stairs and gone, his words echoing in the hollow well.

Alabama originally joined the union in December of 1819. Then, for a brief duration that called itself the War Between the States, it had temporarily seceded. Now, like a piece from a jigsaw puzzle, this more or less trapezoidal shaped land mass was coming figuratively unplugged from the continent as a whole again.

Wench shrugged. Underhand called it. Alabama was in the newsman's bailiwick. BLISS was Wench's baby.

Chapter 7

THE glamorous Valhalla Theatre squatted smugly in the center of Broadway's busiest stretch. Here, the largest unbroken construction of pristine marbled granite in the Western World, office skyscrapers and superbanks fused with each other like a string of paper dolls and, seemingly, grew from the edges of the roadway itself like a monolithic mountain range. Broadway sprawled eight lanes wide in either direction. Shooting north-south, elevated about six stories above Broadway's median, the Zoomway - the supreme temple of humankind's love for motorized transportation - arched in majesty. Amidst this, circular, roughly the diameter of an aircraft carrier, rising almost to the level of the Zoomway, was the Valhalla Theatre.

The Valhalla! How Wench remembered the first time he attended a show at this lavish film palace. Once, it was that: evening wear required, no popcorn, assigned seating, ushers in military dress. The projection screen was as large and as white as an ocean of milk. The dimming lights like nightfall. And the comfort. Vikings may have wanted to go to Valhalla after they died; film goers wanted to live there.

No more. Although its structure may have survived intact, the Valhalla's ambience now reeked of stuff 'em in the seats, crank up the pix, bring on the next batch brand of big business. The theatre had gone pop culture with a vengeance: come as you are, snacks and beverages available in the lobby, smoking sections where designated ....

Wench's taxi pulled up in front of the king of movie houses. He hopped out, handed the driver a five dollar bill.

"Keep it," he said, then "would you look at all those characters itching to get themselves blown up?"

The moviegoers who under normal circumstances would have snaked from the mouth of the Valhalla and slithered down the block and around the corner now formed a pulsating, amorphous mass of rubberneckers, fattened with passers-by.

The taxi only belched exhaust and charged away.

Wench picked up fragments of voices colliding against each other:

"... been waiting three weeks to see this movie ...."

"... don't they just shoot the bastard ...."

"... could at least let us wait inside ...."

"... what about the children ...."

A narrow channel through the crowd had been opened with limited success by the police. Wench fished around in his pockets and produced his press I.D. Bright red for visibility, larger than a playing card, it bore his photograph, thumb print, vital data, and a five centimeter long letter "A" in the lower left hand corner. The "A" meant that Wench was cleared for the highest possible security situations: Federal, military, corporate, police and medical. This was police. Wench flashed the card, accomplishing two things. The cops parted the sea of spectators a little wider, letting him into the empty theatre plaza. The crowd got something else to complain about.

"Hey, Astin." It was Fingerberg, holding his own against the human surge. He had a microcapsule recorder hanging from his shoulder. "Guess you're here for the BLISS demo?"

"Is the truck on its way?" asked Wench.

"Should be." Fingerberg's hat got knocked off by a stray elbow. "Damn. People got no more patience than six-year-olds anymore."

"Don't they know that nut over there has explosives?" Wench remarked.

"Explosives, hell," said Fingerberg, retrieving his gray porkpie off the ground, "they'd race through Armageddon to see that idiot movie."

The Valhalla marquee, always a beckoning focal point even during the off-season, now advertised the year's biggest cinema blockbuster: the musical version of *Bicknell's Cold Physics Souffle*, starring singing idol Jesus Jones. The movie, in its second week, was smashing the charts with a sledgehammer. Soundtrack mCaps and discs were being swept off the shelves with tornadic gusto by consumers, as was the novelization of the movie (not to be confused in any way with the book upon which the movie was based). In fact, the novelization was number one on the *Daily Parade* book list since Thursday.

"Terrific," grumbled Wench.

In contrast to the obstreperous crowd surrounding it, the canopied plaza in front of the theatre was an oasis of peace with a single occupant. The box offices on either side of the

78

semi-circular entryway stood empty. Wench noted, with some sympathy, the small man leaning against the ticket booth, in the shade, on the left. A peculiar contraption strapped to the man's back looked like scuba gear; it wasn't. Paradoxically, next to the man was posted a sign advertising that the air-conditioning within the theatre offered "cool comfort." Indeed.

The man didn't seem all that menacing: bespectacled, balding, about fifty, physically gone to seed with skinny arms, sloped shoulders and bony legs. The bulk of this individual hung squarely in his midsection - belly, butt and waist merged. The man wore a business suit like a plain brown wrapper. He gripped a plastic box in one hand, presumably a detonator. Excitedly he called out something to Wench, making an exaggerated gesture with the other hand.

"You'll have to speak louder!" shouted Wench, walking toward the man as far as safety would permit.

"I said, are you with the papers, too?"

"Yeah!"

The man motioned for Wench to draw even closer.

"Oh no. I'm staying right here," insisted Wench. "You want to make a statement?"

The man nodded.

"I can hear you fine," assured Wench.

The man didn't move from the plaza's far wall. Wench wondered how fast he could run.

"Close this place down!" the man ordered.

"Or you'll destroy it?" Wench added.

"Yes!"

"What for?"

"Because!" The man took one step forward, gingerly. "See the movie! Read the book! Buy the record!" He echoed the pop slogan of the media elite. "That's what this country's come to, you know - a spaced out bunch of sensory junkies! Do anything for a fix. Nobody thinks for themselves anymore. No conversation. No exchange of ideas, except your opinion of a goddam TV show! People today ...." The man paused for a breath. "People today spend half their lives sleeping. Half of the other half of their lives working for somebody else. Whatever time remains -" The man jabbed at his skull. "- they pump their brains full of crap! I know a fellow's gotta eat, and sleep, and I'm no prude, either, understand? But the pace ... where we're going ... I mean, we've sold our souls for a goddam ticket to the movies. And it doesn't end there. It doesn't stop when you leave the theatre, turn off the TV, whatever, to get on with your life. Life's become it! Where's the difference, anymore? I tell you, we gotta shut it down!"

"You could pack up and leave," offered Wench.

"I ain't going to another country!" the man roared back. "I'm no Separatist! That's the damn truth! I live here! I remember how things used to be, and you probably remember, too. It wasn't all that bad then. Yeah, we had problems, but we had more ... well, differences, choices, contradictions, bad and good. Everything's so damned homogenized now. Where's the difference, the bad and good, the chaos? That's it! Where's the damn chaos?"

"Progress - ?"

"You call this progress?" The man indicated the madding, popeyed crowd. "Look at the fools. Look at them! They're going to kill each other anyway to get to see this movie. The hell with me, right? Bet they don't even know who Macallister Bicknell was. Ah, I ought to ..." The man made a move to ignite.

"Hold it! Hold it! We go up in smoke and nobody hears your side of the story. They sweep you up. Call you a crank. The show goes on. Right, buddy?" Wench talked very fast.

The man hesitated.

"Easy now ... you got the stage." Wench was conciliatory.

The man said, "we got to suffer, too, sometimes, you know."

"I know."

"Contentment is easy."

"Apparently."

"I know nobody wants to feel bad, worry, cry, get angry, all that." The man visibly relaxed. So did Wench. "But to make a national priority out of avoidance?"

"Don't want to do that," Wench agreed.

A woman's shrill voice cut through like a scythe. "It's BLISS!

The BLISS truck's coming! I see it!"

The man tensed.

Wench raised up both hands, signaling the bomber to remain stationary, not to do anything rash. Futile, risky perhaps, but, what the hell, the effort worked; the man did as Wench indicated and remained still, for the moment.

81

The boiling population of onlookers changed its tone from resentment to anticipation. "Look! Over there!"

Wench saw it, too. Yellow as a brand new sun. The approaching BLISS truck had a glistening cabover styled tractor that was attached to a medium-size trailer. Festooned with colored lights and a twin set of PA horns, the tractor's doors were plainly marked with distinctive black letters that spelled out "BLISS." The trailer itself was ordinary, except for a massive rectangle of gray ceramic, nearly the height and length of the trailer, affixed to the right side with heavy-duty gripper hooks. A PubVid Unit. The trailer was supporting a PubVid Unit. It was instantly recognized by Wench, and the crowd. The occupants of the truck were going to televise something via closed-circuit video; that was the purpose of a PubVid Unit. The truck rolled up to within inches of the lip of the crowd and squealed officially to a halt.

The crowd split asunder.

Both cab doors flapped open simultaneously. Two men in white coveralls and military hats jumped out. They looked sort of like milkmen. Then a woman stepped out. Her red hair was fixed up in a bob; she wore no hat, nor any makeup. She had on loose slacks, a long-sleeved pullover and a leather bomber jacket covered with badges and insignia like a tourist's steamer trunk. She was young. She was in charge. Wench knew who she was. She knew Wench.

"Astin!" she barked. "Here for the show?"

"Philly Magnon," Wench answered. "Which show are you referring to?"

She pointed to the little man who was threatening the mighty Valhalla. "Him. Bottlethorn."

It made sense that the Government would know the man's name.

Two police squad cars pulled up behind the BLISS truck in the meantime (along with a camera unit from a local TV station). A half dozen cops, brandishing nightsticks, leapt onto the scene with face masks and steely determination. The crowd, subdued more by burning curiosity than anything else, receded like a glacier. More space opened up between Wench and the BLISS truck. Wench quickly made his way to the greater protection of the vehicle.

"Go gently, Magnon," Wench warned. "That guy's a breathing hair trigger."

"Bottlethorn?" she scoffed. "We've got a file on him as thick as a hamsteak. I suppose if we pushed him hard enough, he'd do something drastic. But the bastard's harmless!"

"And you think you're going to BLISS him?"

"Betcha my ass against five bucks we do."

Wench didn't want her ass. Magnon was a soldier of fortune, a political mercenary, and always on the wrong side. Wench had locked horns with Magnon before - when she literally helped to steamroll a toxic waste dump over the habitat of an endangered species of mudworm. That the creatures were "slimy bugs" and not "fuzzy, cuddly things that people can keep as pets" summed up her justification and characterized much of her general attitude. Magnon overflowed with cooperation and the rivalrous camaraderie of an athlete. But she was also boastful and proud of her nefarious achievements.

"How?" Wench asked.

She reached into the cab and yanked out a microphone attached to a long, curlicued wire. "Watch!" She winked at Wench. She spit air into the mike a couple of times to check that it was properly working. Facing the man with the bomb, she dared: "go ahead, Bottlethorn, blow it up!"

"You're nuttier than he is!" Wench cried.

She ignored Wench. She continued: "come on, Bottlethorn. I'm giving you a once in a lifetime opportunity to make the TV news with a blaze of glory. You going to hit that button ... or play games with me all night?" She paused. She scratched at her right arm, impatiently, muttering to herself out of mike range, "shithead, you wouldn't blast off if you were a Roman candle on the Fourth of July." Then, amplifying her voice, she addressed the man in question once again. "Okay! Now listen to me! I'm coming over there! I want to talk to you! No tricks! I'm unarmed, understand? I only want to talk!" Magnon replaced the mike, mentioning to Wench: "now comes the iffy part."

"Well, good luck, then," offered Wench.

"He's safe enough," she figured aloud.

"Even if he refuses BLISS?"

"He doesn't have a choice."

"I thought it was voluntary?" Wench heckled.

She shot him a derisive glance. She placed her hands above her head and proceeded to stride out to the man with the bomb. Prudently at first, then with greater confidence. Magnon took a full minute to get to where Bottlethorn stood.

The crowd hardly budged save for some individuals jockeying for a clearer view. This was better than TV. In fact, against the dusk, which was fading to night like houselights dimming, the Valhalla's exterior spots illuminated the scene as if it actually was on a sound stage.

Wench waited. After all, he wasn't here to fill space between a five car pileup and the sports page; he had much bigger fish to fry, fish which were flapping inside the tractor-trailer.

Yet, Wench wondered if this man Bottlethorn hadn't an arguable case for laying the theatre in ruins, after all. What was it the man postulated? About chaos being a necessary ingredient in human existence? Wench appreciated the logic, or illogic, in it. People, unlike machines, are reactive. Bouncing off unexpected occurrences has led to some of the most remarkable achievements: great books, great inventions, great wars, great mistakes. Bad and good, like the man pointed out, are the halves of creativity. Life itself involves the random action of atoms, molecules, enzymes; sometimes you get heroes, other times you get two-headed snakes. The direct opposite of chaos is order, and where does that lead? To simplicity, where we've been heading for decades. That tired old proverb, "the simpler the life, the happier the soul," has become an anthem! Do we lose to happiness the fuel of creativity, individuality, and the ability to tread the narrow path from banality to brilliance? That does seem to be what people prefer. Maybe, for their own good, they should be handed one of their cherished pleasure domes as rubble, broken metal and twisted glass.

We've got order and contentment, the "good of the people," BLISS. But what begets chaos?

Wench had no time to ponder the answer when loud cheering went up like reverse rain. Magnon, to her credit a master at what she was paid to do, had convinced Bottlethorn to give up the offensive and lay down his weapon. The explosive device, abandoned, rested against the pavement, near the coming attractions. Magnon and Bottlethorn, arm in arm, walked with deliberate solemnity toward the waiting BLISS truck. They resembled a newlywed couple marching down the aisle.

The men in white grabbed the dejected Bottlethorn and ushered him unceremoniously into the trailer.

"Congratulations," Wench said to Magnon. "How'd you do it?"

Magnon reached into her jacket pocket for a pack of coughers, shook one out, lit up, and explained through the corner of her mouth. "Bastard didn't have a choice. I told you. Look. If he blew himself to bits, well, he'd be another ex-screwball which -" she lowered her voice and thumbed at the crowd "- would please those geese no end." She puffed and went on. "The theatre'd be back in biz tomorrow and the movie ... nothing like a little blood and guts to spice up profits!" She took another drag. "He could go to jail. But we ain't talking about a measly couple weeks in a local lock-up. We mean heavy time in Oklahoma Federal. Personally, I'd rather snuff it than draw Okie." She sucked in a deep lungful of smoke, exhaled slowly. "Then there's BLISS. If he goes in for treatment, he's a free man tonight. Hell -" she indicated the

PubVid "- we're going to do it here and now and flash it up on the big screen! You think that crowd wouldn't go ape shit if he strutted out like a freaking man from Mars? They're chomping at the bit to get BLISSed out themselves!"

"Odd coming from you," Wench prompted.

Magnon flipped the butt away and hoisted herself up into the truck. "What should I say? It works. If you want it, you get it. If you don't, you don't. This guy didn't have a choice. I told you. He was doomed from the start. His convictions did him in."

"I'm glad I didn't bet."

"Me too," she teased, "I might have tried to lose. Coming up?" She extended a hand.

"What do you think?" Wench grabbed her hand.

"I think they ought to revoke that damned 'A' card of yours."

"Freedom of the press," Wench insisted as he partly leaped and was partly lifted into the trailer of the yellow BLISS truck.

Chapter 8

THE interior of the trailer, spacious, brightly lit, like a little room on wheels, coincided with what Wench expected to find. The pieced-together, experimental laboratory furnishings did not. Dead center, the focus of several lights and cameras feeding the PubVid inputs, was a leather recliner chair, a good one, a comfortable one. Bottlethorn was sitting in it. He wasn't strapped down or anything like that. As he was the focus of attention, he could have passed for some sort of monarch. But as he was white-knuckling the arms of the chair and bore an exaggerated grimace of trepidation, he would be a very frightened monarch. Behind the chair, a modular wall of polished high-tech smiled: TVs for eyes, a bank of dipole switches for a nose, and a keyboard for a toothy mouth. Other devices Wench could only guess as to their purposes: altogether out of 1950 sci-fi B-picture country!

"War surplus?" Wench kidded.

"Cost cutting," Magnon answered, not amused. "This isn't our standard installation, you know."

She nodded. Her assistants began. One of them took a hypodermic needle from the medical stores and injected Bottlethorn. "THC," Magnon explained, "to calm him. Normally, unnecessary, but this guy's getting staticky. By the way -" she pointed to a TV camera "- we're going on the air now. We'll be using a pre-recorded voice over for a time. You won't be heard ... but you will be seen."

"I'll try not to embarrass myself," promised Wench.

After the narcotic melted his tension, Bottlethorn was plugged up. First, one of the technicians fished into the medical stores for a pair of glossy rubber earstops and blocked up Bottlethorn's hearing. Then they masked Bottlethorn's eyes with oversized goggles that were not intended to improve vision. Most bizarre was the soft, gray banana-like instrument that was shoved into Bottlethorn's mouth an inch or two up to a point where it met a chin cup.

"That looks uncomfortable," Wench commented.

"On the contrary," Magnon smirked, "housewives will love it."

An air tube was stuck into Bottlethorn's nose.

"Oxygen. Don't want him to choke."

Piebald wires sprouting from these devices were sorted and plugged into appropriate jacks on the master control. Dials got dialed, levels checked and switches switched. Wench detected a mild vibration.

Then a cubical contraption, a square diving helmet without a faceplate seemed an apt description, was lowered from the ceiling. It glowed. It looked heavy, but its weight was counterbalanced by a hydraulic arm. It fit snugly over Bottlethorn's head down to the bridge of his nose. The sides of the cube, pristine, offered no hint of purpose except for an LCD indicator rapidly sequencing down from 830.227 ... 830.226 ... 830.225 ... 830.224 .... "That's it!" Magnon declared. "That's it?" "He'll sleep for a few minutes and then be as good as new.

Better, in his case." "Care to fill me in on the tech specs?" asked Wench. "Sure. I can tell you. But you can't print 'em." "What's the deal?"

"The deal," Magnon stressed, "is with the Rooskies. Moscow wants BLISS bad, and they're willing to put up lots of roubles to get it. So ... until the contract is inked, we can't risk any leaks. Savvy?"

Outside, the PubVid blazed the full color image of Bottlethorn snoozing like a contented babe even with so many machines clinging to his head. In close up, this picture, this picture only, was given to the audience. The recorded narrative droned on about painlessness, similarity to an after dinner nap, sensory saturation. The crowd crackled in appreciation.

Minutes earlier, a squad of cops had collected the homemade bomb that Bottlethorn discarded. They took it away in a reinforced van. The Valhalla Theatre subsequently opened its doors to admit patrons to the evening show. Ironically, nobody noticed, or cared. All eyes were fixed on the PubVid.

Inside the trailer, the vibration ceased. Wench heard an electric pop and saw a green light wink up on the monitor. He'd been pumping Magnon, best he could; the talking stopped. One technician made minor adjustments, hummed a tune, and removed the apparatus from Bottlethorn. The other technician slapped Bottlethorn's cheek the way an obstetrician slaps a newborn's bottom; "rise and shine," he intoned.

"You're kidding?" remarked Wench.

Magnon seemed pleased with herself. "what did you expect? Metamorphosis? He'll be right as rain, now." She added as an afterthought: "want to be next?"

"After you."

"I've already tried it," Magnon confessed. "Several times.

But it seems I'm immune."

"Immune?" This was intriguing.

"Yeah. Believe it or not." She dismissed the subject. "They'll solve it in no time, I'm sure. A minor snag." She cocked her head at Bottlethorn, who was stirring. "Check out our prize patient."

The man rubbed him arms, jumped from the recliner, stretched, yawned, examined himself as though trying on a new suit, and announced, "why, I feel so refreshed!"

A victorious cheer broke from the outside crowd like the home team had won the game on a grand slam hit in the bottom of the ninth inning. The recorded narration had ended. The audio feed was now live.

Magnon signaled this fact to Wench. Too bad. Wench would have liked to press her further on the immunity issue, but lack of privacy now made that both imprudent and illegal. Instead, Wench asked Bottlethorn, "do you remember threatening to destroy the theatre?"

The man responded, gladly. "I know you. You're the fellow from the newspaper who stopped me from doing such a terrible thing! Let me thank you." He shook Wench's hand with extra vigor. "I must have been in quite a state to consider a heinous crime like that. You're a brave friend. And -" he spoke to the others in the trailer "- you are all brave, fine people, too!"

"What of the movie?"

"The movie?" Bottlethorn frowned. "No. No. I don't care to see it. Not now, anyway. But that's my business, isn't it? I mean, if others wish to enjoy it, why shouldn't they?" He became apologetic. "I believe I failed to understand that I have no right to dictate more than anybody else. That's where I went wrong, wasn't it?"

Magnon concurred most assuredly.

Bottlethorn sighed as though cleansed from sin.

In his mind, Wench made a wry sign of the cross. He probed deeper. "You were quite adamant about a need for chaos."

"Was I?" The man was puzzled. "Well, I don't imagine I'd recall everything I said, considering. But that's an interesting notion. On the other hand, order gives us irrevocable laws with which we can extrapolate all things, doesn't it? The entire scientific method is based upon order. And is not order more egalitarian? I shall have to think upon it, however. It is certainly worth my time." He rubbed his hands together. "My, but I'm hungry!"

Magnon told him, "we're not holding you."

"I can go?"

"Of course."

"No papers to sign? Affidavits?"

Magnon made a broad gesture, indicating the open rear of the trailer. Like a guest excusing himself early from a cocktail party, the man named Bottlethorn quietly thanked everyone again for their help, shook more hands, bid Wench to visit him if ever the chance arose, and was helped down to the sidewalk. In a few minutes, after humbly acknowledging the accolades from the outside crowd, Bottlethorn hailed a taxi and was swallowed up by the world.

Wench was dumbfounded.

Magnon, taking a seat in the leather recliner, folding her arms against her chest, triumphantly asked Wench: "can we give you a lift back to your office?"

Chapter 9

WENCH brooded for a long time in front of the blank slate monitor of his comm interface. Like a conjurer, he gradually filled the void with characters, his fingers dancing over the keyboard in mystic ritual.

Wench wrote:

There's a brand new feeling pervading the streets and homes of Bigapolis these days. The feeling is rapidly expanding, like a parallel universe. The feeling is reflected as a kind of happy-go-lucky complacency upon the faces of citizens lining up to withdraw money from vending banks, check out their groceries, get into movie theaters. The feeling is responsible for turning traffic jams, once conflagrations of temper and anxiety, into gentle social gatherings. The feeling is especially profound in the family.

The feeling is BLISS.

Biopsychic Lavation for Intensified Stimulation of the Superego. The Yaramon Administration's acclaimed miracle of the decade.

The BLISS Project, hardly launched, is already being hailed as a "high water mark for mankind in this century." BLISS is being compared with the Industrial Revolution of the late 1700s and the Religious Revival of a decade ago. BLISS is certainly popular beyond measure.

In the first days of BLISS, as the yellow trucks swept across the land, statistics seemed to indicate a downward trend in overall crime. Church attendance went up. Furthermore, profits at the box office following the release of major motion pictures, always a reliable indicator of the public welfare, hit unprecedented highs. Quick food restaurants reported they were never busier. This latter development will likely impact positively upon the teen-age unemployment rate, it is believed.

The only question appears to be why the public has embraced BLISS to the extent that it has. Parenthetically, how long will the romance last?

The Yaramon Administration's chief spokesman for the BLISS Project, Dr. Xavier Australia, has likened BLISS to a windshield wiper. He suggests that most people want to see where they are going; in the same manner, they seek direct answers to the major concerns that plague modern day existence. "Society is utterly complicated," Dr. Australia points out. "Of course, we would all like to have the blueprints to this world at our fingertips. But, of the intricately meshed webbing of science, politics, economics, religion and other pursuits around us, it is quite impossible for an individual to know it all. BLISS doesn't reveal; it clarifies. Like removing bugs, scale and dirt from glass, BLISS wipes the mind free of stains."

At first there was a great deal of concern on the part of the Government as to whether or not BLISS would be accepted at all. "Resistance was admittedly high. But that was only because nobody wanted to be first on the block to get something as truly revolutionary as BLISS," Dr. Australia explains. "In time, as people began to see marked improvements in their friends and neighbors, the initial reluctance waned." Indeed, the Government had trouble keeping up with demand. "Right now we are proceeding with a ratio of only one outright avoidance for every 8.7 people who want BLISS," concludes Australia. "This is tremendously satisfying for us, considering that BLISS is, I stress, completely voluntary."

The Government has refused to make public the details concerning the origins and specifications of BLISS, citing "national security." However, former Administration scientists are more open and, at least, more willing to speculate. What BLISS achieves, these authorities contend, is a naturally present, though latent, psychic state within every human brain - somewhat like ESP or the ability to easily memorize huge tracts of printed material. BLISS simply frees the mind from specific acquired inhibitions. In this sense, BLISS adherents are quick to add, the technique in no way manipulates or alters a person's consciousness; BLISS is neither additive nor subtractive.

Further supportive evidence to such claims is spotty and unqualified. Nonetheless, all one need do is take a short walk through any neighborhood in Bigapolis to appreciate, first hand, the obvious consequences of the Government's BLISS Project.

Several case histories, recently made available to the *Daily Parade*, speak for themselves.

Volmer Grybycek, 47-years-old, has been a line maintenance chief with the Bombs Away Munitions Company for the past ten years. His wife, also employed, is a magazine solicitor. The two had been suffering from severe nonorganic depression, the onset of symptoms which coincided with the marriage of their daughter, an only child, to a successful dog food manufacturer. Mrs. Grybycek was largely able to be helped through counseling; Volmer's condition steadily worsened.

In fact, although the wedding had been planned well in advance, even to the point that the Grybyceks lavished a $15,000 reception upon their daughter, after the festivities Volmer Grybycek fell into a 24-hour catatonic withdrawal. He recovered quickly, and even appeared to be improving as the days passed. But, his wife says: "I soon noticed that Volmer was refusing to eat. He lost weight. He began neglecting his job, and showed no interest at all in TV, mowing the lawn, or trimming the hedges. Those hedges had always been his pride and joy!" Volmer Grybycek spent hours moping around his daughter's empty bedroom, crying, and falling asleep on the bed with articles of his daughter's clothing clutched tightly in his arms. At the lowest point in Grybycek's life, he attempted suicide by inhaling carpet cleaner/deodorizer. Fortunately, the chemicals were non-toxic, and Grybycek got only a bad headache. "I was at my wits end," adds his wife.

It was here when BLISS arrived in the Grybyceks' lives. "I was thoroughly amazed at how quick and easy the entire procedure was," Mrs. Grybycek explains. "In no time at all we were on our feet and feeling grand. Why, Volmer, by evening, realized he hadn't lost a daughter but gained a son!"

After one week of BLISS, Volmer Grybycek was going bowling regularly with his daughter and son-in-law. Grybycek enjoys his job much more now and, in fact, is in line for a promotion. He is active in local politics and church activities, recently chairing a fund-raising drive to bring clothing and television to Bornean river people. The Grybyceks also try to go out once a week. They've purchased a state-of-the-art microwave kitchen range, and they earn extra income by renting out their daughter's room to a divinity student. "Life is peachy," admits Grybycek, "thanks to BLISS."

The Grybycek story is not a typical one. Government spokesmen are quick to caution that BLISS is not a curative procedure, and that between 70 and 80 percent of all BLISS treatments achieve far less dramatic results.

More characteristic of the ordinary BLISS subject is Bunni Sue Sartre, 31, a computer administrator with General Hospital Financial Corp. Bunni Sartre faces the same problems the majority of today's upwardly mobile young women do: balancing a career with desires for fulfillment as a wife and mother. The pressures are especially strong in Sartre's case. "Because I am not married," she explains, "my parents are constantly introducing me to eligible orthodontists." Bunni Sartre's life, prior to BLISS, was an anxiety-ridden shuttle from work, to the health and racquet club, to disappointing dates, back to work, and around again. "I tried all sorts of things from yoga, to Dianetics, to crossword puzzles, but nothing offered me answers," she says. "My knowledge of dentistry improved and that was all."

Sartre describes what she felt to be the very nadir of her life. "I gained six pounds!" This led to increased mental anguish which manifested itself as an outbreak of herpes sores on Sartre's legs, arms and face. She reports becoming increasingly introverted and turning to renegade religions for salvation. "I became emotionally involved with an Eastern Flagellant," Sartre continues. "He put me on a strict boiled spinach diet that, oddly enough, retarded the spread of the herpes but left me quite enervated." As a result, Sartre cut her exercise classes and frequently dropped off to sleep at night without having sex. The latter particularly bothered Sartre but, she relates, delighted her boyfriend who considered screwing, eating and other physical acts to be "bad karma."

Sartre was an ideal candidate for BLISS. At first reluctant - "I though you could catch strange diseases from the equipment" - she quickly changed her mind when she noticed the unmistakable glow of well-being on the faces of her girlfriends who'd gotten BLISS. "It was like they were pregnant without being pregnant!" Sartre exclaims.

After treatment, Sartre's own outlook, she describes, lifted like morning after a shift in the wind has blown away the smog. "BLISS lets me see that life is really what you make of it. After all, we are the ones in the driver's seat, aren't we?" Bunni Sartre concentrates on the positive aspects of her life, which objectively hasn't altered too much. "It's how you view things that makes them ultimately satisfying," she points out. Her old boyfriend has entered a monastery. She is currently dating a neurosurgeon whom she regards, with a twinkle in her eye, as a "possible Mr. Right."

BLISS, despite the overwhelming enthusiasm for it across the country, is not without its detractors, however.

Certain high level sources within the scientific community warn that we have not had time to study the effects of BLISS over the long term. These scientists explain that while initially the effects of BLISS might seem miraculous, we could very likely be implanting time bombs within our citizenry, bombs that could go off with disastrous results some five, ten, or even twenty years from now.

Government proponents counter these ominous claims as simply more "end is nigh" jargon from obvious and highly vocal anti-Administrative groups such as the United Separatists, Deviate Radicals and other extremists. According to Dr. Australia: "with new technology, computer projections and biospheric modeling, it is no more necessary to conduct years of experimentation to determine long term medical effects than it is to extensively road test new automotive designs." Biospheric modeling, another Australia brainchild, has taken its own share of the heat lately for its controversial use of rhesus monkeys.

One recent development that is not so easily dusted under the rug is the incidence of immunity. This is an altogether new anomaly, unforseen and potentially damaging to the success of the BLISS project. Few in numbers overall, individuals have been showing up upon whom BLISS treatments simply do not have any effect. The phenomenon is too recent to speculate upon; investigations are now only underway; there is, as a result, no definitive explanation as to why certain people are unadapted to BLISS conversion. "Viral blocking" has been postulated widely as a theory, however; along this avenue, Government scientists are doggedly experimenting, and "preliminary results are most encouraging," say the experts. In the meantime, "I do not see immunity being significant throughout the population," Dr. Australia contends. "It should not hamper the Project in any respect."

The Yaramon Administration has further urged people not to become unduly worried over immunity; the chances of it showing up in an individual are extremely small. Those who are subsequently discovered to be immune have a variety of options until the problem is eliminated. "Immunes" may even freely elect emigration to Alabama.

Immunity, however, may well be a dart thrown at a non-existent target in a lightless room. In an exclusive statement made to this newspaper, Presidential Medal of Freedom winner Gini McReedy of the Yabnir Institute has suggested that no one may actually be immune to BLISS. "Rather," she points out, "susceptibility to the treatment may require a deeply imbedded subconscious combination of desires: that of fitting in with one's peer group; eagerness to conform; a primarily agreeable nature; and, most of all, an inherent yearning for a simpler and less confusing lifestyle." McReedy goes on to state that parameters favoring BLISS may be psychologically rooted within the individual. "The person who thinks he or she fits the BLISS-positive description may, beneath those layers of acceptable social behavior, really be BLISS-negative and will therefore not take to the procedure. The contrary is also valid," contends McReedy.

Government authorities have declined comment on McReedy's hypothesis. Reached by telephone, the Institution for BLISS Management would only issue its official reaction: "we do not choose to give opinions concerning unsupported speculation."

Whatever the future of BLISS may be, one thing is clear. Controversy, debate and sociological divisions engendered by the BLISS Project have only begun to surface. There's an iceberg lurking around somewhere; we've seen the tip.

***

Astin Wench skipped several spaces and hit the number (or pound) symbol several times, indicating the end of his story. It was customary to tagline your work with your last name and "askie" code, but Wench was not in a particularly customary mood.

Chapter 10

INTERRUPTING him, Wench's telephone chirped repeatedly like a demanding crow. Indicator lights showed the call was coming through the video circuits, so Wench punched VTP and routed the signal onto his display terminal - an extra feature with this model that made his work easier. Lowia's face flashed onboard, in black-and-white. "Astin?" she asked. Although there was no way Lowia could afford a video channel with her telephone service, and no pressing demand existed for her to have the luxury, Wench wanted it for her. Using his not unsubstantial influence, he pulled the right wires and secured her a video telephone.

"What's up, hon?"

"You okay?" She noticed his miffed expression.

"Fine. This BLISS thing's riling me is all."

"That's why I called. The truck's up the street ."

"Forget it!" Wench stiffened.

"No! You don't order me ... " She also bristled.

"I'm sorry."

"You're not being fair. We talked about how my analysis wasn't having much effect. If I continue like this, I'm going to crack up or kill myself between these damn pills and the coughers. Astin, honey, I don't see the harm in at least giving it a try. Maybe BLISS can help me. You know Beverli down the block? She got it last night. I spoke to her a little while ago and, honestly, Astin, she isn't any cabbage! I swear!"

Wench squirmed. Lowia stressed the point that stuck in his belly all morning like an undigested clove of garlic. Early reports were indicating, contrary to all the previous authoritative finger-wagging, BLISS did not produce automatons. Hell, Wench only now finished his own virtual goddam written endorsement of the procedure! However, that proverbial nose-for-news gremlin within him was nagging away at Wench's plumbing, too: something ain't right. He had no answer for Lowia.

"Shit!"

"You shouldn't use language like that on video," cajoled Lowia, softening, smiling, cheering him marginally.

"Look," he compromised, "you've gone this long without BLISS. Let's give it a few more days, okay? I need more time to look into it. If I can't come up with solid counter indications by the weekend, well, we'll consider it. But please give me more time."

She seemed satisfied. She sighed. "Okay," she groaned in agreement. "See you later?"

"Later, honey. Love you."

"Me too!"

Lowia's picture popped out. The display terminal presented a blank face to Wench, the little blinking cursor mutely informing him that the article he'd written had been translated into electronic bits and sent, simultaneously, downstairs to the composing room and across the hall to the Managing Editor's office. It was even now being prepared for the evening edition. It was a good story. Wench knew it was a good story.

Chapter 11

THE yellow truck practically blocked the road. The way it cavalierly nosed against the curb in front of Lowia's apartment house, allowing enough room for another car to squeeze past and no more, gave the impression that it was really something special. To most people, the BLISS truck was special.

Not to Wench.

Seeing the lemon-colored vehicle with BLISS painted on its sides in bold, black letters, he cursed under his breath and doubled his pace. Lowia promised she wouldn't do anything rash before consulting with him! Easy does it. There were, he rationalized, other tenants in the building.

He scaled the three exterior cement stairs in a single bound, reaching the front door that opened to a roomy inner hallway accessing the several individual apartments. This was where children often parked their bicycles and mothers their baby carriages. As Wench burst in, he nearly knocked down one of the two clad-in-white-uniform, squeaky clean, crew-cut BLISS technicians who were on their way out. They carried with them their leather equipment bags and document cases.

"Whoa, there, pardner," one tech said like he'd been roping dogies all his life.

"Out of my way," Wench groused.

"Just doin' my job," replied the tech. "Maybe we oughta have a look at your head why we're still here. That's some attitude you're carrying around."

"Aw, let him be," the second tech drawled.

The front door banged shut behind the BLISS technicians as they exited, jabbering. This left only the woman who occupied the apartment adjacent to Lowia's, a middle-aged, attractive black woman, standing halfway in and halfway out of the hallway, arms crossed on her bosom, leaning on her own open front door, facing Wench. Evidently it was her premises from whence the two technicians had departed.

"Don't you worry, Mr. Wench," she assured loudly. "Your lady friend is going to be fine, if you ask me."

Wench froze. "They treated her?"

"Lucky woman," the other nodded her head in agreement.

"Lucky?"

The black woman continued. "She took like a charm. Ain't going to have any more trouble, I tell you. Life of Riley. Not like me. Those boys told me I was one of them immunes, and they even tried twice to give me the treatment. But no way I'm going to see a better world while I'm alive. It ain't fair, I tell you. I don't know what I'm going to do, now. It ain't fair for me to be left behind with an unimproved brain. Figure maybe I ought to go down to Alabama with them other immunes and folks who don't want the BLISS treatment. My sister's in Alabama; she moved there last week. I could stay with her for a while. What do you say, Mr. Wench? Think I ought to go down to Alabama?"

Wench had to laugh. "You're immune? You're bitching because you're immune?" Flabbergasted, he added: "go anywhere you like. Go to Alabama. For chrissake, go to Venezuela!"

"Why should I go there?" The black woman sighed. "They ain't even got BLISS in Venezuela .... I don't know." She walked back into her own apartment and closed the door quietly.

Wench did not know what to expect next.

Usually he knocked and stood outside Lowia's apartment, politely waiting until she let him in. It was a habit, formed when he was dating her, that stuck, regardless of her many mild admonishments to him otherwise since they had become a, well, couple. Now he used his keycard.

The door was unlocked anyway.

"Daddy's home!" Lowia singsonged brightly, as Wench practically fell into the room.

She was sitting on a plain wooden chair, the television flickering before her like an electronic fireplace, her little daughter cradled in her lap. Lowia had on brand new jeans, pink sneakers, and a spiffy purple blouse that Wench didn't remember she owned. He short-cropped hair, blow-dried, was puffed out to twice its normal thickness. With only a hint of lipstick, glinting silver earrings and clear, happy eyes, Lowia looked terrific. The baby, too, seemed more cherubic.

"Say hello to Daddy," Lowia directed.

"Hi, Daddy!" the baby squealed.

For quite obvious reasons the little girl had some time ago concluded that Wench was "Daddy." Although this wasn't the biological fact, Wench and Lowia naturally assumed, sooner or later, it would become a legal fact: they let the child have her way, even encouraged her.

"Are you two all right?" he asked.

"Why shouldn't we be?"

Wench gestured toward the outside door. "The BLISS truck. It was here. Your neighbor told me you got it."

"Well, we did!"

"We?"

"Children can get BLISS, too ..." Lowia said, then tauntingly, "or weren't you aware of that, mister science writer?"

"And?"

"And you are wrong!" she crowed. Gently, she lowered her baby to the floor. She rose from the chair. The toddler crawled off to play.

The TV announcer was in a dither about the much touted Christian Weight Loss Diet (pray pounds away!) which promised an anorexic figure in weeks without harmful side effects. When heard the familiar jingly accompaniment. He noticed that Lowia seemed positively glowing with high-fiber, polyunsaturated, rich in vitamins good health herself - sensibly fuller figured, though. Could Wench have been mistaken concerning BLISS?

"You mean you don't feel any different?"

"Of course I feel different," Lowia chided. "Better than I've felt in months." She squirmed up against Wench, draping one arm around his neck, adding: "feel better this way, too." She pecked him on the mouth, illustrating her meaning pointedly. Then she danced away like a pixie. "Look" she changed the subject, showed him an empty ashtray. "No butts. Haven't had a cougher in hours. And you know something else? I don't want one."

"Will it last?" Wench injected doubt.

Lowia ignored the remark. She trotted into the small bathroom, opened the medicine cabinet, and

108

withdrew a plastic vial of tranquilizers. With theatrical emphasis, she undid the childproof top and let the handful of ruddy capsules tumble into the sink. "Don't need these, either," she pronounced.

Wench, caught in the whirlwind, went to her. Almost out of a sense of reward, or perhaps delight, their lips met. She kissed him feverishly, clinging to him, and it seemed to Wench as though she was drawing energy from him: an enjoyable embrace, by all means, yet very much one-sided.

"You want a bite?" she asked.

Wench licked his teeth and pretended to go for her ear. She pushed him off.

"Something to eat ... from the kitchen," she giggled.

"That's housewifely of you."

Lowia danced away to whip up a snack for him. Wench wandered back to the living room where the TV monitor continued to cast a multi-colored incandescence. She was having a better time than he was.

Across the video screen, a cartoon chicken paraded, dressed like Uncle Sam, to a pop rock background beat. Mixed voices chorused patriotically:

Lickity Chicken is A-number-one.
Naturally bred for each daughter and son!
We serve with pride:
Nuggets, burgers and fried.
So c'mon in and thrive at the red, white and blue!

"We should try that one day," Lowia called out, referring to the commercial. "I hear it's supposed to be quite good."

109

"Lickity Chicken?" The name alone implied culinary doom. Wench expected no response, and got none. An uneasy premonition, translated as his nose for news, bothered him, like two frames of a stereo image not properly aligned.

No, BLISS certainly hadn't affected Lowia the way Wench envisioned, with trepidation, it might. One half of him groped in an unlit dungeon, among the spiders and dust, pawing frantically around for the keycard to the gate and release. Another half of him, like a little boy praying for the safe return of a lost pet, hoped for evidence that the Yaramon Administration's heart was in the right place. Clutching straws for peace of mind? At least let BLISS not be fully potent.

Anxieties quelled, later, as Wench and Lowia shared a meal, laughing, reveling in a family setting. And later still, after they both tucked their daughter into bed, bidding the child good night, they watched some TV. Lowia wanted to see *Cheri Goes to Church, Part II* that was being aired; a light entertainment was the operative word. Wench condescended.

Comfortable, they went to bed. Lowia wanted sex.

She propped herself upright, rump on a pillow, back against the headboard, with her delicious legs, knees up, alluringly displayed. She wore only a yellow tee-shirt that came down to her waist. Her femininity was, thus, teasingly revealed. If she were a flower, the bees would know precisely where to home. At the same time, Wench, in briefs, sat on the edge of the bed. He was rapidly becoming uncomfortable in his garment - pleasantly so. He

110

reached over to remove his girlfriend's thin covering.

She stopped him. "Not yet," she insisted softly.

He tried to take off his shorts but Lowia quickly stopped him again, scolding coyly, "that's for me to do ... in my own sweet time."

"What then?" Wench asked.

"Don't rush it, honey." This was to be her show.

She flopped back down on the bed, inviting Wench to merge. He did. Lowia, stretched out completely beneath Wench in what Wench often referred to as "a perfect fit," purred and parted her legs ever so slightly. She parted her mouth, letting him explore with his tongue. Wench was on target at both locations, and he wiggled against her, a fishy wiggle: she enjoyed it immeasurably.

She raised her arms, interrupting the long kiss, and cooed, "you can unwrap me now."

Wench eagerly obliged, shucking the thin cotton cloth from her body in a single, swift motion. Lowia was not large-breasted, but each mound, the size of a scoop of ice cream, was perfectly formed and topped with an elegant nipple. Wench liked to stare at them in wonderment.

"Do me!" Lowia ordered.

"No kidding." With artistry, Wench placed the tip of his tongue against her right ear, tracing a line to her lobe which he then lovingly toyed with until she got goose bumps all over her neck. He ran his tongue down to her shoulder, followed the path of her pectoral muscle, and halted where the flesh of her breast began to rise. In a deliberately paced spiral, Wench's tongue worked 'round and 'round Lowia's breast, ascending, wending its way to the

111

roseate summit. Lowia arched her back to facilitate the climb, sighing with each circuit.

In a kiss, Wench took the nipple. He laved it, suckled it, blew a little warm air over it, and she whined. Already, elsewhere, Lowia was enlarging, moistening, preparing ....

"Having a good time?" Wench whispered.

"Glad you are here," she breathed.

Wench did magic to her. Time became irrelevant. Wench played a symphony with the folds and curves and angles of her well-tempered body. Movement followed movement as the music swelled deep within her. It was like chords, arpeggios, crescendos of sensuality bursting from her every inch. Wench was in glory as the composer of her ecstasy. She was glory incarnate. In fact she had already climaxed, once, a small orgasm but certain proof that both of them, this time, would touch the stars.

Gently, she urged him pause.

Wench raised his head and met her imploring stare. Like mind reading, it took no words from her, hardly a gesture, for him to realize she was calling attention to his own ready instrument, still wrapped up. He reached down to release the stallion from the stall.

"No, silly," she teased. She wrestled him over on his back. Then she straddled him, pinning him down by the shoulders. "My turn."

Lowia kissed him full on the mouth. Using her lips and tongue, she attempted to work her way down his body in much the same fashion that Wench had inflamed her. But Lowia's efforts were

112

endearingly impatient. She was face to face with his BVD'S in only three kisses.

"Oh my!" Lowia remarked.

Taking the waistband between her fingers and thumbs, Lowia delicately pulled the garment out and away from Wench's full-blooming manhood (so as not to hurt him). She yanked the shorts quickly down his legs, off, threw them aside. Wench, unencumbered, presented himself at attention to Lowia. She was not unappreciative.

She caressed his inner thighs, purposely avoiding contact with his genitals. It drove Wench mad; he loved it. Slowly, she petted him, in smooth arcs from one thigh up and across his stomach to the other thigh, back and forth, this time titillating Wench's sex. He pulsed. He parted his legs farther, begging her to take him. She held her hand beneath his scrotum, fondling him there for a while, then ran her fingers along the measure of his stiffened shaft and lovingly manipulated its crown. She kissed it.

Wench closed his eyes, awash in an erotic ocean, waiting ....

"Fuck me." She shattered his pleasure. Flinging herself on top of him, she commanded, "fuck me!"

"What?"

"Now!" She insisted, whorishly positioning herself within penetration range, practically plugging into him.

"Fuck me," she fervently repeated a third time.

She had to be teasing. "More," Wench whined like a little boy who wasn't ready to put away his toys.

Lowia nibbled on his ear, wiggling aggressively, anxiously. "I can't wait," she gasped, mauling him, bouncing her little ass up and down. "I'm gonna bust!"

Wench surrendered. Was there something of an aphrodisiac in BLISS? Wench pondered for the fleetest of moments. She had aroused him to a much higher level than he realized. So no more messing around. He'd best get on with the mating biz or, what with her gyrating the way she was, Old Faithful was liable to erupt anyway.

The two quickly switched positions: Wench, on top, adjusted himself with his hands beneath the small of Lowia's back in the manner she preferred; Lowia hooked her heels to his legs. He connected in a wink.

And with biological bliss, anyway, Wench planted his seed within Lowia Lilli. The two lovers made a single, blazing orgasm. Wench had no idea how long, locked together, they rocketed through the universe. This was, however, a trip to write home about.

Back on earth, Lowia was pleading. "Make me come again."

"Already?"

"What's wrong with that?"

"Nothing," he agreed, adding, "if you prime the pump."

"You're plenty primed," she said. "I can feel you."

"You know what I mean," Wench pouted.

She was not about to delight his body with the varying pleasures he lusted after. She became unfamiliarly selfish, with a stranglehold on him, insisting, "no. Fuck me again. I want to come again. You owe me."

This bothered Wench. But not much. He was still hard. And was Lowia correct? All those evenings that she let him spend his passion in her, so many ways, out of love. Wasn't that love? Was this love?

Wench held Lowia firmly and resumed churning within her. He thought only of her, concentrating upon what she desired of him and, slowly, surely, carried her to another breath-taking climax. But this time he did not share her joy. That was okay, too.

The bodies separated. Lowia rolled over onto her stomach and murmured, "thank you, lover," before drifting into semi-consciousness and the satisfied sleep of the spent.

Wench could not rest. He stared at the ceiling for a very long time. Silly. Any man's ego would puff to the size of a dirigible as a result of getting a woman off the way he had, and more than once to boot. Still, something didn't click ....

Lowia breathed quite heavily now. Wench got out of bed and, without turning on any lights, felt around for his shorts. Quietly, he dressed, except for his shoes. Carrying them, Wench walked from the master bedroom into the living room.

The clock said two a.m. After all their lovemaking, Wench assumed it was closer to dawn. But the clock said two a.m. The late, late newsgossip was beginning on Channel 7, so Wench waved on the television monitor, keeping the volume very low in order not to disturb his girlfriend or her child.

Nearly exhausted, he dropped into the fat recliner.

115

The TV lit up, imaging a large blue-and-white tour bus revving and fuming in front of Bigapolis Terminal. A line of people, like a centipede trying to work its way through a tiny hole in a wall, were boarding the bus. Some of the passengers carried overnight cases; others toted shopping bags. Wench noticed that a disproportionately large number of people on line where of minority groups. The destination window on the bus revealed: ALABAMA. The picture had been "recorded earlier," according to a subtitle, and at the left of the screen, Wench saw and heard a perky brunette TV correspondent deliver the facts.

" ... as another busload of emigrants prepares for their long journey to Alabama. Since the ratification, by majority vote, of President Yaramon's insightful proposition, establishing an independent United Separatist state, hundreds of citizens have been departing from this very spot day and night. There appears to be quite a number of them. The emigrants are all men and women whom, it must be pointed out, have either been unable to appreciate, are sadly immune to, or remain opposed to the Government's BLISS Project. Although none of these emigrants have agreed to speak to us on camera, we do understand that they believe their lives will become more satisfying once they are settled in their new homes. For their sakes, we certainly hope so. Recent legislation, you will recall, brands each and every one of these people an outlaw, persona non grata, the minute they cross the Alabama border. Any unauthorized return to this country is, of course, a criminal act, punishable by a $50,000 fine or up to 15 years in jail. I know I am

116

speaking for us all when I wish these hardy souls a bon voyage.

This is Mandi Pottawattamie reporting for Channel 7 newsgossip."

Wench never cared too much for "boob-tube journalism" nor the chorus line correspondents who practiced it. The bulk of TV news, he judged, bore little difference from the game shows that occupied the lion's share of broadcast time. It was look and see what's behind curtain number three: a fully appointed camper/trailer; a six-alarm apartment fire; another war? The audiences gasped and applauded. Reality and contrivance blurred into an indistinguishable middle ground.

He folded his arms against his chest in tacit disgruntlement. But he wasn't about to book passage on the next charter out of town. The Lickity Chicken commercial was coming on again. Wench waved off the TV. He put on his shoes and quietly left Lowia's apartment, locking the door behind him, pocketing the keycard, making his way down the stairs to the street outside. The most disconcerting thing was, somehow he knew, Lowia would not be upset when she awoke in the morning to find him gone.

Chapter 12

THE sidewalk forked in two directions: to the local bus stop on the corner; and up a steep incline to a lonely hilltop overlooking a valley. Because Wench needed to think, he did not go to the bus stop.

The hilltop would serve as it had done frequently, and Wench headed for it. The cool night invigorated him. He soon reached the spot where the pavement melted into the grass, and he sat down. He inhaled the chilled air, looking around, assuring himself that he was, no surprise, alone.

A yellow BLISS truck stood parked for the night in a driveway far below.

Understanding came together. Piece by piece, Wench realized the whole stinking mess.

BLISS was the nucleus.

BLISS was what everybody wanted, and BLISS was what everybody got. He didn't know exactly why, but it didn't matter much. He figured that so-called civilized man had become a complacent sonofabitch. Like a long distance runner grabbing a breather, humanity decided to sit on a rock and ponder the vast distances it had come. In doing this, the running is altered, no longer toward a goal. The original reason for the sprint is obscured. Why not take time out for good behavior?

Time out. BLISS offers time out. In the blaring of a billion 39-inch megachrome TVs demanding that we "see the movie, play the recording, read the book, buy the slacks, eat the food, go to church, screw our spouses, and take a shit," the Government governs and the people are ... that's all. We get what we want. We want what we get. Blame nobody. Blame is unimportant. Blame does not compute.

Immunity does.

Yaramon's mind-tinkerers hadn't taken into account, it is doubtful that they even considered the possibility of, immunity. Which isn't the same as resistance. Over time, resistance wears down and we all dine at the local Lickity Chicken, or submit to BLISS in one form or another. But immunity is forever.

The Government couldn't allow large number of such individuals to walk among us, it dawned on Wench. Look at Lowia's neighbor. The woman desperately wanted BLISS and became outraged when the treatment didn't work. How many more like her might there be?

BLISS may be optional, but immunity eliminates options. Resisters can be compromised, coerced or controlled. Immunes promise only conflict. Unrest among the immune population - BLISS riots? - would put too much of a strain on the development of a neat, ordered, smug society. The Government wouldn't want that. Hell, the entire BLISSed out country wouldn't want that.

What a way to become extinct. That's the irony. BLISS wasn't forced down our throats like an invasion from outer space. We welcomed it with open arms. You can't really point a righteous finger at the Moralists.

It makes too much sense, then, that those devils in New Washington choreographed the Haddon Heights uprising. They pounced upon the opportunity to effect a clean excision of troublemakers. Flawless. The incident reminded Wench of jujitsu - giving way to the strength and weight of an opponent to defeat that opponent. The United Separatist Action was unshakeable. The bloody riot of the Haddon Heights demonstration wasn't incited to "put down anti-BLISS forces," as many thought. If it did squelch a handful of potential pains-in-Yaramon's-neck, well, that would merely be a bonus. The massacre was intended to catalyze all opposing forces into a congealed mob that could be plucked out of society like a lump from gravy. Wench saw it as plain as the constellation Orion. Yaramon didn't even have to do his own plucking.

The Administration "gave way." In fact, they gave Alabama away. Ostensibly bowing to DropOut Party pressure, they let the state be turned into an independent nation. But in reality the Government was springing a trap door through which the manipulated mass of counter-Moralist humanity plunged like an eight ball in the corner pocket.

First Separatists emigrated; now immunes were "allowed" to change addresses.

Before long, the discovery of a protester, resister or the inevitable immune in our midst will be no more threatening than the presence of an irascible flea on the back of a buffalo. If the thundering ruminant desires to plunge headlong off the top of a convenient mesa, what in hell is the flea going to do about it? Negotiate?

It was becoming a perfect world for BLISS, an easy highway for the yellow trucks to traverse north and south, coast to coast. Most of the population, giddy as children on the eve of their birthdays, awaited in sparkling anticipation the arrival of the new miracle at their doors. Nothing was ever going to change for them again, they thanked god and Yaramon. They'd always have jobs to go to, jobs which they would enjoy, receive terrific satisfaction from, enabling them to afford all the wonders of the modern age: self-cleaning blue jeans, audio-visual implants, test tube lobsters, and so forth. Happiness would be permanent.

Wench was not ready to throw a change of underwear and a toothbrush into an overnight bag, pack up his comm interface, stuff everything into the trunk of a rented car, and floor it along the Zoomway to the Separatists' southern homeland. Not yet.

The night shone uncommonly black. Moonless, cloudless, the dome of outer space, freckled with stars, that hung over the steep hilltop where Wench sat thinking seemed remarkably near. One could excuse a person for believing that all those other worlds out there might actually hear you if only you shouted loudly enough. In the valley below, the closely nestled single-family homes and low-rise apartment buildings mingled their fire colored incandescent lights into a suburban soup. Those people undoubtedly would hear him, if Wench shouted loudly enough.

He got to his feet and kicked at a rock planted firmly in the soil. He kicked the rock a second time. He turned toward the sleeping valley, the cold universe. He thought about Lowia and then he shouted.

121

"Damn you, Yaramon! Damn you! Damn you to hell!"

Chapter 13

ON a spring Tuesday morning, the Government closed down the offices and laboratories of Genetique Health Products, Middletown, New York. The reason given for this action was that the firm had been conducting biohazardous experiments without proper licensing or safety precautions, but the reason was unimportant. Ever since the Government enacted its "secular medical plan" (as they called it), nationalizing all doctors, hospitals, research facilities and birth control clinics under an umbrella welfare program (combining the Red Cross with the Blue Cross into a Purple Cross because they liked the symbolism), people wildly applauded continued efforts to take doctoring out of the hands of the private sector. After all, had not the multi-billion dollar health care industry been largely responsible, in the past, for blackmailing the population with threats of diseases and lingering death? Hadn't physicians channeled their efforts primarily into lucrative plastic surgery techniques and the writing of diet books while individuals continued to succumb to cancers and coronaries? The closing of Genetique was, if anything at all, news that people responded to with a rip-snorting "good for them," or "about time!"

What made this incident worth a second glance, if anyone cared at all enough to read past the opening paragraphs of the reports that were printed in most of the newspapers (little mention was made on TV), was that a couple of research scientists in the employ of Genetique had managed to disappear without a trace. The two doctors had vanished with - and this itself was only speculation - notes, records, even samples of materials having to do with extremely confidential "designer germ" experimentation. It was suspected that the missing researchers, working for three years on infectious diseases, fled to Alabama, taking the goods with them. They may have been allied with a fringe religious cult. True or not, this escape, when brought to light, aroused national ire. Under "secular medicine," no group or individual was allowed to maintain such a cloud of secrecy over their projects, let alone abscond with the entire kit and caboodle in the night like love struck elopers. Who knew into what hands that valuable research might now be delivered? The public had a right to feel outraged.

Chapter 14

ON the following spring Thursday morning, Astin Wench and Mars Gumbo were plotting delivery of their own design. They shared coffee by the corner window of their favorite Italian restaurant watering hole cum hangout, illuminated by the break of day. This suited Wench fine; things were becoming too gloomy, as far as he was concerned.

His relationship with Lowia was, for instance, idyllic, looking at it objectively. Everything pleased the woman since BLISS entered her life. She cast aside the drugs and coughers with nary a jitter. She divided her being into an ordered and (to her) joyous existence consisting of time with her daughter, work, and time with Wench. The latter, in fact, she thrived on. Subjectively, though, Wench felt he'd traded-off their previously precarious sex life for the role of a faithful, warm and reliable dildo. Lowia's underlying selfishness was the trouble: she loved her work; she loved taking care of the child; she loved the mothering, the housewifing, the careerwomaning; she loved the loving.

The BLISS story grew. As the Government's "revolutionary new process" soaked its way deeper into the national fiber, Wench reported on its forward march via the printed page, garnering prominent bylines as he did so. He got personal publicity; he became an authority, too, which enabled him to publish the occasional editorial and appear on TV talk shows. His opinions concerning

125

BLISS weren't, by any stretch of the imagination, laudatory. Nonetheless, Government spokesmen rarely bristled or objected to his taking such a pronounced anti-BLISS stance. They didn't have to: the public usually responded for them with a flood of letters-to-the-editor roundly condemning Wench, calling him everything from the anti-Christ to a dupe of left-wing anarchists. Some letters (one or two per month) actually sided with him. But the upshot was that Astin Wench became, himself, "news." His very name helped keep the presses rolling merrily along, readership, out of pure curiosity as to what verbal shenanigans the fellow would get up to next, high, and advertising rates climbing. On the job, as at home, Wench felt distinctly used.

Things were darkening, all right, and quickly.

When he first got the message that Gumbo was up to no good, Wench wanted to do a little dance of celebration. The time had come to reach beyond the keys of his comm interface. The pen may once have been mightier than the sword, but that held true when people believed what they read in the newspapers. Now they only had faith in television, which was real. "Meet me you-know-where in forty minutes," the familiar voice said, and Wench needed no other inducement to go, despite the early hour.

Gumbo poured a half cup of steaming liquid down his throat in one gulp.

"You'll burn yourself."

"Not me, Chief! Got an iron-clad gut." Gumbo wiped his beard with the broadside of his hand. His eyes fired up, however, as he explained to Wench, "it's that Genetique business."

Wench nodded. "Yeah, closed down for hazardous experimentation without a license, wasn't it?"

"Hazardous, my foot!" Gumbo got conspiratorial. "Except for some boring aggie stuff, the bulk of their research was targeted at the common cold. They were pussyfooting around with influenza. Sneezing and runny noses. The Feds slammed the door on them for that?"

Wench forked a muffin. "An excuse. That's all. It sounds good and gets them lots of hand clapping from the fawning masses. Come on, Mars, you know the Government's taking over the entire medical structure of the country bit by bit. I can't believe you got me out of bed in the middle of the night for this ... ?"

"It's seven a.m., Chief."

One of the differences between the two reporters was that Wench was a confirmed night owl. Gumbo was also a night owl, and a day owl, and an afternoon owl - it often appeared to Wench that his comrade, Gumbo, required no sleep whatsoever.

"O.K. So?"

The senior editor, ever bight-eyed and bushy-chinned, drove home his point. "So ... the Government's 'secularizing' all the labs."

"I know that!"

"But they aren't shutting them down. Not every one of them. Look. I made a list of the private research facilities that have been closed since the whole 'secular medicine' nonsense began - well, a partial list. Anyway, that's good enough." Gumbo handed a wrinkled sheet of printer paper to Wench. On the paper, in longhand, some twenty-three names of institutes and companies had been hastily inked. Genetique headed the column.

Wench wasn't certain what grand revelation an assortment of company names was supposed to offer, except perhaps an acrostic spelling of WE ARE NOT ALONE, or the like. Some of the firms' names he recognized, aside from Genetique. The others were mysteries. "I give up," he conceded.

Gumbo ran his finger down the listing. "These places, in one way or another, were all working on influenza. They were all engaged in researching common, contagious viral disease!"

"Maybe the Government thinks monies would be better spent on curing more serious, more debilitating illness. That is the line they've been spouting. After all, take two aspirin, call me in the morning ... that's always been the cure for sniffles. No?"

"No."

Gumbo double-checked over his shoulder to see if anybody was eavesdropping: of course, the place was nearly deserted. Too early. Satisfied, Gumbo leaned in closer to Wench and withdrew another folded document from his pocket. He laid it flat on the table and quietly slid it under Wench's nose. Sketched out on the paper, a sheet of Genetique letterhead, was an incomplete chemical formula and fragmentary drawings of a protein that, even with his limited knowledge of microbiology, Wench recognized as a virus. Not a living, breathing (figuratively speaking) virus, but a germ-in-progress, a man-made molecule. The sketch included a subunit "capsomere" diagram, which may or may not have been conclusive all by itself, but the distinctive "nucleocapsid" pencil drawing that filled the bottom of the page proved it.

"Where in hell'd you get this?"

"Under a monkey cage."

"What?"

"Wait - " Gumbo snatched the papers, both of them, refolded them and put them in his pocket. "How's your muffin?" he asked.

"Fresh."

"More coffee?" He didn't wait for a reply. Gumbo signaled the waitress to bring the pot over for refills. Sandi didn't come on duty until the lunch crowd descended. The morning waitress was a girl, a high school student probably earning pocket money. Gumbo remained silent until the kid topped off both their mugs, then dismissed her with a cheery, "thanks, hon!"

"You were saying?" Wench asked impatiently.

Gumbo modulated his voice. "I told you." He stole a bite of Wench's muffin. "The labs that were shut down, closed, out of business, finito, all had viral research work going. It piqued my inquiring mind no end. I figured to stir the waters a bit." He stirred his coffee. "I didn't know if I'd come up with anything more than a lot of wasted time. Anyway, last night I dropped in on Genetique, after midnight ... the old secret agent gig."

"Tem-te-dum-dum. Te-te-dum-te-dum." Wench mimicked the theme music from a popular spy series.

Gumbo appreciated it.

"Genetique labs is a compact, two-story structure of gray slabstone and glass. It sits atop a grassy rise smack in the middle of proverbial nowhere. A three-meter high chain wire fence skirts the property, with only a padlocked gate. Of course, because the facility was hurriedly vacated, there's no sign of what other security measures may once have been employed."

"That's of singular importance?" Wench needled Gumbo's polished delivery.

"Bear with me, Chief," Gumbo urged.

"I take it you broke into the lab?"

"Easily. But, you know I've always had a talent for picking locks."

Wench quietly slipped his coffee, intent upon Gumbo.

"The place drowned in emptiness. You know. It gave off that jangling sensation of some enormous activity recently snatched away, like a rally after the crowd's gone home. The place had been cleared out so instantly, the aura hadn't even had time to dissipate. I swear I could feel ghosts at each turn. Water faucets dripped. Fluorescent ceiling lamps rocked imperceptibly from their moorings. Somebody had left a telephone, an old pushbutton model, off the hook with the hold button punched in and glowing red. I made my way into the main lab, a windowless chamber with only the single entrance. Six worktables graced the center of the room in two parallel rows, three times three. One wall bore stacks of animal cages and metal cabinets. The place had been ransacked; what struck me, however, was the way the place had been ransacked. Most of the animal cages were empty, one or two of them had been dashed to the floor. But a couple of cages still contained rats and hadn't been touched. The same was true of the cabinets. Weird. Expensive microscopes stood undusted next to smashed beakers. One cabinet was rifled down to the paint. Another was chock full of immaculate lab ware."

Wench shrugged. "Whoever took what wanted only what they took."

"Precisely!"

"It still doesn't explain why the lab was closed."

"There's more. Remember your description of the BLISS equipment in the yellow trucks?"

Wench nodded.

"On one of the tables, I found an overturned metallic box, real smooth, roughly the size of a microwave oven, looked kind of like one, too. A door on the side of the thing hung ajar. Along another side I noticed an LCD readout, busted, stuck at eight-three-oh-point-something, and several audio-visual leads that had been clumsily ripped away."

"Coincidence."

"I thought so, too, Chief. So I looked inside the thing and, you know, I found some brown hairs. Monkey hairs!"

"They were microwaving apes?"

"My zoology isn't up to the level of making snap identifications from a handful of bristles," Gumbo continued unabashed. "Of course, I did write that series of articles on forensics two years ago. I knew they weren't human hairs. So I rummaged through the empty cages for more

131

evidence. That's when I found that partial sketch of a virus protein ... "

"Under a monkey cage."

"Some scientist's doodle more than not, destined to be crumpled up and tossed away, instead getting used as makeshift cage liner-or misplaced. Fortuitous, whatever the explanation."

"It's still very much apples and orang-utans."

"I know," agreed Gumbo. "So I snatched that $3,000 microscope that was obligingly left behind, carted everything to the *Daily Parade's* voluminous research library, opened a text on simian biology to the appropriate page, and took a real long gander at those hairs."

"Monkey?"

"Rhesus positive, Chief!"

By now, the activity of people on the street outside the restaurant, under the growing warmth of the morning sun, catalyzed into the beginning minutes of rush hour. With increasing frequency, the front door of the eatery gasped open and jingled shut as early risers came and went for coffee, Italian pastries, a quiet spot to meditate before the hectic pace of the workday fell down upon them. The conspiratorial bubble, if there was one, enveloping Wench and Gumbo, quietly popped. But any lack of privacy they may have now felt was unfounded, and they knew it. The lean gentleman in a cloth overcoat stiffly seated at the table next to them, wholly absorbed in an illustrated, large-print, pop fiction paperback, could care less about monkey hairs or viruses. If Wench and Gumbo were to vociferously plot an overthrow of the Yaramon government, the man would probably move to another table.

It was sweet to pretend. Wench and Gumbo hunched closer together, mothering their coffee mugs.

"You mean," Wench gathered, "they may have actually been working on BLISS at Genetique ... a privately-owned lab?"

"Makes sense," said Gumbo. "Viruses. Biospheric modeling. They'd have to use biospheric modeling to test other forms of BLISS." He slurped his coffee thoughtfully. "I don't like it."

"Don't like what?"

"What all of this implies."

"Which is?"

"An immunosuppressive germ," guessed Gumbo, "capable of transmitting BLISS."

Wench whistled.

All of a sudden he felt an uncomfortable draft that did not emanate from the opening and closing front door. It came with the realization that BLISS, as of now, was carried inelegantly and most deliberately in noisy yellow trucks. It had to be wanted. It was wanted, wholeheartedly, the statistics proved loud and clear like church bells on a still, cool morning. Yet, if the Government had a way to literally spray BLISS into the wind, pass it from warm body to warm body in an uncovered cough, allow it to rage across the nation like an errant contagion ...

"No," insisted Wench.

"No?"

"Why close down the lab, if that were the case?"

"The runaway doctors?"

"The Government's crazy, not vengeful," said Wench.

Gumbo raised a perplexed eyebrow.

Wench ran a finger around the rim of his coffee mug. "Unless - "

The chatter of a cash register interrupted him. The bartender, a man of rotund girth and wit known to everyone as Al, with skin so slick it appeared as if he washed with carnauba wax instead of soap, in starchy whites, checked out a customer. Al, humming and chuckling merrily to himself, reached up behind the bar and waved on a late model 39-inch megachrome TV, the only feature of the entire establishment less than ten years old. The TV was propped on a high shelf. Al cooed in satisfaction as a commercial began.

(Wench's Law specifically stated that if you turned on any television monitor to any channel at any hour, the odds of hitting into a commercial were about 67 percent, or two out of three. The chances of finding a commercial on every channel was an astonishing fifty-fifty.)

On the TV, simple black letters against a yellow background spelled, and a fatherly announcer asked, "WHAT CAN BLISS DO FOR YOU?" Quick cut. An auburn-haired young mother, holding her child, glimpses of a nondescript play yard in the background, answered, "BLISS had made me a better parent, a better homemaker and a better wife. I am contented and satisfied with my role, and take great pride in doing my share for my family and my community. My life has never been better!" Quick cut. A burly man wearing a plaid flannel shirt, jeans, work boots and hard hat, one foot hoisted onto a small stack of lumber, answered, "this job used to get to me, y'know. Kept putting in time and sweat and thought I wasn't getting nothing out of it. Well, BLISS shows me the benefits I'm getting. It's much more than a paycheck, y'know. It's being part of this great land. It's being a part of humanity." Quick cut. Two smartly-scrubbed college students, a young man and a young woman, stopped and turned. The young man, several textbooks tucked under his arm, answered. "I know what I want from life. BLISS has given me the direction, and the ambition I need to get there. No surprises. No wavering." The young woman answered, "we're on our way!" Freeze frame. It shrunk down to fill the lower left quadrant of the TV screen. At the same time, the upper left and upper right quadrants wiped in stills (like putting back slices of pie) of the young mother and the construction worker. The lower right quadrant remained black, then grew a yellow question mark. The announcer asked, "what about you? These people know where they are going. Can you be as certain about yourself?" Lap dissolve to a yellow BLISS truck at dawn. The sun, an orange tennis ball, bounced up behind the vehicle. The announcer said, "if life's got you circling in a whirlpool of anxiety, confusion and fear, BLISS can set you back on the straight course. With BLISS, everything is possible. With BLISS, contentment is a reality. With BLISS, in the name of the Reverend Yaramon, the sun will shine from coast to coast!" Gushy, hymnal music swelled into a fadeout.

The next commercial began right away, selling automobiles for the low, low, lowest prices in town ...

Al the bartender wiped the counter top with broad, circular strokes, positively glowing.

Wench two-handed his coffee mug up to his lips and took a pensive swig. "... unless we're analyzing this entire business ass backwards and upside down."

"Got a hunch, Chief?" asked Gumbo.

"Perhaps. How many scientists would you estimate haven't exactly been turning double cartwheels in unbridled joy over the BLISS Project?"

"Bunches."

This was true. In virtual similarity to the community of scientists who took a vocal, often demonstrative stand against nuclear arms proliferation years ago, when the country was installing multi-headed ICBMs in every mall and churchyard, today's physicians, chemists and other PhDs maintained one of the strongest, unified coalitions against BLISS since the

U.S.A. This was an underlying reason (though hardly publicized) why the Government hastened to "secularize" medicine, and all of science, to the full extent of the law.

Wench's eyes twinkled. "Pretend you're Yaramon," he suggested to Gumbo.

"Geez, Chief, do I have to?"

"What would you do if you got wind of the fact that certain independent labs, contracted, let's say, to work on BLISS, instead were formulating a cure, a vaccine, to stop BLISS ... to prevent it ... to reverse it!"

The answer was as plain as cement. It was as exhilarating as snow in August. Gumbo slammed the tabletop with his fist; the mugs jumped; nobody else in the restaurant did. "Close them down quicker than a spring tornado! Ship the docs to Prudhoe Bay! Annihilate the notes! Chief, you know what this means?"

Wench knew full well what it meant. It meant that the weapon he needed, the instrument of his vow, the payback, (what gratifying words!) was at least a dim hope. But it also meant, Wench said gravely, revealing the flip side of the coin, "that the Government's going to tightening the thumbscrews. If we're right about our speculations, we won't be the first to know. You, me, the entire anti-BLISS cause, up to now benevolently allowed to play the part of loyal opposition, could become a very endangered species."

Visions of Alabama danced in their heads.

Chapter 15

TRUE to form, the Yaramon Administration soon released the following videocard:

"During the past several months in which your Government has been implementing Biopsychic Lavation for Intensified Stimulation of the Superego (BLISS), the support and encouraging response from you, the people, has been truly overwhelming. We are indeed happy to report that families, entire communities all across this blessed nation of ours, have discovered a new contentment and joy in their day-to-day lives. We are further pleased to announce that our preliminary objectives, set well before the Project had even begun, appear to be nearing realization. Much needless worry, fear, and anxiety has already vanished, you may even say evaporated, from the national consciousness. This is significant. Freed from our primitive inhibitions, we can develop our minds and move onto higher levels of self-satisfaction.

"We are also aware that a large number of you still harbor doubts concerning the BLISS project. These doubts have hardly been abrogated and may even have been magnified by a malicious rumor now being spread by an irreligious group of anarchists. This rumor-that a mild illness, no more uncomfortable than a 24-hour cold, can counteract the effects of BLISS and render a person immune to additional treatment-could not be farther from the truth!

"To begin with, there is no way to reverse the effects of BLISS, since BLISS is a subtractive procedure, essentially accelerating within the human mind what nature has already put into motion. Can you return a removed appendix? Can a person who has lost a limb regenerate a new one? Can you grow younger? As for 'catching' an immunity to BLISS, we again reply that this is nonsense. In truth, we are all aware of those unfortunate individuals among us who are inherently resistant to BLISS. The good news is that our scientists are steadily working toward that day when everybody, yes, everybody, can enjoy the benefits of this blithe new world.

"Any gossip you may hear to the contrary should be summarily dismissed in the same vein as UFO sightings, or the periodic lies that our beloved President has fallen victim to a fatal tragedy. You may, on the other hand, obtain news that your Government is bulldoggedly endeavoring to root out and squash those rumormongers and terrorists who seek to disrupt the BLISS Project with their seditious deeds. Believe this! And also have faith that, in the name of the Reverend Yaramon, the sun will shine from coast to coast."

The word, on television, in the newspapers, over the radio, posted on billboards, and letter mailed to every citizen of voting age, fell with the power and glory of gospel. Almost.

Chapter 16

WENCH made a crumpled ball of the Government flyer that had been stuffed into his mailbox and deliberately tossed it out of Gumbo's three-year-old candy apple blue Uranus Mark V Turboboom coupe.

"Litterbug," accused Gumbo.

Wench squirmed in the leather-lined bucket seat. "Besides you and me, who else in this BLISSed out world is going to give a damn?" He was in a petulant mood.

"Perhaps, where we're headed ..." Gumbo decided it would be best not to start anything at the moment. Let him be.

Gumbo was earnestly attired for driving, from head to toe, outfitted in crepe-soled suede shoes, tan chinos and a striking blue nylon, zippered jacket (to match his car) over a green tee-shirt. He completed his "look" with streamlined sunshades. He wore no cap. Sometimes he wore a cap when driving; this time he did not. Wench, less decorous in a crimson pullover, jeans and sneakers, fiddled with the air vent.

The low-slung three-seater streaked over the monotonous gray highway in quiet urgency, no fumes and barely an audible whine emanating from the vehicle's power module. Red and pale green indicator signals sparkled across the dashboard, offering a plethora of continually updated information. The midday air itself, gushing past the half-opened windows of the car, smelled of adventure. Airy harpsichord music danced out of the laserdisc player. Gumbo reached down for the black T-shaped gearshift jutting from the floor and firmly threw the car into third. The car responded with an accordant growl and, as if being gently thumped against the rear by the heel of a gargantuan hand, accelerated swiftly from 70 to a cruising speed of near 100 kph. Gumbo veered the little Turboboom left, into the faster lane. Red warning markers - they looked like roadside lollipops- whipped past, indicating that the blacktopped on-ramp to the Interstate Zoomway lay ahead. Gently rising over a half-kilometer incline to merge and allow access to the ultra high speed thoroughfare, the on-ramp itself split into two lanes: one gave non-stop direct entry; the other led to a checkpoint where motorists with one-time or temporary Zoomway passes had to halt for clearance. Gumbo, of course, would not need to brake.

Seconds before making the on-ramp, Gumbo hoisted the soap bar shaped CB mike close to his lips, held down the thumb switch, simultaneously cutting the volume of the 'disker, and barked authoritatively: "Gumbo. Askie 9J2846. On approach."

A moment of pause with an electric pop came through, then he heard the tinny response: "... jay two eight four. We have you on visual. You are cleared for Zoomway. You may proceed. Thank you."

Gumbo replaced the mike. The music resumed. Reaching the peak of the incline, now level with the Zoomway itself, the on-ramp became an acceleration lane that would eventually bring

141

vehicles into the mainstream of traffic. Gumbo again reached for the gearshift and thrust it all the way forward. A very large indicator light on the dashboard glowed TURBO in pure white. The car growled like a lion in heat and Gumbo, comfortably held within the bucket seat, felt partial g-force pressure as the car inexorably impelled forward, faster-130 kph, 150 kph, 160 kph, 190 kph, 250 kph... The blue Turboboom was now on the Zoomway, heading for Syracuse.

The trip would only take a couple of hours. Gumbo became entirely absorbed in driving; the almost druglike exhilaration he got out of pushing his vehicle to the max was nothing new, and one of his few vices. Wench, in contrast, folded his arms across his chest, wiggled into as relaxed a position as possible in the seat, and closed his eyes. Perhaps he could rest. The Zoomway may be about as fast as anybody could want, but the scenery leaves a lot to be desired.

Wench was in another universe. With the windows now tightly sealed against the excessive air velocity produced by the high speed, the automobile's interior took on an unworldly quality. The dashboard indicators monitoring "life support" - temp, oxy, hum, press - further enhanced the effect. Except for delicate notes from the harpsichord disc, the odd silence was like being in outer space. (Wench had taken a short flight into space, once.) The outside dimension reeled past him in a liquid, surrealistic ribbon.

Their destination, Syracuse, had at one time been a teeming, thriving city of skyscrapers, enormous power demands, and an upscale

142

population domiciled in vast suburbs. Then the city, like so many other cities, declined, for the usual reasons. Syracuse still functioned all right, but a dirty patina replaced the promising shine. The city now contained the highest concentration of Freeyares in the whole Northeast. Representatives of the Order had contacted Wench, which was a most extraordinary occurrence all by itself, to say the least. The Freeyares, reputedly, had made only one other official request of a member of "lay" society throughout their entire seventy-four year history. For the second time they'd broken their imposed isolationism and, with a moderate degree of clandestineness, requested that Wench meet with a quorum of Freeyares in Syracuse. It was okay for him to bring along Gumbo.

Wench had no idea what the Freeyares wanted; they refused to give him a clue. It was logical to assume, though, that these people wouldn't violate their most sacred tenet unless the reason was pretty damned earthshattering. At first, Wench surmised that the Government might be starting to climb all over the Freeyares backs, but this didn't make any sense. If true, what could Wench do about it, anyway? Above all, the Freeyares were a "separatist" faction in the truest sense of the word, and the Government had nothing to fear from them. Wench would simply have to wait and see. As the music played on, he dozed.

***

In two hours sharp, Gumbo awakened Wench with a loud imitation of an electric bass guitar.

143

Gumbo had switched to jazz fusion and was boisterously bumping his palms against the top of the steering wheel as he vocalized along with the heavy metal beat. They were tooling into the main drag of Syracuse' seedy south side. Wench recognized some of the dilapidated buildings.

"Where to now, Chief?" Gumbo asked.

Wench cracked a window to blow the fog out of his head. Recalling the Freeyares' instructions, he said, "make a right on Halstead Street, then a couple of blocks east."

"Gotcha."

The Turboboom rolled with the stealth of a stalking predator, made the right turn effortlessly, and quietly proceeded for two and one half blocks before coming to a final halt in front of a gathering of street people. The pedestrians, expressing quite some curiosity, were tattered, but not unkempt, and two of them wore open metal trapezoids (the symbol of their religion) on a chain around their necks. Freeyares. The oldest of the lot, probably a Sanhedrist, as Freeyares termed their high counselors, wore holey jeans, a poncho cut from a brown blanket, a simple beanie to protect his head; he looked altogether like a Franciscan monk. He soundlessly shuffled up to Wench's side of the car in the openhanded, obeisant pose that Freeyares used for begging. This was the agreed upon sign. For if Wench was not Wench, the Freeyares would give nothing away.

Wench offered the leader a dollar bill, as directed. "We came as soon as the rain stopped," he recited.

"The storm was indeed fierce," the cleric replied.

"I'm Wench."

"I am known as Huddigger Freeyare."

"And I'm glad this codswallop is over with," declared Gumbo, bouncing from the car.

Traditionally, upon joining the Order, Freeyare apostates kept their former last name as a first name and adopted the communal surname of Freeyare. The wizened Sanhedrist took the money (which wasn't agreed upon, but what the heck) and gestured for Wench and Gumbo to follow. The Freeyare leader, accompanied by his gentle entourage, passed into an unimpressive red brick warehouse. Wench stepped out of the Turboboom, slammed the door shut behind him, and raised an eyebrow in Gumbo's direction.

"After you," Gumbo insisted.

They followed the leader.

Within a monochrome, cold smelling arena framed by cinder block walls, an uneven cement floor and a single letterbox opening high near the ceiling that served more as an air hole than a window, ten shoddy sectarians and two reporters mingled hesitantly. There were opposing doors: the heavy front door through which they'd all entered, now shut and bolted; a rear door, partly opened, was guarded by a squatty Freeyare with more hair on his chin than his head, in sandals, gray slacks and a dashiki. A table had been made, to one side, of wooden crates, covered with cloth, and laid with the sacred articles of Freeyare faith-the book, the glove and the garlic. Huddigger, the revered high prelate, turned away from the congregation, placed his hands upon the table, and solemnly lowered his head. The other Freeyares bowed their heads, too, clasping soiled hands against devout breasts. Wench and Gumbo, not knowing what to do, did nothing. The magic words were uttered by ten sonorous voices in sloppy unison. "Attaboy. Oolitzu. Vobiscum." The meeting, official, sanctioned, cleansed, purified, could begin.

"You will permit us our respects," Huddigger said, backing away from the table, his hands withdrawing into the folds of the poncho.

"I guess."

"We don't have time for a High Mass, Chief," Gumbo whispered.

"Service, not Mass," Huddigger corrected.

"Nonetheless," Wench urged politely, "time is precious."

Huddigger raised a hand, fingers heavenward, palm outward, and assured them, "I intend to come directly to the point."

There was a brief preamble/prayer first. Then, Huddigger Freeyare cleared his throat and adjusted his tattered gown. He fixed his neckpiece so that what little light there was shone brightly off the surface of the metal trapezoid.

"We are pariahs," he began matter-of-factly, "social outcasts, untouchables, to use an obviously paradoxical phrase. It is a condition to which our sect has long aspired, and cultivated, within society as a whole. For it is not enough, we believe, to merely live outside of the temporal world. We must go beyond humility. We must denigrate ourselves, often court martyrdom, encourage the chastisement, punishment and oppression of the population to

146

achieve spiritual fulfillment. Certain now-defunct historical sects, like the Flagellants of the seventeenth century, had the right idea but went about it the wrong way. Punishment, to be effective, cannot be self-inflicted. It must be earned. Additionally, the methods must not involve any direct intercourse with profane society. And thus we exist; an existence that commands no greater attention than that of a tree or a rock. We beg because any other form of procuring subsistence has a stigma of social acceptance, which is unacceptable to us. Mendicancy has fine historical precedents.

"We've heard all this before." Gumbo interjected.

Wench elbowed his colleague.

The Freeyare leader continued: "we've been greatly successful - for decades. We wear the wounds and bruises from an unloving world proudly. Our Order cherishes its time-honored reputation of being gloriously abused. How many teenaged bands have roamed the midnight streets in search of a solitary Freeyare to torture and cudgel? What citizen has not, at least once, succumbed to the irresistible temptation to deliver a solid kick in a tender zone to a brother begging for alms? Police officers routinely rout us from our shelters and leave us cut and bleeding in the gutters. We thrive on it; our souls glide along the great spiral of life toward the center point of godlike perfection."

Wench fidgeted.

"You've heard all of this, too, of course, I know," Huddigger intoned.

Wench nodded.

Gumbo, who sometime before had taken a micro DVM camera out of his hip pocket and switched it on, now checked to make sure it was recording properly. The red LED glowed brilliantly.

The Freeyare Sanhedrist continued: "the Government's BLISS Project is neutralizing our religion! I don't imply abolishment. A concerted effort of extermination, unsolicited by us, would be tantamount to deliverance - instant nirvana for every Freeyare on this planet. Rather, BLISS is inextricably removing our sectarian ability to achieve perfection. Our souls are in danger of becoming eternally locked within a purgatory of oblivion. And why, you might ask? Because BLISS is fostering benign indifference. The inhumanity of it all!"

Gumbo sighed sympathetically.

Huddigger continued: "BLISS has scarcely made people more charitable, lest you think the Government's touted miracle has us waist deep in bequests and brotherly love, a dreadful situation we could exploit. No, friends, we remain neglected. But we are not oppressed. Not swiped at. Not spat upon. Not beaten up. We aren't even cursed at any longer, for God's sake. Our mortal souls, the ghosts of our forebears, cry out for drastic remedy! Oh, heresy!"

"Heresy?" Wench asked.

"Yes. Our faith has recently become ravaged by some among us who would question our teachings, it grieves me to admit." Huddigger solemnly shook his head. "However, the heretics may be our salvation. Yours, too. That is the purpose for which I have summoned you here. Seek out the heretics, my friend. I cannot. Go to their sacrilegious meeting

148

places. I shall not. Find the one who carries with him the knowledge of the world."

"Who's that?" Wench wanted to know.

The Sanhedrist continued, woefully: "only once before in the whole history of the Freeyares has outside contact been required. We fear the fruits, this time, if we are successful. But we dread what must be the outcome of a second violation of dogma even more, if we are not. It is in your hands, my friend."

"What is?" Wench was getting irritated.

Huddigger Freeyare, practically in tears, moaned, "there remains for us but the Ultimate Sacrifice."

"Not again?" Gumbo remarked.

"This time we mean it," Huddigger assured.

Freeyares had often threatened mass suicide, at least on seventy-two known occasions during the past seventy-four years. It was the sect's favorite (if only) indulgence, effected to elicit guilt. A knee-jerk reaction, the threat rarely worked. Gumbo played along. So did Wench, unable to make heads or tails of the heretic business.

"To the last man and woman?" Gumbo wondered. (There were, he knew, some practicing lady Freeyares around, though not many.)

"How come?" asked Wench.

"Suffer a lifetime of indignity with no hope of redemption ever? Non-life followed by un-death? Thank you, no, my friends. Better to have it done with at once, I think."

"That would condemn you throughout eternity," said Wench, "dissolve your religion. You'd never get to heaven."

"Nirvana."

"You'd never get there."

"The Ultimate Sacrifice," Huddigger agreed.

The other Freeyares held their hands, palm within palm, by their stomachs, bowing their heads, as if in prayer. They stood around uncomfortably, letting the weight of the air cling to them like a bad smell. Wench felt his arms and the back of his neck grow prickly. Gumbo clicked off his micro DVM, carefully replacing it in his hip pocket as he muttered under his breath to Wench (like an embarrassed guest) "maybe we ought to get - "

"Police!"

With a bang and a blow, the front door exploded out.

"Freeze!"

Nobody did.

Gumbo swerved, saw a brutish, hired killer step into the doorway. The cop, glabrous but with tufts of rough hair, like epaulets, topping his shoulders, was about the size and shape of a Minotaur, give or take an inch. He was naked from the waist up except for a pair of leather suspenders from which (the right one) a polished, silver patrolman's badge dangled. He wore denim uniform pants and police issue shoes. He hoisted an ugly, angular dieselgun, larger itself than one of the tinier Freeyares now scurrying for the back exit. Freeyares, despite years of indoctrination, never could completely overcome human instinct. Then, why should they?

A second policeman, probably of higher rank than the first policeman because he didn't bear the same bloodthirsty aura about him, wearing a wrinkle resistant, polyester version of the standard

150

uniform, pressed in from behind. He also toted a dieselgun. Weighty, double-barreled instruments of impartial slaughter, dieselguns incorporated an internal combustion engine fueled by a gas tank within the stock. Instead of driving pistons, the engines fired stainless steel darts (or dumdums, depending upon the degree of mayhem one desired). Cartridges were not required, so dieselguns could carry thousands of rounds. They could deliver up to 1,500 RPMs at full burst. As field weapons, dieselguns were inaccurate, too heavy to control, and wasteful. In close quarters, though, they were terrifyingly effective.

"Diesels!" someone screamed an alarm.

Gumbo drove to meager protection behind an oversized wooden packing crate; the crate had stenciled upon it in faded blue letters, "COMFORT"; the coincidence did not escape Gumbo's attention; fortunately, the police were not after Gumbo. Like a jack-in-the-box, Gumbo kept popping out from behind his cover and carried on a bizarre shouting match with the backup cop:

"You're out of bounds!"

"Keep your fuckin' head down!"

"This is private property!"

"None of your business!"

"I'm with the press!"

"Drop it!"

Wench had stiffened in fear, meanwhile. A miasmic bubble welled in his gut, sickening him over what he had no idea was about to happen. When it did, it happened around him. He was an island. A rapid series of gunshots. An odor of brimstone and machine oil. All the coloring drained

151

out of the room. He saw one Freeyare literally rocket off the ground, impelled by an unseen power. The little sectary dashed against the back wall, his shoulder ripping away from his body in a burst of gore. Another Freeyare, the one with beard and dashiki, crumpled at the middle and dropped like a toppled domino to the floor, emitting a long, gurgling growl that ultimately quieted. Wench at the same time saw a chunk of red flesh fly away from Huddigger Freeyare's left side. Huddigger screamed and collapsed in a frenzy on the ground, jerking his legs as if riding a phantom bicycle. The Sanhedrist did not die immediately.

"Somebody call a MediBus!"

The urgent voice rang above the gunfire. It was Wench. Almost involuntarily shouting. He knew full well that Freeyares stood as much chance of receiving emergency aid as they did of getting their own TV show. It had nothing to do with health benefits. But, humanity and compassion must have their shining moments.

Huddigger, on the other hand, biting dust, coughing up blood, shook his head as best he could. "No, no," he argued, "let my spirit go."

Impetuously, Wench scrambled to the side of the fallen prelate, though realizing there was unlikely anything he could do for the man, and in reckless disregard of the potential (seemingly distant) danger to himself. Huddigger reached for Wench's offered hand, drawing the reporter closer. Wench expected grief. Rather, the Freeyare beamed, beamed beatifically as a glorious peace spread over his face. He whispered: "joy, oh joy, a martyr's joy. I go to perfection." But before the man went, he

152

calmly delivered his final word into Wench's receptive ear: "Archimedes."

In the rapidly developing silence, Wench pondered the name. It meant nothing to him.

The carnage had ended. Two dead, one injured, and the others escaped into the streets.

The bulky policeman chuckled, admiring his handiwork.

"Why?" Wench asked in pitiful outrage. Cops routinely beat up Freeyares. It was a fact of life. But they didn't slaughter them.

"I guess you could say they was in the way." The cop showed his yellow teeth, swung the death machine to within inches of Wench's nose. "Mister Wench."

"You know me?"

"That's why we's here, Mister Wench."

A punch of nausea hit Wench like a right cross.

"Alive," the cop emphasized, "so don't get staticky."

The impact proved to be temporary.

"Now." The cop rolled his tongue around his teeth. "Ya comin'? Or we gonna carry ya'? Mister Wench."

Wench, with no choice but to obey, really, followed the leather thonged policeman out of the building, into the street, and into a waiting squad car, the big red-and-yellow swivel light on the car roof turning his face alternatively crimson and jaundiced. Wench noted with some puzzlement, before he was whisked away, that although the policemen were well aware of the presence of Gumbo - Gumbo had even stepped out from behind his protective box and tried to say something to

Wench - they showed very little interest in his friend. Gumbo would have to drive home alone.

154

Chapter 17

THE trial of Astin W. Wench made all of the newspapers, including the *Daily Parade*. It did little to mitigate Wench's growing consternation. It clawed at each and every one of his nerve fibers until he burned to pummel somebody, even a friend. Being the center of a public mockery, prosecuted for nebulous and trumped-up charges, accused of breaching the national security, indicted for spying - that was a crime unto itself. Furthermore, rain, on the day the trial concluded, splashed down in loud, weighty droplets that could be heard impacting with painful finality from within the locked confines of the courtroom itself. The day had been forecast partly cloudy.

The only real support Wench received was from Mars Gumbo. Gumbo sat faithfully by Wench's side throughout the entire tribulation. He was a St. Bernard of a fellow, a one-man rooting section, shoveling out encouragement with one hand and doling up heaping spoonfuls of consolation with the other.

This day, the final day of the trial: Gumbo wore his best pullover cardigan of subdued Republican brown, revealing the knot of a tie at his neck (no longer yellow, the color of BLISS). His combed and trimmed beard glowed. He shielded his mouth with the side of his hand and confided to Wench, "a ridiculous publicity charade, Chief. They think they can water your fire by embarrassing you, that's all. They've been itching to come down on what

155

piddling anti-BLISS movement there is in this country for months. Pinhead dancing by pinheads. You know that as well as I do. When this is all over Yaramon will strut around crowing like the rooster who laid the hen that laid the golden egg. Hell, you can go back to your desk and get weeks more column fodder out of it all!"

So why wasn't the Administration strutting?

Wench was not overly relieved. "Thanks for the info."

"Anything else?" asked Gumbo, semper paratus.

"Did you check the VideoDoc to see if I've made prime time?" Wench, at least, kept his wit.

The major networks would not, of course, pre-empt any of their hugely successful sitcoms, soaps or gossipers for something as mundane as a sedition & spy trial: however, one of the local Government feeds did offer a half-hour capsulization of general court proceedings each evening prior to the Moralist Sundown Penance. The VideoDoc, in fact, on the override, selecting "last minute," signaled this with an impressive WENCH CASE, in caps. Gumbo slapped down yesterday's hard copy on the table in front of Wench, indicating the particular entry with a forefinger.

Not indicative of a strutting Administration, either.

Wench complained. "It still doesn't wash."

"The trial or the coverage? We know the trial's a sham."

Wench passed on Gumbo's comment. He determined that if the Government really, truly wanted public mockery, they weren't doing their damnest to get it. They were giving, say, 50 percent, 55 percent effort at the most. Christ! Nobody had even written a pop tune about him, Wench must have muttered, semi-audibly.

"Why do you want a song?" Gumbo asked. He'd apparently forgotten about the power of positive hyping.

"Forget it," groused Wench.

No strutting so far as he could see.

The Government wasn't skimping on courtroom facilities, however. For this esteemed occasion, they commandeered the Fallgood Memorial Chancery: a massive arena of waxed, costly lumber, bannisters lathed by ancient artisans, and decorative railings that commemorated great events in political science. The ceiling was so high, clouds often formed there. The place even smelled like a national anthem. Certainly this was the public quarter from that to propagate TV exposure and press coverage. After all, those run-of-the-mill, laminated plywood, fluorescent lighted courtrooms of the hoi polloi that echoed vehemently and trudgingly with years of "$50 fine, next case" would hardly be appropriate. This was indeed the proper milieu for Wench's trial. If strutting was the intention.

On the last day of the trial, Wench was probably oversensitive about the way he perceived his own newsworthiness. Still, Wench ruminated, in his spankingly tailored camel suit, sitting behind the enormously bulky *table a defendeur* that could easily double for a parking space, there was something decidedly out of joint about this whole affair.

Gumbo, on Wench's right, continued to cast eyes and ears about in an effort to snare other juicy juridical tidbits. On Wench's left spread the high priced lawyer from the firm of Lemwalt, Zumwalt and Shumwalt, retained by the *Daily Parade* to get its reporters out of sticky situations. Across the room, at the *table a demandeur*, the plaintiff's table, the Government's seat, inch for inch as impressive as the furniture behind which Wench and his team huddled, if not even a foot larger, a covey of black-and-white Yaramon appointed attorneys brooded. They could hardly be seen above the stacks of papers and dockets that topped the table like miniature skyscrapers.

"All blank, Chief," Gumbo whispered. "White as snow and strictly for show."

"Then why isn't the show on the networks?" Wench could scarcely get the inconsistency out of his mind.

"During a ratings war?"

"Seems to me," Wench concluded, "the Feds don't really want my name up lights."

"Maybe they're saving you for better things." Gumbo's response was supposed to be sarcastic.

The judge gavelled limply. He sat in a marbled and ivory banc that was encrusted with filigrees and little bas-relief symbols of justice. Actually, banc was hardly the appropriate word for the structure, although that is indeed what the judge's bench was, legally. Added to that, in his fashionable scarlet robes of dark brown trim, with a horseshoe of white-turning-to-gray shoulder length hair semi circumnavigating his head, the judge resembled a god. All the magistrate needed was a halo, for which an overhead lamp, beaming reverently down from the cathedral ceiling, provided a suitable substitute. Wench noticed that if you angled your head to get a clear look at the judge, the lamp did seem to cast a pre-Raphaelite nebula; otherwise, the lamp got in your eyes and it was difficult to see the judge in any respect. He wondered how TV cameras dealt with the phenomenon, but there was only one camera present.

Wench scanned the dark stained, worn, gallery pews. They were as empty as ballpark bleachers during the last week of the season with the home team struggling to stay above last place. A few vagabonds had managed to find their way in out of the rain. Some newspaper reporters lackadaisically scribbled notes; they had to be here. Notably absent was Wench's lady. Lowia told him, though, blissfully confident, that he'd nothing to worry about (really?), and that she'd like to attend. But, having so much to do, and TV programs to catch up on ... she'd be with him "in spirit, all the way." She perkily pecked him on the cheek and sent him packing off like a schoolchild going to classes. Wench expected no more from her.

Wench stood accused of three counts of seditionary acts against the nation (why three counts was a mystery), two counts of incitement to riot, and one count (only one?) of espionage. That's how the Government interpreted his activities with the Syracuse Freeyares at the time of his arrest. Those two police officers who apprehended him, the cops who left behind that picturesque tableau of death and transfiguration, uttered not a clue to Wench during the long drive back to Bigapolis. They eschewed the Zoomway, in favor of a "leisurely" trip. It wasn't that they said nothing, either; they said nothing to Wench. The senior cop steered the car, carefully, attentively, quite professionally, in fact. The other one cradled his dieselgun tenderly in his lap, caressing the ugly machine periodically with a well-oiled rag. He'd make a half-sigh, half-whine as he stroked the gun muzzle. This bothered Wench. Also upsetting to Wench: when not doting upon his weapon, the beefy cop would jab an elbow into his partner's ribs and boast, "ya see the way those jerks blew apart like melons when I plugged 'em?" or "ain't we got time to roust another bunch-a dem holy bums?" or comments along these lines. Wench rode in the back seat. There were, of course, no back doors and the back windows were all barred. At least Wench was not handcuffed, which, in a way, was a blessing; he could sleep. When they roared up to the Tenth Precinct, siren ululating, blinkers oscillating, they gave the distinct impression that Wench was either a head of state or a serial murderer, or both. The two cops sort of rolled from the car. The beefy officer with the damnable cannon opened the door for Wench and patiently waited while the prisoner exited. Then the cop jammed the dieselgun's muzzle into Wench's back to the extent that it hurt. Uncomfortably, Wench led the procession into the station house. The paperwork was ready and waiting for him: indictments, hearing dates, plea affidavits, bail bonds ... All Wench had to do was sign his name and he could go home, until the trial.

And here it was. Day the last. Not lengthy as such proceedings usually go. But the trial managed to drag and draw out long enough, what with the Government layering fiction upon fiction. Wench was frazzled. He felt as if he'd already served a life sentence.

Gumbo remained peppery. Gumbo was not having his ass hauled up before kin and country. But what would Wench have done without him? Gumbo combed his fingers through his beard several times, then, animatedly, repeated, "here we go, here we go," indicating action from the judge.

Wench looked up.

The judge glowered down at Wench.

The magistrate then tapped unskillfully at a terminal keyboard recently installed in the high bench. Modern computer and telecommunications hardware permeated all judicial proceedings nowadays. Although one couldn't always see the machinery, it was assuredly there. It was used in lieu of a live jury - that civic duty became significantly easier and more palatable if a person could serve on-line. It was used to tap into public records with the speed of light, affording less delay and adjournments. It was used as the judge was now using it.

After examining the monitor at his right for a minute, the judge remarked, "I see that you haven't been attending very many movies, lately."

"I read a lot," replied Wench.

"But I see - " The judge motioned casually for the defendant to stand up. Wench got to his feet. "I see no references," the judge continued, "to any purchases of bestsellers at all within the past two years."

"No. No novelizations," Wench granted. "I read books."

"You do?" The judge paused to study the VDT monitor. He made a few quick snorts through his nostrils and reasserted his gaze at Wench. "I can't find any copies of receipts showing that you bought any pop recordings, current laserdiscs or music videos, either?"

"I have one of the finest collections of vintage jazz and '40s Big Band hits in the city!" Wench boasted.

"You may," retorted the judge, "but that is hardly in keeping with our most recent national policy - see the movie, read the book, buy the record. It can hardly bode well for the outcome of your case. Have you no socially redeeming evidence to offer?"

The judge waited for a reply.

Wench had none, right away. Gumbo nudged him and stage whispered, "tell him you're a big fan of Jesus Jones!"

Wench resisted. Let's get the damned farce over and done with, he thought. He said, "can we just get to the verdict, your honor?"

"As you wish," answered the judge.

"Good," said Wench.

Gumbo sighed, disapprovingly.

Another advantage of computerization in the courtroom was that it expanded the defendant's right to a jury of his peers in ways that brought patriotic tears to the eyes of constitutional interpreters. It had long been argued that one dozen adults, a mere twelve men and women, who managed to survive the rigorous jury selection processes of the modern legal system were, it turned out oftentimes, peers as much as bytes are butterflies. The famous case of Gill v. Yugo, in which it was discovered after the fact that nine of the jurors were illegitimate children of the plaintiff, clearly pointed up the inequities of "egg carton" litigation. Data processing, with real time computer access of the masses, made it possible for the accused to be tried and judged by thousands. The overwhelming democracy of the concept set a battalion of flags waving from sea to sea, and the bill proposing the fundamental change, P.L. 7734-40, became law in the blink of a microchip.

"Let's see." The judge harumphed and cleared his throat. He pecked at the bottom row of the interface keypad as though the technology were all new to him. (And may well have been, considering the high turnover rate in Moralist bench appointments.) After a moment or two of noiseless binary conjuring, the computer displayed the verdict to the judge. The judge faced Wench squarely and said, like he was reading the side panel from a family-size box of breakfast cereal, "according to this, you've been found guilty as charged of all counts. What do you say to that?"

"Nothing," Wench responded.

Gumbo grabbed Wench excitedly by the wrist, tugging and urging, "come on, Chief. This is your big moment. You've got to say something."

"No. This isn't right."

"Of course it isn't. It's a monkey trial. A stunt."

"I mean, they're up to something."

"What?"

"I don't know," said Wench. "I have a feeling."

The judge gavelled. Inquired: "are you two conferring? Making a statement? Kindly let the court in on it, gentlemen."

"One sec, your honor," Gumbo begged.

The judge was patient.

During all of this, the fancy lawyer retained by the *Daily Parade* from Lemwalt, etc., made broad sweeping doodles on a pad of lined, legal-size paper. He drew moustaches and bold dollar signs and wrote his name in different styles. The battery of attorneys representing the Government, however, conferred. They voiced no objections. That's when the monitor from the bench, still at maximum power, shrieked out a demanding tone signal, a continuous b-flat above middle c.

The judge hammered loudly. The courtroom silenced asymptotically to the point that it was possible to hear the ambient air, stirred up by circulation vents, eddying. The rain, too, continued to beat down outside. The computer had ceased whining; the judge tapped on the keypad, made an error, tapped again. He read carefully whatever the message was that was so important the computer had to scream so insistently like a little boy needing to go to the little boy's room. The judge consulted with the bailiff. The bailiff, appearing confused, pointed to the terminal. The judge also seemed baffled.

Wench did not feel altogether well.

"Maybe you got a pardon?" suggested Gumbo.

The bailiff, scratching his head, ambled laboriously across the courtroom to the pair of husky security officers who were flexing their muscles under a framed portrait of President

Yaramon. Wench wondered why peons of power are always built like Surf City lifeguards. The two officers made their way over to the defendant's table. Wench figured out why. He felt doomed, nauseous and doomed.

The judge raised his voice. "Very irregular," he remarked. "I'm not entirely sure it is even legal. There is precedent, of course, but I'd still urge the defendant's attorney to press for an immediate appeal. In fact, I'd declare this a mistrial myself if not for the fact that the defendant has been found guilty by an overwhelming vote of 70 percent in favor, 16 percent opposed and 14 percent undecided. I don't know what to make of it, really, except to inform you. I'm truly sorry, Mr. Wench, but it is my unpleasant duty to report that an Executive Order has been transmitted to me. It requests ... no, it directs ... that I sentence you to the maximum penalty for the crimes of which you have been convicted. I'm awfully sorry. It's death!" the judge frowned.

Wench panicked.

The officers of the court pounced.

Gumbo bellowed at length.

But Wench was too stunned to hear anything except his heart pounding against his ribs.

Chapter 18

RIOTS seldom broke out anymore. With a solid two-thirds-plus backing of the electorate behind everything the Government did, from declaring war to picking its nose, and most of the Separatists gone to Alabama or packing their bags to catch the next bus to Alabama, the vocal opposition that remained was as watered down as a bottle of temperance beer. BLISS had done far more to keep everyone's blood pressure low than 200 years of medical science. Nonetheless, some things could still be counted on to engender a modified version of discontent among the population. Lottery fraud, last minute cancellations of rock concerts, school busing ...

The death penalty, in a trade-off agreement with the anti-abortion lobbyists many years ago, had been abolished, except in extreme cases (the same with abortion). Nobody had been executed by the state in recent memory. Nobody had been aborted, either. Wench's trial, hardly an extreme case, would, as the Government intended, draft a subtle and cautionary note to those who would dare oppugn the BLISS project. At the same time, by playing down the trial, the Government was cleverly obviating any potential outrage from its contented constituency. Neat as surgery; you never know; why take chances. This, which was what nagged at the back of Wench's mind throughout the ordeal, was what he rationalized, and was what he now believed. To his credit, Wench was half correct.

Wench desperately denied his fate, however. Battling off attacks of rage, depression, resignation and abject terror, Wench clung to the certainty that he would not die. Fear produced and unusual syndrome: nervousness, cold, and the uncanny ability to certify that he'd come out of the situation in good shape. Emotional Novocain. So Wench wasn't yet ready to wail or weep or gnash his teeth. He did kick at a foraging cockroach. He told himself again and again that the Yaramon Administration would have nothing to gain from his too early demise.

The holding cage that Wench tenanted was little more than a foul, restroom-size cubicle with steel bars for a door.

Lowia visited him the day before yesterday. She had worn her flouncy blue dress, the pretty one, the one that came down to her knees and flared open at the neck; it wasn't designed to conceal her figure. Since BLISS, Lowia vowed that she would dress more femininely. Not that she didn't dress like a woman before. She meant that she'd wear clothing that was more feminine. Thus, the dress. She clutched her handbag (also a practice of recent adoption) and, despite BLISS, sobbed: "you could have told me. I thought we were a couple ... you know, like husband and wife, almost. Now what am I supposed to do? What do I say to the neighbors? And my daughter's got to put up with this at school, too! You haven't been fair to us. You've seen yourself what BLISS has done for me. Why couldn't you leave it alone? If you don't like BLISS, nobody's forcing you to have it. But you go and mess things up for everybody, get yourself in trouble, and make me and my kid look ridiculous. Now I've got to find a new apartment, maybe even a new job, and alone, too, with you locked away here and probably never coming out, like a criminal. You don't love me. You don't love my daughter. All you care about is your damned newspaper and your damned stupid causes!" With that, Lowia's tears flowed like a summer shower.

Gumbo's visit was far more affirmative. He embraced Wench in camaraderie across the tiny counter that divided them. Within the nearly vacant rotunda, red and white posters commanded ALL HANDS ON TABLE. Wench and Gumbo ignored the signs. They also paid no heed to the superintendent guard stationed in the corner like a church icon. Security at prisons was exceedingly lax. Besides, Wench, the sole inmate, wasn't dangerous.

With the enthusiasm of a student about to embark upon spring break, Gumbo regaled Wench with the logistics of a citywide protest he was organizing. It included a one-day strike by newsmen and other members of Wench's union that would bring the media "to a standstill that'll have those BLISSed out potato heads scattering like wind-up toys at a flea market!" he said. He assured Wench that the appeal was "working, Chief, working." He brought Wench copies of the newspaper and some antique VHS videocassettes (that the prisoner was allowed to have). He asked, genuinely concerned, tenderly, "you hanging in okay?" The two men split a large moment of knowing quiet, saying nothing. There was nothing they dared say. Wench and Gumbo understood.

That happened yesterday.

Wench paced off his three meter by four meter windowless cubicle, wearing the same clothes, needing to wash his hair, wishing he could wash his hands. It's the little things that tear down a person's resolve.

Today, they came to get him at fifteen minutes past eight o'clock in the morning. Fifteen past eight. Too early for anything. Never mind the fact that Wench couldn't sleep and, as far as he was concerned, it was the middle of the night. Not a reasonable hour. Not the proper time for a showdown.

Three men strode to Wench's little cell. They had the gaits of bankers on their way to the vaults. They were freshly attired, neat, and certainly looked like they'd gotten a full, rejuvenating night's sleep. One of the men was gray: gray hair, gray suit, gray faced. He'd probably never even seen the sun because he worked for the Government and spent all his time moling around the halls of justice. The other two men, one black and one white, Wench wasn't sure about. As Wench had come to take for granted, these two men were muscular, taller than the Government official. The white man wore a black Homburg, a black suit, black shirt, and completely black eyeglasses (not sunglasses). The black man wore a white Homburg, a white suit, white shirt, and white glasses (even to the lenses). Wench couldn't figure out how either man saw the world clearly; it didn't matter. Mr. Gray drew an accordion folded piece of legal length computer printout from his jacket pocket and announced succinctly, while his twin sidekicks methodically opened Wench's jail door, "by further Executive Order you are to be taken herewith to a place of sentencing."

That was it. This was it. The jig was up. God save the jig.

Wench felt electroshock. One million bubbles of numbing tingle cascaded up his legs and shot into his brain. His gyroscope fell off its hinges. He forgot to breathe. He forgot how to breathe. But presence of mind, somewhere, like a mouse in a labyrinth, reacted to the impending doom. Wench backed away as far as he could and groped with an unfeeling hand for something solid - made contact with one of the bulky, old style videocassettes that Gumbo had brought. Wench functioned out of pure instinct. Any port in a storm.

"Hey, guys," he pleaded, "slow down a minute, will you please? Give a man a chance to catch his breath? Okay? Please. Not so close. I need more time. Give me some more time, a few more minutes, five minutes, okay, please? Come on, guys."

The metal grating heaved aside with an arthritic creak, and Wench smelled polyester inching nearer and nearer. He could taste his own stomach. It was bitter. He spasmed. His brain lit up.

"Fuck you, cocksuckers!" Wench changed his tone of voice.

Wench swung his arm around with as much speed and strength as he could muster, driving the angular corner of the videocassette sharply into the black man's white glasses. He heard a crunch. The cassette snapped apart and the reel of tape it contained spun into the air, unthreading all the while as it tumbled to the concrete floor. The black man vented a saliva-filled scream, clutched at his face, and keeled over, hitting against the right wall with his back, slipping down onto his knees. The others watched, more surprised than anything else. Some blood oozed out from between the black man's fingers.

"Get back!" Wench threatened. He held onto the remains of the deadly videocassette. He trembled, felt hot, had some difficulty catching air.

The white man in the black suit (what sort of officials were these guys, anyway?) angrily fumbled around inside his jacket and whipped out a tin-plated handgun - cheap, foppish, but effective.

"No," ordered Mr. Gray, quickly, staying the white man from firing, "don't spoil things."

Wench, wide-eyed, gulped.

The white man drawled, "but the guy's crazy." He insisted upon pointing the pistol at Wench.

Wench, in turn, held up the broken videocassette, defensively, like a switchblade.

"Put that thing down," Mr. Gray told Wench, paternally, soothingly. "Use your head. You aren't going to get out of here with a shard of plastic, now, are you? So go easy on yourself. You want to be shot dead right here? By the toilet? Slowly?"

The man had a point. Not much of a point, Wench thought, but valid. With no choices available, time became the option by default. Buy time ... minutes, even seconds. Buy low, sell high. Who knows? Time was all Wench had. He loosed his grip and let the broken videocassette clatter to the floor.

They took Wench. Delicately, almost consolatively, Mr. Gray and the white knight supported Wench. Side by side, arm in arm, in no particular hurry (which was fine with him), they paraded Wench from his cell and into the yellow-lit corridor where they turned him and headed him to forever.

Time careened around Wench like a whirligig. The corridor lamps sprouted rainbows. The floor became alive. Wench saw himself, a puppet. The puppet spoke, apologetically, "I'm really sorry, you guys."

"It's all right"

"Will he be okay?" Wench referred to the black man.

"Yeah. You only gashed his skull. Messy. The poor fool never could stand pain."

"Not too good with it myself!"

Wench experienced a fresh surge of panic, ripe and strong.

He tensed against it, but his captors only held him tighter.

"Come on. Show 'em you're a man!"

Drop my drawers? Wench was getting farther away from himself. His voice, curling, whined, "I didn't do anything. I really didn't do anything. I really didn't do anything. I really didn't -"

Wench screamed.

In front, a large black door stood between Wench and all the time he had left. Automatically, the door hissed and slid aside, revealing an ocherous chamber containing rows and rows of gauges and dials and metering instruments. Two windows loomed directly ahead. In the very center of the room was a leather armchair, with straps. On the chair rested a metal skullcap with sinuous wires extruding out, and down, and plugged into dark sockets. Wench thought the room looked like an airplane cockpit. Wench was drifting in and out of the scene, however, and was able to notice such things. At one point he even saw two men force his thrashing, resisting body into the frightening chamber and onto the chair. Wench's mouth was open and Wench saw his lips quivering, but he couldn't hear anything come out.

Wench's gaze floated beyond the glass windows and he witnessed a most peculiar thing! In the cold, cold gallery of observers sat Mars Gumbo. Gumbo was smiling, giving him the thumbs up sign! Now that was a bizarre thing for his best friend to do ....

They're killing me, you sonofabitch!

An intense pinprick whipped Wench's consciousness back into his body, like a vacuum cleaner sucking up dust. Wench howled unrestrainedly while a white-frocked medic, called in the last minute, injected some vile fluid into his biceps. Wench swung out to strike; his nerves didn't serve him and the effort failed. Nothing obeyed. Faces leered at Wench from out of the sky. The world, like an egg, cracked open. Wench, like a yolk, fell out. Wench was in another dimension and his mind was trying to run away from him, but he reached out and grabbed his consciousness with both hands and held onto it despite the tumbling and spinning as undefined forces limning his space tugged and pulsed; Wench clutched his mind even tighter to his breast and wouldn't let go of the familiar fuzzy thing no matter how deep or how far he continued to rocket toward the edge of the universe ....

It was his mind!

Chapter 19

HIS mind, Wench's, roused.

He felt the tugs and folds of his clothing: a swarm of angry pinches. His mouth was chalky. His skin prickled. He could smell tangy, wormy earth through the pervading sweet odor of half-rotted wood. He rolled over, allowing the back of his right forearm to flop across his brow. Grunting, he felt miserable.

Wench had fallen asleep, in spite of good reasons not to. Maybe they'd drugged him, he pondered as he wiped the inside of his mouth with his tongue, put something in the water. His head ached.

He unsealed a rheumy eye, focusing involuntarily on the depressing image of the underside of a corrugated tin roof. A brown spider was doing a lousy job of constructing a web in the corner - probably felt as bad as Wench did. Good morning, young arachnid, whoever you are. Coffee? One lump or two? And how's the wife and larvae? Excuse me, that's right, wife and spiderlings.

A brief shower marched past, typical of early Alabama mornings. The rain drummed a tattoo on the woodshed roof, a rhythm from the clouds, reveille for the new world. The droplets tripped in nines, it seemed; three to the measure, in triple time. Three times three is nine. It takes nine months of gestation to hatch a brand new Homo Sapiens. There used to be nine planets in the solar system. Ludwig van Beethoven wrote nine symphonies before he met his own composer. A regulation game of baseball is played in nine innings. There are nine Muses. The proverbial cat has nine proverbial lives. There are nine boxes in a grid of tic-tac-toe. There are nine zeroes in one billion. There are nine square feet to the square yard. There are nine years between Wench's last memory and today ....

"Dammit!"

The spider scurried to safety.

In an instant, like a mental fillip, Wench knew the gist of his situation, and he did not like it one bit. He startled, as though he'd poked his finger into an electrical outlet. He inhaled in panic, only to gag on a mouthful of musty air. Gripping the side of his cot to keep from pitching over into madness, he sprung to a sitting position. Lowia! Was it nine years since he'd even spoken to her?

"Hey! Get me out of here!"

He swung his feet round and planted them on the cold, hard earth. He attempted to stand, but the blood rushed from his head too quickly under gravity's immediate pull and his surroundings banked too sharply left, causing him to collapse rather ungainly back upon the cot, narrowly missing it completely. Wench paused until his internal gyroscope got back on track, then stood up with greater confidence.

"You guys! Anybody there?"

The woodshed wasn't nearly as large as it appeared to Wench when he was flat on his back. The pitcher of water that they'd set out for him the previous night (day?) remained on the ground by the foot of the cot, half full, beside an empty plate. He reconnoitered some more. The shed itself was no

176

maximum security prison by a long shot. At most, the little wood door was probably fixed with a simple hasp and padlock. However, as Wench didn't even have a paper clip on his person, and had barely enough strength at the moment to take a piss, he might as well be incarcerated in Okie Federal.

"Get me out of here. Please?" Wench used a more imploring tone, this time.

Nothing.

He tried his legs. Success. He walked to the woodshed door and tried muscling that. The door bore no handle, however, he could get a fairly good grip on one of the worn vertical slats and jostle the door in and out. It did move, but it was obviously pinned to the jamb by something stronger than Wench. "Yep. A padlock," he muttered. He forced the door harder, tentatively threw a shoulder against the stubborn barricade. His center of balance started to come unglued; the door stuck fast. Wench stopped and returned quickly to the cot, sat down to regain his composure. How long was he to be trapped here?

Fortunately, it was morning and some thin cracks of daylight squeezed through the woodshed's haphazardly planked walls. If he concentrated, he could hear distant sounds of activity, meager links with an outside world.

Like his cellmate, the spider, Wench spun a web. He remembered precisely nothing of the alleged nine year lacuna in the text of his life, which was odd. His trial seemed like yesterday: to Wench, for all intents and purposes, was yesterday. A rational man would have called his captors liars; Wench could not so easily dismiss the physical evidence apparent in his face, his hands, his body. It was called aging, and time could be read most truthfully in his wrinkles, grayed hair, physique. Again he thought of Lowia, his love, and liquid filled his eyes.

What happened to her? Here was a mystery that gnawed at him to the quick. His only consolation, and poor consolation, was that Lowia, under the spell of BLISS, would cope with his absence far better than he could. Score one for BLISS, Wench chuckled inwardly. Although, didn't the doctor, whatshisname, mention something about Wench in ... "deep" BLISS? Is that what happened? Instead of giving him the ultimate pink slip, shutting his power off for eternity, they BLISSed him out? Why? Why that way? Why couldn't he remember any part of it, goddammit?

"What's that?"

Wench startled at some too close noises, metallic jingling, muffled speech. The woodshed door creaked open like a picket fence gate, allowing gallons of daylight to pour in. Wench turned.

"Thought I've been hearing a white man in a woodpile," announced the doctor, jocularly.

Backlit as the man was, his large-featured face, silver and white mottled beard trimmed neatly enough to be erroneously described as unshaven, and Schnauzer-like head of hair could be clearly discerned. The doctor's black skin glowed; his smile soothed; the man had a most comforting visage, to be sure. The doctor wore plain clothing and around his neck hung a stethoscope like an albatross.

"Afraid I've forgotten your name, doc," Wench said.

"Titus Archimedes. If you wish, call me Archie. Everyone else around here does, although I can't admit to having particular fondness for the moniker myself. How're you feeling this morning?"

"Fine ... uh ... Archie ... uh ... I got questions."

"Okay." The doctor approached Wench the way a dog breeder might approach a valuable bitch, and proceeded to undertake a series of clinical ministrations - eyes, tongue, heart, pulse, cough, again, reflexes, hair, that sort of thing. "Ask away." Wench noted that the doctor spoke an interesting blend of rhetoric, slang and academia with an ever so Midwestern accent. The doctor ordered Wench to unbutton. Wench did, and the doctor began thumping vigorously on Wench's chest.

"Where the hell was I for nine years?"

The thumps thumped to a thumping halt.

"Some question!"

"Well?"

Methodically, the doctor folded up his stethoscope and, seeing that there wasn't an end table on which to put it, hung it back around his neck. "You were in Deep BLISS, like I explained."

Was Deep BLISS a bus stop? Wench, irritated, complained: "My neighbor is in BLISS. The paperboy is in BLISS. My girlfriend is in BLISS. Millions of people are BLISSed out all over the damn country and I don't know of a single case of nine year, slam-bang amnesia among the lot of them!"

"Deep BLISS. It's a relatively new procedure," the doctor elaborated, gesturing for Wench to cool his temper. "We didn't know about it for a long time, either."

179

"And ... ?"

"Apparently, it's as close as you can get to perfect brainwashing. It wholly strips the individual of every vestige of free will, but, unlike regular BLISS, leaves ability and talent intact."

"You mean the country's full of - "

"Heavens, no!" corrected the doctor. "The Government couldn't administer to millions of functional zombies. For the average citizen, BLISS is adequate. Deep BLISS is reserved for special circumstances."

"I'm a special circumstance?"

The doctor beamed proudly and placed a manly hand on Wench's shoulder. "You were - " He selected the adjective carefully. " - notorious. Who better to make an example of than the national spokesman against BLISS, no?"

"But they didn't kill me," Wench pointed out.

"I know; you said. I reviewed your media last night."

"Anything good?"

"Following your trial and the controversial death sentence that, by the way, had the majority of the population - 70 percent of them, anyway - licking their chops in anticipation of a juicy weenie roast, excuse the expression, the Yaramon Administration benevolently declared hither and yon that, if you volunteered, your sentence would be commuted to BLISS."

"What?"

"My boy, you volunteered," the doctor said.

"I did?"

"Well, your computer image did, on the telly, several times a day. Everybody thought you were

180

going in for the standard BLISS and blow-dry. Nobody had an inkling that Deep BLISS existed. God, you should have heard your sycophantic swearing in the day after, pledging your all to Yaramon and his thugees like they had cured you of the seven greatest plagues of man. It's on videocard. We might even have a copy here. If you like ... "

"What are you saying?" Wench interrupted.

"You weren't acting under your own volition."

"Out with it!"

"You *are* a clean slate. Good lord, you wound up working for them."

"Yaramon!"

The doctor nodded. "Secretary of something or other, I think, writing movies."

"You're kidding."

"Well, propaganda films at first. *The Yaramon Chronicles* was your best effort, I felt. Although the critics roundly favored your *Save the Unconceived Children*, and *Zygotes: Save the Unconceived Children, Part II*. It made a lot of money and the theme song topped the charts for months. Unprecedented."

"Did I compose the theme song, too?"

"Nope."

"Thought not."

Wench flashed back to a particularly unsettling memoir of his freshman year at college, when he hung a major Saturday night drunk, and the next morning his best friend told him how he'd lustily proclaimed his undying love for a co-ed he'd only dated once, and chipped a tooth, though events of that evening remained an everlasting blank to

181

Wench. Funny he should think of that. He never had the tooth repaired; his tongue found the fracture.

"But wait a minute. Rewind. Why the ruse? If the Government had in mind to BLISS me out, why didn't they give me the option for real? I mean, anything's better than snuffing it."

"Offhand, I'd surmise it had to do with the fear factor."

"I was scared all right."

"Which is probably why they didn't tell you. Helluva thing to put a man through."

Wench looked puzzled.

"BLISS, you understand, is psychologically similar to hypnotism, in many respects. For one, it is virtually impossible to BLISS out a person against his or her will. Unless that person is scared."

"Fear."

"Correct. And the more terrorized the subject, the more effective the BLISS treatment. We can only, as yet, theorize as to the causal relationship. However, maximum fear -"

"Fear of death equals Deep BLISS."

"That appears to be the story."

"Joke was on me, eh?"

"Helluva thing to put a man through."

Wench inquired, "what about natural immunity? Does this fear stuff obliterate that, too?"

"No. Immunes are still immune. A kiss is still a kiss."

Wench glanced past the doctor, which was convenient as the doctor had, in fact, directed him to look straight ahead in order to examine his neural responses. Wench stared through the wide open shed door onto the broad expanse of sloppily tended lawn outside. His view was limited, framed like a picture; nonetheless, he could make out a leafy tree or two, people, and machinery tiny and silent in perspective, moving like mites along the back of the horizon. Occasionally, a broad-shouldered guardsman would step in front of the door, obscuring the scene, making certain that nothing untoward was happening within the confines of the shed. Evidently, the guard had been pacing this way, back and forth, throughout the entire conversation Wench was having with the doctor. The guard toted a gun.

"And the amnesia?" Wench asked.

"For some reason," the doctor continued, "and we don't know why, either - maybe due to temporary synaptic routing, memory layering - a patient brought out of Deep BLISS can't recall anything that occurred while under Deep BLISS. Has no memory of the experience, far as we can tell. The brain disc sort of erases itself. That is, if the person survives re-emergence at all."

"Survives?"

The doctor sighed. "We lose too many. So we don't do too many." He smiled, immeasurably satisfied. "But we didn't lose you. You're fine!"

Fine? Wench swallowed the word as if it were a bitter caplet. Virtually an entire decade had been ripped from his life like so many square pages torn out of a desktop calendar. In movies, you get at least that image, if not a two-minute montage of lap dissolves. Hell, all Wench had to show for the past 3,285 days, give or take a Sunday, was a lousy suit that he wouldn't buy on a bet, and a potbelly. Fine?

183

The doctor unfolded his full six-foot-two height, rolled back his shirt sleeves that had loosened during the examination, and adjusted his wire-framed eyeglasses. (Wench didn't remember if the doctor had worn glasses at their previous encounter; perhaps the man only used them occasionally, for reading, or house calls.) The doctor turned to leave. Wench wouldn't have any of that.

"Doc ... ? Archie!"

The doctor caught himself in mid-step, spun, raised a brow.

"I appreciate everything you've done for me." Wench felt silly, like he was accepting an award. "But -"

"We try."

"Why?" Wipe that absurd smile off your face! "Why do you try? What are you trying? What in hell is going on here? Doc, I've been living a whole other man's life the past nine years and I don't have the foggiest idea what I've been eating for breakfast. One day I'm plucked out of my existence like a damn mushroom at harvest, scared shitless, and the next thing I know is I'm way down South in the land of cotton trying to catch up on a fistful of birthdays. I need more than a lesson in modern science."

The doctor seemed disappointed. "I figured you, a former reporter, would appreciate an honest assessment."

"I do, only - "

"Everything else will be told to you as soon as the Guv'ner returns."

This was new. The Guv'ner? Governor? Capital G? As in somebody in charge of the store? There

184

was a certain irony to it: Wench, a refugee, captive, escapee, what you will, being told to wait for the Governor on the magnolia-scented grounds of a leftover antebellum plantation somewhere in the heart of Dixie. Wench half-expected an inflated old gentleman sporting lace, four-in-hand tie and a goatee to come galloping in on a gleaming carriage, its thin wheels going tic-a-tic-a-tic against the gravel. Wench shook the crazy illusion from his mind.

"You okay?"

"Sure," replied Wench, "just thinking."

"Well. Guv'ner'll be back any moment. He went to Birmingham to shoot some rock music discs. Likes to get involved, you know."

There was a brief detention in the flow of time, like the clockworks jammed and then started up once again. Wench wondered: "Am I stuck here?"

"In the shed? Only until he gets back."

Him again. "One more thing?"

"What's that?" the doctor asked, eager to be of help.

"You wouldn't have any information about a woman named Lowia Lilli, would you?"

The doctor smiled widely, as if he knew the answer to the final question on *Quiz for Gold*. He laughed under his breath, mouth closed, two or three puffs of amusement snorting from his nose: a response that heralded very good news indeed. He said: "you married her."

"Married?"

"Years ago." The doctor signaled for time out with an open right hand, raising it up and forward. "Please, no more," he insisted. "The Guv'ner wants

185

to fill you in on the details. And I did promise him."
The doctor departed quietly, on rubber soles. He left
the door ajar.

"Oh?"

Wench couldn't have been more effectively
immobilized. For about a minute, anyway. Then
reflex took charge. Unable to absorb anymore,
propelled by instinct, he threw himself at the door.
What happened next was pure circumstance:

The single guard was into the "forth" leg of his
back-and-forth pacing, that is, approaching the
woodshed entrance from the right. The door itself
was hinged on the right, meaning that it would
swing open toward that direction. When Wench hit
the door in blind fury, adrenalin pumped, driven by
superhuman rage (the effect well-known in medical
literature), the door shot to the right like a catapult.
The door and the guard met halfway. Though
massive himself, the guard was no match for the
slamming action of the door. Neither did the guard
expect to be stricken by such an obstacle. He
expelled all his breath in a voluble, pained oof, lost
his balance as one leg came up off the ground, and
teeter tottered drunkenly on the other. Then, like a
sawn through tree, he fell. The gun the guard was
carrying flew out of his hands and landed several
feet away on the ground with a solid thunk. It did
not discharge.

The doctor, probably on his way back to the
makeshift hospital, meanwhile, turned around at the
first spark of commotion and saw the guard
knocked for a loop as Wench barreled out of the
woodshed, choleric as the devil.

186

Wench spotted the weapon. The guard was still too shaken to react. In no time, Wench scooped up the firearm, cradled it in his arms, positioned himself with his back toward the deserted shed, faced the dawn, and pointed the weapon primarily at the recovering guard because, determined Wench, the doctor didn't pose any serious threat. He was, of course, right. The doctor simply watched the little drama unfold, hands in his pockets, rocking on his heels, tut-tutting in mild disapprobation.

What else could Wench do? "Everybody freeze!" he ordered.

"You haven't even seen the Guv'ner, yet."

Wench bristled. He knew he had taken a monumentally stupid chance breaking out of the woodshed. But that was the animal in him, his shadow fury, caged once, long manipulated, finally exploding. Sheer chance had placed the unfortunate guardsman in the right place at the wrong time. Fate placed the gun in Wench's trembling hands. It wasn't his fault. However, he chose not to think about what the outcome might have been thirty seconds sooner, five seconds later. Despite the edge, the advantage with him at this moment, he didn't know what to do next. That scared him. This place was likely infested with armed Separatists. Was he going to blast his way out with a solitary, medium-range rifle? There was all of Alabama to consider, as well, between him and home. Was he attempting to go home? Did he want to go home? One thing he knew: for whatever reason, the Separatists wanted him to stay. They would not hurt him.

"All right," Wench snapped. "I give up. Who in hell is the Governor?"

The doctor pointed to an amorphous shape growing in size and, as it did, congealing into a distinctive outline, approaching from the horizon. "That's him."

Wench heard the sound of an engine, first as a barely audible hum, then a distant roar, then a shattering cacophony of banging pistons, grinding gears and unmuffled internal combustion. It was an old, gas-fueled engine, and not one that was very well maintained. It was coming closer, at top speed.

When he could recognize what it was, Wench saw a truck - a pickup truck, rusted, splotches of oxide all over the metal body like automotive carbuncles. It was dented in so many places it looked as if it had been hammered into shape. Only one of the truck's eyes worked, and that headlamp was cracked. As the vehicle jounced and squealed its way nearer, Wench made out the driver leaning hysterically on the horn, blasting it emphatically as if armistice had been declared. There was something familiar about the driver.

The pickup popped like a cartoon cannon and stopped dead, close enough to Wench for him to touch the hood. Instead, he dropped his weapon. Even after nine whole years, there could be no mistake. It certainly was ...

The driver wrestled his way out of the truck. Sure, the once bearlike silhouette had degenerated a good deal to flab. Sure, the beard, once the vibrant hue of a late summer sunset, looked now like broom straw. Time hadn't been altogether kind to this man, either. But the raw energy was still there, and no passage of years could erase or contort this welcome figure which greeted Wench now, which had greeted Wench so many times back in Bigapolis and kept him buoyant to the bitter end. Wench wanted to let out a whoop that would fill the sky.

"How ya' doing, Chief? Long time no see," cackled Governor Mars Gumbo.

Chapter 20

WENCH had been living a double life; that is to say, while the original Wench was put on hold, the BLISS version of Wench flowered. He was a personality detour, a fork in the road of entity. Though the new Wench remained aware of the old Wench (and thought himself the better, by comparison), the old Wench, subjectively, was in stasis, something like hitting a brick wall with your eyes closed under water at midnight.

During these years, the Yaramon Administration took the country in hand and somnambulated forth with all the due haste of a paperweight precipitating gently to the bottom of a barrel of mud. A cloying pall of contentment bathed the land; one could even smell it.

BLISS technology, as technology is wont, improved, miniaturized, came down in cost. The procedure simplified to the point that it could be administered from the panel windows of those familiar yellow trucks, by a single tech with a day's training, while eager communicants pressed in from curbside, wearing designer tee-shirts, sandals, robes & curlers, holding pet dogs on leashes as the animals pissed and barked, everybody waiting for their lives. BLISS techs, observers frequently noted, could be likened to old-fashioned ice cream vendors. The trucks even took to heralding their presence with a catchy tune played through a loudspeaker over and over: " ... a better life ... dad, kid and wife ... " went part of it.

Application, the ritual of giving the masses their dosages of BLISS, had evolved into one painless swallow of a bland medication followed by the pressing of a clamshell size disc of yellow copper against the subject's temple for about the length of time it took to recite "in the name of the Reverend Yaramon, the sun will shine from coast to coast," all in a compact movement. This was strikingly similar to an evangelistic laying on of hands. The parallel was certainly not lost to a wildly enthusiastic public, many of whom took BLISS more than once.

Although a single "immersion" - the authorities doted on jargon the way the population doted on BLISS - was all that was necessary to achieve the full, duration-indeterminate effects of the procedure, people quickly discovered that additional "immersions" produced an extremely pleasurable feeling of bodily well-being - a high, a "walking return to the womb," one devotee put it - that lasted for several hours, easily long enough to get a person through to the evening's first prime time TV picks. Television, in fact, and fast food, and sex, if indulged in following a fresh juicing of BLISS, could be greatly enhanced. Especially sex.

(The Moralists turned a blind eye to the aphrodisiac qualities of BLISS; sexual attitudes invariably produced more babies. With more babies came a whole raft of Moralist supported side effects: parental responsibility, job security, credit card applications, and so forth.)

The appearance of BLISS trucks on the streets, schoolyards and shopping malls of the nation multiplied like yellow jackets swarming around a pizza parlor on a hot afternoon.

Key to the improved BLISS technique was the discovery of CH-20 by a lesser chemist in Government employ. The discovery of the substance was not so important as the fact that CH-20, a restricted pharmaceutical derived from a plant alkaloid, was a major export of Trinidad and Tobago.

This led to the war for Trinidad and Tobago.

Ever since the island republic had elected Mostafa Guypan as its presidente, it had been teetering on the ideological fence separating the New East from the West, too often giving every indication that it was about to plunge irretrievably headlong into the lap of the "other side." Throughout this precarious balancing act, however, Trinidad and Tobago managed to continue its strong trade ties with the democratic nations. Trinidad and Tobago was a major exporter of pre-packaged pu-pu platters and Steely Rock, in addition to that very classified botanical extract that, when refined according to the Feldman-Sykes Reaction as published in Heluva. Chem. Acta, 39, yielded the invaluable CH-20. In order to prevent possible cutoff of supplies, an unthinkable likelihood should Trinidad and Tobago fall under New Eastern domination (not to mention what would happen to the lucrative Euro BLISS market should the Russians secure their own source of secret alkaloid), the Yaramon Administration promptly bulldozed through Congress a foreign aid package supporting a covert guerilla war against the Port of Spain regime.

It was called a regime; the instigation of veiled hostilities was not a difficult political maneuver to effect. The argument, clearly and presently, was that by keeping Trinidad and Tobago pre-occupied (or semi-occupied) with an internal struggle against the "Contra Skeptics," as they were christened by their leaders who were based, undercover, in a rooming house in downtown Bismarck and from which they gave frequent press briefings, the country would have no time or funds with which to stabilize. At best, Presidente Guypan would be overthrown in favor of a Yaramon puppet. At worst, Trinidad and Tobago would be cast into a politico-socio-economic quagmire from which it would never recover. That was the thinking.

Unfortunately, everybody involved had completely forgotten about an obscure defense pact Trinidad and Tobago had signed with the United Kingdom decades ago. Technically, the treaty was still binding (even though England's Prime Minister overtly sided with Yaramon on the issue of covert activity). So, in order not to provoke an international incident which would surely have wreaked havoc with television scheduling and advertising revenue globally, the U.K. made a deal, sub rosa, with Trinidad and Tobago. They, the U.K., would sell the party of the second part, Trinidad and Tobago, DeLong-Harrier fighter planes at wholesale if the island republic wouldn't insist upon full treaty compliance. The latter didn't. The former shipped. The war could be safely engaged. The world breathed a sigh of relief. The conflict, it was expected, would smolder, seemingly without end, like a glowing charcoal, and the precious fount of

193

CH-20 would continue to flow, provided the war kept clear of the crops.

Plant damage turned out not to be the next tile in the rapidly falling queue of dominoes. The British planes, it was discovered to the chagrin of all concerned, were "damnably effective fighting machines!" With the kind of nationalistic zeal infusing the Trinidad and Tobago pilots that only occurs when a downtrodden minor league nation gets the opportunity to clash horns with one of the majors, the Guypan army swiftly took the upper hand.

Yaramon winced. Britain, essentially, shrugged her shoulders noncommittally. Congress refused to send in troops. What's more, the Yaramon Administration was prevented from organizing a rock concert or a telethon to raise money in support of the "Contra Skeptics" because the rebels, although open and above board (sharing room and board in Bismarck, ND), were covert, and a national fund-raising campaign would breech this secrecy. Such a move, the Secretary of State proclaimed, would not be legal, either. Or moral.

But ...

Great discoveries have a way of popping up in the right places at the right times; it's more certainty than serendipity. The automobile, it has been posited, became readily available at the precise moment when the horse lost its charm and practicality as a means of individual transportation. Yaramon himself often admitted that the widespread acceptance of interpersonal television peaked propitiously at the time his own Moralist

Party was ready, and able, to leap into political prominence.

With the war in Trinidad and Tobago going badly, then, it was no wonder that somebody developed a way to synthesize CH-20. Some might even insist it was written.

In fact, Dr. Meri Mammalia, Ph.D., FACS, working feverishly day and night, not even breaking for lunch or to answer her telephone, discovered that not only could CH-20 be synthesized, but the essential ingredients in the synthesis were obtainable from several plants indigenous to the New Jersey Meadowlands! Furthermore, Feldman-Sykes had overlooked the obvious catalyst. Synthesis could be accomplished with minimal added expense for some cheap lab ware, in an ordinary kitchen.

This was good news, indeed. Dr. Mammalia was awarded a huge grant and Feldman-Sykes were relegated to the alchemists' archives. They were outshone by the new and lauded Mammalia Synthesis that was milked for all it was worth by the scientific establishment and sensationalized by the Society for Women in Laboratories.

The covert war for Trinidad and Tobago could at last be terminated, much to the relief of the Yaramon Administration. The skirmish was a bust, anyway. Nobody had paid very much attention to those two tepid islands in the Caribbean. And, despite BLISS, the residents of quiet, communal Bismarck were increasingly perturbed over the boisterous activities of the "Contra Skeptics" based in their town. UHF and microwave reception often suffered as a direct result, complained homeowners.

Children were reluctant to go out of doors. The hens refused to lay. Many people swore they had seen flying saucers.

Nonetheless, Yaramon was hardly about to mince quietly away from the shores of Trinidad and Tobago like the boy who'd been caught dropping eggs off the roof. In Executive Session, it was determined that the Administration wouldn't carry an unwon war on its back throughout recorded future history. The honorable solution: bomb Trinidad and Tobago to hell and back with impunity. This was a stroke of political genius. There would no longer be any concern about Trinidad and Tobago going New Easternist, capitalist or anywhere inbetweenist - the country would be too busy suffering. At the same time, missionaries from the major Moralist Parishes could be dispatched to Trinidad and Tobago on pious and humanitarian grounds, to give succor, to give paperback bibles, and to give the folks back home plenty of opportunities to pat themselves on the back for their unselfish devotion to the underprivileged. Of course, the plant crop from which CH-20 alkaloid was derived would be wholly decimated, maybe eradicated. No matter anymore. In fact, this was the piece de resistance for the Yaramon Administration to rain fire and brimstone (in a very authentic sense) upon Trinidad and Tobago. Congress also approved the raids. According to informed sources, Russia had no native plants from which CH-20 could be extracted.

Bombs fell like spring hail.

At this point, it must be reiterated that fortuitousness is not a demonstrable belief. The whims of mass taste, while as light and variable as a midmorning breeze, can and have been charted with predictable exactitude, give or take a few percentage points. (See *Up Your Accuracy*, by Stephani Bucket; Colonic Press, Boston.) The shoe, here, was simply on the other foot. The Yaramon Administration failed to take into account the evidence plainly around it, and lost the competitive edge. Steely Rock was climbing the charts faster than a thief being chased upstairs. A craze was brewing, albeit untested. Opportunity, like virginity, once lost, cannot be gotten back.

Steely Rock, a heavily syncopated form of light pop music incorporating Caribbean steel drum idioms with Reggae influences, was taken to heart (and ear) by the consuming masses in a way no musical genre had ever been. The lyrical qualities of Steely Rock, singable rhymes that told of the plights, hopes and promises of the common folk, reverberated through all market segments, elevators and car stereos. The appeal, truly, was universal. The father of Steely Rock, if any single entertainer could be credited with generating this latest musical phenomenon, was twenty-seven year old Simon Eye, going by the stage name of Brother Simon. In fact, declared one nationally syndicated music critic: "Brother Simon's star already approaches none other than that of the legendary Jesus Jones in magnitude. How long before we have two bright lights of the highest order in music is not the question; we must ask ourselves when the wizard of Steely Rock will blaze in the firmament all by himself." Alas, this was never to be.

Eye (like the majority of Steely Rock musicians) was from Trinidad and Tobago.

When the bombs obliterated these islands, the CH-20 producing vegetation was immolated well beyond nature's capacity to regenerate it, true. Trinidad and Tobago's pre-packaged pu-pu platter export industry was also dealt a fatal blow; few people cared. What nobody, from Capitol Hill to the homemaker shopping in Food-O-Rama, ever expected was that Steely Rock would be crippled in its prime. In fact, Simon Eye himself, working on his eagerly awaited Steely Rock opera, was blasted to smithereens in mid-note. B-flat, F, E, C - boom! That much of a fragment was uncovered in the wreckage following the raids. A great loss.

For a time it appeared as if the world might never recover. The Steely Rock tap had run dry; a frightful situation, it was worse than the Television Strikes of a previous decade. Yellow BLISS trucks jaggedly ran and reran their routes all across the country, working double and triple shifts, in a hectic attempt to stave off taedium vitae on a massive scale. Hospitals swelled beyond their capacities under epidemics of the blahs. In desperation, some people even went to libraries. Cases of catatonia were doggedly treated. Movie theaters remained open around the clock throughout the crisis.

The Separatists in Alabama, meanwhile, monitored these events with a great deal of solicitude. They were largely unaffected by the rest of the country's throes of ennui; however, they had their own problems. They missed the good life. Hell, even saints, historically, were known to indulge in pleasures. Separatists weren't saints.

They did what men and women (men and men, et cetera) have always done. Alabama farmland proved bountiful and, in this respect, the Separatists developed self-sufficiency. But neither soil (nor sex) could prevent Alabama from becoming technology poor. Video equipment broke down; microwave ovens malfunctioned; the latest entertainments were not to be had, anywhere. This is what increasingly bothered the Separatists like an unscratchable itch. They were politically, economically and socially motivated; they were not beyond enjoying a rousing "actioner" in true color and quadrasound. People are the same all over. Have your cake and eat it, too. The fundamental things still apply.

But necessity (and here's another adage for you) is the mother, or at least the adopted caregiver, of invention. The country was not wallowing in the depths of its deprivations two months when, quite intentionally, Separatist Curtis "Leppy" Lepidoptera left his small farm in Tallapoosa County, during a three-day heat wave, for the border, taking quite a risk. He could have been heavily fined, without warning, if caught outside of Alabama, "Leppy" well knew. It was a calculated risk. "Leppy" had the solution to everyone's problems. "Leppy's" parents, his grandparents on both sides, in fact, his entire family tree back to the roots, sprouted from Trinidad and Tobago. "Leppy" was a musician, a composer of merit, and a student of Steely Rock. The poetry of his forebears was in his blood.

"Leppy" was apprehended at the border by two burly patrolmen in dirty green coveralls who wanted to castrate him on the spot; the world might never have been the same. Fortunately, the patrolmen were deeply bored themselves, enduring the same malaise that had stricken half the continent. So they opted to drag "Leppy" kicking and pleading back to headquarters where the entire crew could work on him slowly. Kill the entire afternoon, they anticipated. There, "Leppy" managed to convince the Captain, a rabid Steely Rock afficionado, to at least listen to some of what he'd written before they pulled out his arms. "Leppy" had written six Steely Rock singles, a Steely Rock symphony (something new), and a funeral dirge in honor of Simon Eye. The world was saved. So was "Leppy."

Events had conspired to mold history in such a curious, at first exasperating, fashion that what followed may have been only a matter of time. Whatever, this is how an entire industry was born. This is how history was processed. This is how Separatist Alabama and the rest of the nation to which it was still, if in geography only, attached shook symbolic hands and became friends - business partners, anyway. Alabama, because BLISS was anathema to creativity, because BLISS was voluntary, because emigration was a viable alternative, found itself thick with a creamy layer of unapplied expressionism like a bottle of unhomogenized milk. This bred irritability; it is possible to, say, sit under a magnolia tree by a babbling brook and write out poetry in longhand, but it isn't very rewarding. Alabama's artists got restless. Everyone else simply got ornery from too many reruns.

Steely Rock was the cure; it had been the cause, now it was the cure, and it opened the floodgates. In

Alabama, every illustrator with a cartoon or comic, every writer with a pulp fiction, every musician with a chart buster, every film maker with a camera soon beat a path to the border traders - those quick-buck investors who, seeing a hot property, bought low and sold high. Serious "art" wasn't in great demand, but work was work, wasn't it? Soon it was even legal.

The Yaramon Administration acted quickly to take full credit, of course. In a televised address to the nation, it was revealed that: one, the Government had been prodigiously "uncovering" local talent all along; and, two, Reverend Yaramon, who had graciously conceded independence to Alabama in the first place, now had authored an historic trade agreement with the sovereign state. In return for music, movies, videos, comic books, novelizations, and other entertainments, Alabama would get hard technology, cable TV, and a Lickity Chicken franchise. In other words, Alabama received an economy, money, jobs, take-out pizza, televised wrestling; it exported seven-part miniseries (to run Mondays through Sundays), Top 40, illustrated large-print romances ... somewhere along the line, Eric Emm even invented the enormously popular dukhorbortsy wheel.

Congress flirted with the notion that creative Separatists ought to be offered lucrative contracts, and amnesty, to live and work outside of Alabama. The idea rattled around for a while, like a loose grape, eventually getting squashed. The basic tenets of Separatism hadn't changed, after all, nor the quintessential reasons for granting independence to the state in the first place. Why roil calmed waters?

Saner minds prevailed. The Trade Pact was best. It worked.

Later, even the border restrictions were loosened.

"And that's when you were finally able to get me out?" wondered Wench.

They were sitting in the middle of a sun drenched dining hall that was one of the larger rooms within the mansion to which they had taken Wench, arm-in-arm, following the joyous reunion at the woodshed. Wrinkled glass panes, framed in dark wood molding, ran the length and height of three walls. The fourth wall, the entryway, displayed a faded oil painting of a man long since deceased. The solid wood floor didn't even creak; it supported an enormous, mahogany, stained and filigreed oak table surrounded by an eclectic scattering of chairs. The chair in which Mars Gumbo stuffed himself was broad backed, with heavy arm supports, and was cushioned in genuine leather. Doing all the talking in his usual spirited manner that had not diminished over the years, Gumbo resembled a Tudor period monarch on the throne. The chicken leg he nibbled at as he explained events to Wench only enhanced his kingly visage. They'd ordered food brought in the moment they'd entered the room, suspecting that Wench would appreciate a solid meal. They also brought him a change of clothing, assuming he'd want to get out of his conspicuous evening wear. They were quite right, on both counts; Wench showered and ate a full dinner.

Wench stretched, feeling more comfortable in the sneakers, belted denim jeans and roomy green sweatshirt they'd scrounged up. Sated, he crouched atop a straight-backed dining chair, one knee tucked against his chest with his arms wrapped around the bent leg, listening intently to his old friend's narrative. Archimedes leaned against a sideboard that was empty except for his half-drained mug of beer. It was the heavy part of the afternoon now and the windows were taking on the same color as aged lager.

Gumbo squirmed in his chair. "Not exactly," he admitted.

"Oh?"

Gumbo laid down his chicken leg. "Everything I've told you happened within two, three years of your trial."

"Two, three years?" Wench bolted upright. "You left me dangling like a damn worm on a hook for five more?"

"Six."

Wench eye's widened. He flushed. "five, six ... what the hell were you waiting for? An engraved invitation - "

"Hold your horses, Chief. It wasn't so easy. We didn't know how to bring people out of BLISS until a couple years ago. Besides, you were working for them! You were married! We hadn't an iota as to the extent of your conversion: how much was BLISS, how much was you. In any case, we couldn't run the risk of jeopardizing our entire enterprise for one man, no matter how much I urged. Can you follow me, Chief?"

Wench was not sure. "Then why did you pull me out at all?" he asked.

"We had to."

Wench gave his friend a very quizzical look.

Archimedes cast his eyes heavenward, as if the clouds were about to burst.

Gumbo responded to Wench, defensively: "you were going to get us all murdered!"

Chapter 21

ABUTTING the sideboard, a late model, 37-inch television monitor with direct satellite dish feed, stereo sound capability and mahogany finish kept its own counsel. Upon Gumbo's nod, Archimedes waved the set to life. It glowed lime. The doctor then touched the proper code into a flat remote and the set winked once. It revealed a spaceman's eye view of the Western hemisphere, cloud shrouded. Archimedes touched the remote again. The TV beeped. The doctor pressed a bulbous finger against the screen itself, roughly obscuring the state of Texas. The TV stopped beeping and deliberately zoomed in on that area of the hemisphere. Texas filled up the entire screen. Archimedes tapped the remote; the image froze; he touched in another two-letter code; the image was instantly overlaid with graphic isobars and color-keyed pressure systems. Archimedes smiled at his handiwork.

"Take a look," Gumbo directed Wench.

Wench scrutinized the monitor. He stepped right up to it and, with its cold light bathing his face, gently traced along one of the more prominent isobars with his index finger. Wench could read a meteorological surface map with the best of them. "If this is correct," he mused, pausing to fully interpret the data, "if this is correct ... then the climate has shifted, again." Wench turned to Gumbo, student facing teacher, insightfully. "This means Texas is re-inhabitable."

"Is and was," Gumbo declared.

Wench, curious, sat down. "What's it got to do with me?"

Gumbo explained. With broad and animated gestures, he told the story of how the Great Heat Wave (older than an entire generation) cooled. The displaced people of the Lone Star State, en masse, virtually the same day, hour, second that the weather reports hit like happy lightning, charged for their four-wheel-drive vans. Flags flew. So did footballs, football helmets, and double-barreled shotguns. The smell of barbecue and near beer almost overcame the odor of gasoline. In a lemming-like wave of humanity, Texans, returning to their promised land, hauled up young ones, old ones, bank accounts, stakes (and steaks) and funneled into the paved arteries going South. Celebration was a 1,700 kilometer long tailgate party. Traffic was backed up for counties. Radiators boiled over; so did tempers.

"You don't want to provoke Texans," said Wench.

"Precisely."

Which is why a brand new leg of the Zoomway, linking Bigapolis with Houston, became the order of the day, a la carte, with chaps on. Signed, sealed and promised by the Yaramon Administration, amidst loudly drawled cheers and applause, the new Zoomway, christened the Santa Anna Annex, also meant that "the sun will shine from coast to coast" now included the Gulf Coast.

"So?"

"The first law of the Zoomway, Chief: the shortest distance between two points - "

"Bigapolis. Houston."

"Is a straight line."

"Through the top of Alabama!"

In order for the Government to accomplish this miracle of modern civil engineering, and genuine crowd pleaser, to boot, it was necessary to first obtain one of two things: road access rights through Alabama, or Alabama.

But government is an odd duck, a prophet once remarked. He knew of what he spoke. The Yaramon Administration had several alternatives spread before it like a buffet dinner, and could easily have selected any entree. The main leg of the Zoomway extension could have been projected from Chicago to Houston, and wouldn't need to slice through Alabama at all. A road access treaty with the independent state could have been negotiated, much the same way the Trade Pact had been hatched. There was even talk of returning Texas to Mexico as a birthday present (felicitas navidad!), thus, sidestepping the issue altogether. The latter notion was absurd; Texans were so Moral. Besides, travel from Bigapolis to Houston and back, before the drought (B.D.), was etched in loving memory. It had been an essential factor of national life, and would be so again. The route of the new Zoomway was, literally and figuratively, cast in cement: a commandment, no less.

It must be peripherally detailed that plenty of loud voices in Congress had always opposed granting independence to Alabama. No matter that the popular referendum showed 70 percent in favor, 16 percent against, and 14 percent undecided. With adequate hype, scientifically disseminated ... what a golden opportunity to admit the state to the Union, for the third time.

Then there were the Separatists themselves. They weren't exactly in solidarity forever concerning the proposed Zoomway. Some Alabamans jubilated that the Santa Anna Annex would pump oodles of toll dollars into state coffers; they hailed the project. Others insisted that the Zoomway would only transmogrify their beloved home into a major theme park or, at best, another Staten Island; they hated it. In short, the Separatists were "uncompromising, implacable and virtually impossible to deal with," said Government spokesmen as they walked away from the bargaining table even before coffee was served.

Threats proved useless; the Administration dared not imperil the delicate trade balance that existed between the country and Alabama. Force was unthinkable; the Administration could not risk another Trinidad and Tobago. The Zoomway to Texas looked stuck.

"Till there was you," said Gumbo.

"What did I do now?" groaned Wench.

"Boffo box office," replied Archimedes.

A smash in ultrascreen and wallsound, the highest grossing commercial film to date, in fact, *Adventures in Blondland*, written, directed, edited and photographed to a large extent, although not scored, by Astin W. Wench, was also the turning point, depending upon whose side of the border one happened to reside. Wench also wrote a book, based on the movie, which sold very well. The enormously popular soundtrack was composed by Jesus Jones, mentioned in passing only because the aging rock star was the other "recruit" in Yaramon's talent stables. The important fact was that Wench no longer made propaganda. He was in the Big Time. Capital B. As in Deep BLISS. As in Balance of Trade.

"As in," Gumbo stressed, "if Yaramon's boys don't need us anymore, they can build their Zoomway over our dead bodies."

Archimedes calmly handed Wench a wrinkled page of coated paper. It was a secret document; it said so. In all capital letters, in non-repro blue ink, under the heading PRODIGAL SON, was typed: CONFIRMING EFFECTIVENESS SELF-SUFFICIENCY RE POPULAR MEDIA INITIATE MOBI-LIZATION COBINED FORCES TARGETING MONTGOMERY, BRIMINGHAM, HUNTSVILLE, RALPH. Almost all capital letters. The fax, somehow, had fallen into Separatist hands, fortunately, depending upon whose side of the border one happened to reside.

Wench read and whistled. "Ralph?"

"A small burg near Tuscaloosa. We keep our computers there," informed Archimedes.

"See? We had to yank you out. Like I said, you would have got us all butchered. Indirectly." Gumbo philosophized: "you are only one man, but the road to wreck and ruin begins with only one man. Nip the Yaramon brain trust in the bud, that's what we had to do. Hey." He snapped his fingers, inspired. "It's kind of like corporate raiding on a bigger scale."

"How'd you do it?" Wench asked.

"You weren't confined."

Wench found it difficult to be grateful. "You pulled me out to save your miserable economy? You let me wallow in BLISS for years, then pull me out because I made a lousy movie?"

"A good movie," said Archimedes.

"You don't understand," Gumbo pointed out. "The Separatist Consuls wanted to kill you. Dispatch a hit squad. I changed their minds. I promised them you'd work for us."

"Not a chance."

"You'd have it good here," Gumbo explained. "You'd be well paid. Have your own office. A liberal vacation package. Generous health benefits."

Wench paused like a thundercloud before it breaks loose. He stiffened, reddened, then let it pour. "Jeez, Gumbo, you sit on your goddam ass trying to sell me a job like a goddam employment agency! I've been floating around in zombieland for nine years, dancing to Yaramon's music, doing who knows what to help the bastards. I'm not happy about it; at least I have an excuse. You came here, for whatever reason. All right. I'll buy that. But do you have to play go-between for these malcontents and those BLISSed out nincompoops? Do you have to drag me in? Holy cats, Gumbo, what the hell happened to you? What's your excuse? Why have you changed?"

Gumbo stuttered.

Wench headed for the door like an irate husband. If he had a hat, he would have put it on. He reached for the brass knob, yanked the door open. It swung easily on its oversized, greased hinges, without a squeak. Wench stormed out of the room and into the hallway like a bull out of hell, let alone a bat. Dire purpose had come over him; it could be seen in his eyes. As a fuel, dire purpose has no equal. Wench was running pure. He once had a vow; now the vow had shape and form.

"Where you going?"

"Home!"

Chapter 22

THE hall, long and polished and studded with windows on one side and doors on the other, was the firing chamber to the bullet that was Wench. Luckily, Archimedes had shot after him. Archimedes took a firm and unthreatening grip upon Wench's forearm before the latter burst through the front door and into an open encampment of none too sympathetic Separatists. Troops of militants could be heard swarming outside like hornets, as deadly, as touchy. Their stings were more potent.

"Don't be an idiot," advised the doctor.

"You, too?"

"Hell, I don't care what you want. As a physician, though, I hate to see you toss your life into the gutter like it was an empty tin of fish."

"Look," Wench stated firmly," I've got to do two things. I've got to do them! If I don't, what the hell's the use of having a damned life, fish or no fish. I've got to find Lowia. I have to see her. Then, I have a score to settle with those damn bastards and their damn BLISS. Nine years of scores. If I get killed trying, you, nobody can deny me that right."

"Revenge?"

"It's as good a reason as any. Besides," Wench swore, "BLISS is no damn good!"

"So you say."

A Separatist militiaman, meanwhile, chewing phrenetically on the butt of a black stogie, pressed his face close to the front door glass panel, peering inside, overwhelmed with curiosity. Archimedes acknowledged the man with a reassuring smile, sending him away on the rest of his rounds.

"Awful lot of guards around here," Wench muttered, "thick as flies."

"It's the Governor's Mansion," Archimedes explained.

He suggested the two of them step into a bay windowed but still private, and less exposed, antechamber where, in another century, Southern belles entertained Southern beaus. It wasn't a large room. The seats, a single long bench really, jutted from the wood framed wall. The windows were stained glass, which is why it wasn't easy to see either in or out. Musty cushions covered the bench; however, an enormous potted Ficus tree had been plopped squarely in the center and had to be moved aside. Wench, for a fleeting moment, had a vision of going to confession. Archimedes' sometimes clerical attitude prompted this religious deja vu. The cloistered quarters helped.

The doctor shut the door behind them and spat "Shangri-La!" as if it were a dirty word.

"Who?"

"Utopia. Arcadia, now. Everybody wants it. Even here they believe this will last forever." Archimedes made himself comfortable and continued. "You need to understand the long haul. See history in terms of geologic time. Ah, these momentary flurries of political trends mean little, have less effect. Sure, perhaps half a generation of a single population may benefit from what we do, or suffer. How many generations have been born, have grown and re-seeded the planet since the beginning of time? You can make an argument, you realize, that, taking the next million or so years into account, BLISS isn't very significant. I mean, it's not worth breaking a sweat over. It's like war, upheaval, natural disaster. You know what those are? They're hiccups. That's what. You hiccup and, for a fraction of a moment, your body jerks, you can't talk, you can't breathe, see or even think properly. So what? The hiccup lasts for only the least of micro moments and then you are fine again. Really, you can hiccup while driving a car, hiccup while you are doing heart surgery ... hell, you can even hiccup while making love and it doesn't interfere with a damn thing! Does anybody fret over the potential of hiccupping. I ask you? Agonize over that nanosecond when they will be incapacitated? No. Of course not. And this planet isn't concerned about BLISS, Separatist Alabama or the crazy climate, either. Earth hiccups. Life hiccups. That's all. The human race - not the population right now - but the whole human race from our Pleistocene beginnings to our infinite future doesn't give a hoot what's aired on TV tonight. Should we? What the hell can our piddling efforts accomplish in terms of eons, anyway?"

"Nuclear extermination?" Wench wondered.

"Accidents happen."

"Then what do we do?"

"Nothing!" Archimedes declared. "That is exactly my point. The swarming masses out there, 70 percent of them, anyway, clamored like hungry chicks for BLISS. And they got it. They got their opiate. They got their pablum, too. It is an exceedingly contented world; more importantly, it is a world of their making. You don't approve? Fine. It will pass. Chaos shall return. But do you have the right to impose your will on the masses, right or wrong, benevolent or malign? Whose concept of order is proper, or appropriate? Is any? Is chaos the only real truth, the only real nature? I ask you."

Wench pondered Archimedes' rhetoric. It was, given enough latitude, valid in the purely objective, idealized sense. But deep within himself, Wench held his own truth. Lowia. BLISS. Nine years ....

"Who reckons for me?" asked Wench.

"Personally?"

"Give me that!"

"Go," ceded Archimedes, "if you're imbecilic enough to demand selfish vengeance, although I doubt you'll make it past the north perimeter of this plantation by yourself. Return to your family, by all means; you may succeed in that much. But leave the world to writhe and contort in its own misery, should it choose. We bring pain down on our own heads aplenty: that status is very, very quo. Always has been. Maybe it is true. Perhaps, in a way, suffering is the only means by which we can achieve nirvana."

There was an echo of familiarity in the doctor's words. Wench dislodged a stubborn memory. "You almost sound like a Freeyare," he remarked.

Archimedes, with the attitude of a child who half desires and half refuses to reveal a secret, extracted a small metal trapezoid from his shirt pocket. If he'd guessed that Wench knew more of the secret than he cared to reveal, the doctor may have changed his mind. But he showed the symbol to Wench.

"You are a Freeyare!"

Realization followed. It bounced off the shiny medallion and rattled around in Wench's head like a roulette marble until it came to rest on the jackpot.

Huddigger ... beamed beatifically as a glorious peace spread over his face. He whispered: "Joy, oh joy, a martyr's joy. I go to perfection." But before the man went, he calmly delivered his final word into Wench's receptive ear: "Archimedes."

"You," Wench bounced up, "are Archimedes!"

The doctor appeared puzzled.

Wench, agitated, didn't hear the knocking at the door, or assumed it was fate. The doctor heard a very solid, real enough rapping, and reached out to unlatch the shut portal. It swung aside. Mars Gumbo stood in front of the entryway, an old carbine strapped to his right shoulder, a pair of mismatched handguns tucked into an ammunition belt that girded his not unsubstantial waist. He wore brown corduroys, a brown lumberjack shirt and brown boots. He resembled a comic book version of Pancho Villa. Wench cared little about the resemblance; he pointed a finger at the doctor and continued to shout, "Archimedes! Archimedes!"

"I know," agreed Gumbo in a slightly bewildered tone, "but we call him Archie."

"You don't understand. Syracuse. The day I was arrested. The Freeyares. He's one of them. He's the Archimedes!"

"How many are there?" asked Gumbo.

"Just me," said Archimedes. "But I'm not a Freeyare. I was one. Once."

Gumbo learned long ago never to take Wench for a fool too long. With all due respect, he lifted

216

the carbine from his shoulder, set the weapon down aslant against the door jamb with the muzzle pointing ceiling-ward, and urged the doctor, candidly: "go on."

Wench panted.

Archimedes insisted, "I'm in the dark. I was reasoning with the guy when I happened to reveal that I, at one time, had been associated with the Order of Freeyare Souls."

"You never told me that," said Gumbo.

"It didn't seem important."

"Important?" Wench blurted. "Huddigger spoke your name before he died."

"Will you stop picking up from where you left off?" Gumbo chided Wench. "I swear, you're like a time machine." Then he turned to Archimedes and, perturbation rising volcanically in his throat, said, "Look. I got two dozen angry Separatists outside who'd love to sink their fangs into a Freeyare. It's crowded and stuffy in here. What's more, I'm short of patience and getting tired. I suggest that you fill me in on this cozy tete-à-tete. Quickly."

"But - "

"Quickly!"

"I don't - "

"Now!"

Archimedes did the best he could. He seemed visibly averse to discuss his association with the Freeyares. His reasons were good, but he had no choice; that's what comes of playing "remember when" with a time machine.

He sighed, almost resignedly. "We must begin with the Large Schism ..."

The Large Schism was already an established fact when the Syracuse enclave of Freeyares summoned Wench to that fateful and, for many, fatal meeting nearly a decade ago. At the time, however, the Large Schism was not discussed openly. Freeyares certainly wouldn't allow their internal bickering to become a matter of public record. Thus, Wench, and the world as it was, had no inkling of the ideological split, initiated by a plethora of other factors, catapulted into a terrible reality by BLISS, that was tearing the Freeyares apart. The history books now clearly bear this out.

" ... Freeyares could not tolerate benign indifference," said Archimedes. "Their entire credo and religious existence depended upon oppression. Without that, without healthy persecution, they had no alternative. Scripture commanded an awesome response."

"The Ultimate Solution," recited Wench.

Archimedes nodded. "But there were those within the Freeyare organization who sought to redefine Scripture. Whether in response to holy enlightenment, as they claimed, or simply to save their own skins, these protesters, heretics some called them, branched away from the orthodox sectarian body and founded the Reform Freeyares. Their views on persecution were less punishing; their beliefs concerning intercourse with the outside world less isolating; what's more, they held that they had divine right to monkey with temporal affairs."

"I see," Wench was developing the full picture. He said to Archimedes: "you were a Reform Freeyare."

218

"I ... yes ... " Archimedes continued more guardedly. "The Reform Freeyares pursued unwaveringly every combative avenue they could in their crusade against BLISS. But they always ran smack into dead ends, in more ways than one. The exigencies of the outside world hardly mattered to them, obviously. Results warranted any means, and - "

"The virus!" exulted Wench.

"What?" bellowed Gumbo.

Wench smacked his right fist into his left hand. He quoted his undiluted past. "*The heretics may be our salvation. Find the one who carries with him the knowledge of the world.* Archie's a biochemist. What else could he have been doing as a Reform Freeyare? You were cooking up an anti-BLISS germ, weren't you? That's why Huddigger gave you his dying breath."

"What's why?" asked Gumbo.

"Because Huddigger knew a Reform victory over BLISS meant reconciliation of all Freeyares," Wench crowed. He had hit the bull's-eye.

Archimedes threw up his arms in frustration, like a cornered felon. He protested vainly, "it's not what you think. Christ, it didn't even work!"

Gumbo wrenched a pistol from his belt and emphatically poked the weapon into Archimedes' sternum. He growled, "tell us how it didn't work."

The doctor let out his breath. "All right," he confessed. "I was working on such an organism. Ages ago. First as a Government employee, then as a Reform Freeyare, and now ... now I'm out of it. I'm no longer involved. Hell, I haven't looked at a virus in years."

"This guy's got more careers than a guidance counselor," Wench wisecracked.

"Go on," Gumbo prodded.

Archimedes complied. "It was a fluke. An accident. A real deus ex machina like the kind they don't make anymore. We, I mean the Government scientists, were synthesizing a virus all right. We had this silly notion that a bug could lick immunity. Early tests suggested we were on the right path, but, boy, did we take a wrong turn! The virus didn't even slow immunity; you know what, though? Damned if it didn't transmit BLISS. Well, needless to say, the Administration went bananas. A germ like that? How're you going to stop it? Within a few months, some fitful sneezing, trade winds being favorable, at the height of the tourist season, why the entire world would be awash in BLISS whether it wanted to be or not. So ... Damn the immunes, full speed ahead! Trouble was, midway in our research, the virus up and mutates, as viruses will do. Contrary to our objectives, we found ourselves knee-deep in a strain of anti-BLISS molecules." Archimedes shook his head, laughed ironically. "Well, the Government promptly axed that baby. And how. They destroyed the labs, the notes, the cultures, even some of the more outspoken scientists. Those of us who managed to escape the wrath - "

"Us?"

"Me. Coward. Others. Coward and I had been attending Freeyare proselytizing sessions. The Reform movement needed help; we needed to hide. That's it."

"You developed an antidote to BLISS and tell me that's it?" Wench complained loudly.

"It was another big, fat zero. A failure," Archimedes explained. "It cured, sure, but then it killed. The side effects were deadly."

"It couldn't be tamed?"

"I don't know. Maybe. Not by me alone. Not here." Archimedes squirmed, rubbed the back of his neck nervously, and made some guttural noises. "Ah, you might as well know. All the research, cultures and equipment were confiscated by Coward when I left the Order. Hell, I don't know if any of the stuff still exists. Or if he does."

"Then let's go find out," demanded Gumbo.

"Let's go?" asked Wench.

"Why do you think I'm carrying all this artillery?"

"I was wondering about that."

"If you insist upon chasing off after wild geese," Gumbo said, "I suppose I ought to tail along, keep you out of mischief. Can't have you getting yourself bumped off, or re-indoctrinated into the Yaramon camp. Not now. Besides ... aw, hell, Astin ... I haven't changed!"

"Thanks," Wench said, heartily.

Gumbo grumbled something.

Archimedes added, " ... in Okie Fed."

They both looked at the doctor. He volunteered, "Coward Santiago is in Oklahoma Federal. Last I heard, anyhow." He paused. "Dammit. You'd better take me along, too. You'd never get inside the place. The Reforms have become a pretty nasty bunch."

"In prison?" asked Wench.

"It isn't a prison any longer," said Gumbo. "It was closed down eight years ago."

"Then what are they doing there?"

"Hiding," said Archimedes.

The Separatists were changing shifts outside. Evening had ridden in on a gentle breeze, as it always did, and there was noise and bustle as the day guards exchanged places with the night guards. Wench, Gumbo and Archimedes exited the mansion like three old pals on a carousal. Against the dimming light, they blended into the surroundings. In the pervading sounds, smells and activities, they projected no indication that they might be preparing to embark on an adventure that, if successful, would assuredly alter the economy and entire way of life in independent Alabama. This was coincidental, not intentional. Regardless, had their plans been discovered, the three would certainly have been apprehended, or worse. The conspirators agreed to depart first thing in the morning. Archimedes strolled off toward his surgery to pack a duffel bag. As the Southern sun buried its head below the horizon, Wench and Gumbo went for a little walk to discuss the nature of democracy.

"How'd you get to be Governor, anyway?" Wench asked.

"Free elections, Chief."

"Is that all you're going to say?"

"No. Actually, I came here after I was fired from the newspaper. Heard this place was looking for some creative minds and keen ideas. Or was it vice versa?"

"The paper canned you?" Wench was astounded.

"Not at first. They offered me a fat salary increase, an immediate bonus, and my own office ...

to stay on as Diet Editor! What does a Diet Editor do?"

"Who became Science Editor?"

"Nobody. They wiped out the department, along with the City Desk and the International Section. The *Daily Parade* is now the hottest pop gossip, scandalmonging rag north of Huntsville. Circulation's in the millions, Chief. And here I am."

"Governor?" Wench prompted.

"When I first got here, the artists were in sorry disarray. Intra-state competition was fierce; nobody was getting a decent living wage for their work. There was a guild, in name only. I helped put some teeth into the thing and strengthened its bargaining power with the Yaramon Administration. I became president of the guild and, a year later, Governor of the State."

"Didn't think you were all that interested in politics," Wench remarked.

"I'm not," admitted Gumbo. "The job's more of a sinecure. I get to live in the Governor's Mansion and the Separatists get a warm body to blame should things become staticky."

"Why do it, then?"

"Keeps me off the streets."

223

Chapter 23

OKLAHOMA Federal Penitentiary for Wayward Men and Women was a tedious and uncomfortable drive from Alabama, primarily because the Zoomway didn't go there. The Zoomway went to Maine, The Torontoes, Detroit and Chicago. In fact, if plotted on a map, the Zoomway resembled nothing as much as a skeletal right-hand splayed out over Bigapolis, covering quite a broad patch of the Northeast Corridor. The thumb stretched down to Atlanta. The four lanky fingers touched northern destinations. But the Zoomway didn't go anywhere close to the Southwest, as yet, and existing roads to the region had badly deteriorated over the years of drought. Traffic signs were long gone, or stolen. Even the car radio, at best, was mute; at worst, it crackled angrily.

Driving west, Gumbo, Wench and Archimedes found themselves ever barreling into the sun, that oppressive visual reminder of the gaseous hell that lay beyond the thin skin of their automobile. Even though the climate had begun to moderate, it was still pretty hot out. But they were in an air-conditioned capsule, confident that the life support systems of the Uranus Mark V Turboboom coupe would not let them down. Gumbo's car had gotten older, the candy apple blue a shade or two duller, the chassis dented and scratched in a gracefully aged manner. Gumbo testified to the vehicle's enduring reliability: "they don't make 'em like this anymore."

He was right. They'd crossed the border into Mississippi early, before sunup (4:43 a.m., eastern standard time), by veering off the road and driving through open country. The land was mostly flat; the Turboboom had traction and horsepower enough to scale any of the small hills they encountered. In this way, by driving in the dark, with the headlamps off, they were able to get out of Alabama unnoticed. By the time the Separatists realized they had fled, reaction - indignation, anger, whatever - would be academic. Gumbo wouldn't be Governor; he'd abdicated his office the moment the car's front bumper edged over the political boundary. Wench and Archimedes would be fugitives from two nations, a condition which Wench virtually relished, and to which Archimedes politely resigned himself.

They'd upset the status quo, you see. In essence, they'd triggered a nibbling away process at the ties that bound Alabama to the Yaramon Administration. Unification by a mere pledge of alliance is a gossamer thread, rent with a whisper. Chains of economic dependence are difficult to break. Once forged, they require extraordinary forces to undo. This can prove both positive and negative. On one side, commerce sure beats combat as a means of dealing with a hostile neighbor. On the other side, economics, q.v., the tampering with, can get you blown away.

Wench and Gumbo hadn't the fullest comprehension of what effects their excursion would eventually have upon the continent at large, though they certainly intended to have some impact.

225

The Separatists were paranoid enough to consider only the worst. And the Yaramon Administration had always held Mars Gumbo highly suspect, anyway.

With the radio off, conversation flourished. Archimedes took up the entire back seat, his arms folded under his head, and his legs crooked up. In his herringbone sport jacket and gray slacks (no tie), he appeared more refined then rebellious. He posited: "if you two do come up with this counteragent to BLISS that you're looking for, who's the villain?"

"What do you mean?" asked Gumbo.

"I mean ... people want BLISS." Archimedes began the discussion. "The procedure's never been involuntary, and people swarm to it like flies to an open garbage can. Conversely, the method we have to bring people out of BLISS hasn't exactly been taken to the public bosom by an overwhelming margin."

"It's sloppy," said Wench.

"But this virus you're after could wipe out BLISS on a universal scale," argued Archimedes.

"I know."

"Folks aren't going to like that."

"They won't have a choice."

"My god! You're worse than Yaramon."

"He started it."

"He gave the people what they wanted."

"And screwed me royally for nine years."

"You broke the law."

"A bad law," Wench maintained.

"Maybe. But you broke it and you could have fried."

"They lost Gumbo his job, too," Wench insisted. "His way of life. You aren't exactly the apple of their eyes, either, you know, Archie."

"Beefs. Private beefs," Archimedes replied. "Good ones, granted, but," he raised the issue, "do we have the right to retribution from an entire population?"

"Can we wait until we get to Okie Federal to decide?" Gumbo squelched the debate with a mallet. "We may find nothing there but discolored bricks. Or worse. Or a band of Yaramon's angels with dieselguns coming for to carry us all into the arms of everlasting BLISS." He seemed to mock the very dreadful connotation his paraphrased verse implied. It was intentional. They knew the risks; they drove on, anyway.

As milky dawn shifted through turquoise day into rusty evening, then blackened, the Turboboom shot across Mississippi and most of Arkansas, ferret like in its determination to get where it was going. With less than half a day's travel time remaining, the adventurers parked and slept uncovered against the surface of the planet, blanketed by the see-through atmosphere, looking at outer space.

They arrived within distant view of Okie Federal the next day at 2:01 p.m., eastern standard time, according to Gumbo's watch. Wench never wore a watch, and Archimedes had peculiarly unconcerned opinions about time. He said it flowed, which was enough for him. Gumbo, though, liked dials, meters, instruments that measured.

The Federal Pen poked up from the unbroken horizon. The clayey structure took on a sanguine tinge in the light. The buckwheat colored land, long parched, had a noticeable convexity. From the vantage of the travelers, Okie Federal resembled a pimple on a clean-shaven cheek. Closer up - they pulled in closer to their destination with extreme caution - the prison could be more accurately delineated as three twelve-story brick buildings. Each was T-shaped, with the heads of each T forming a non-touching equilateral triangle around a center court. Many windows in the buildings were broken. A chain-link fence, topped with razorwire scalloping, originally built to circumnavigate the prison, stood in vestigial pieces, now. The quietude had also deteriorated, gnawed through and roughened by the aggravated chirrs and rattlings of hidden vermin.

The Turboboom's engine stilled; the car doors cracked, hissed and yawned open; the travelers got out of the car and stood around in the yellow bath of solar energy. The atmosphere took some getting used to; it appeared lifeless, that is, devoid of any sentient beings.

Gumbo kicked away an oversized, furry ant that had red markings on its abdomen. "Deserted," he spat.

"Not necessarily," said Archimedes.

Oklahoma Federal was built near the shores of Lake Texoma, in the very southern plain of the state. It was not a maximum security prison; mostly, it was a gulag for political criminals and malcontents. It featured seventy kilometers of razed flatlands all around. Escape was never completely impossible, but, because daily temperatures soared into the low 110s (mid 40s C.), and the no-man's-land thrived with scorpions, spiders and snakes, few had ever tried to flee. Nevertheless, the prison was ultimately shut down; BLISS saw to that. BLISS enabled 70 percent of the inmate population to become rehabilitated and tailored to fit back into society. Another 16 percent were allowed to emigrate to Alabama, where they became Separatist border guards or local bureaucrats. The remaining 14 percent were deemed insignificant and simply ignored, allowed to roam free. Okie Federal went to seed, the plowed land moat never recovered, and insect life experienced a baby boom.

At one point during the past several years, Reform Freeyares secretly occupied the vacated buildings, and nobody cared, or bothered to care. This part of the country was egregiously uninviting, except, apparently, to Reform Freeyares.

Archimedes signaled for his two companions to remain behind while he alone broached the nearest jutting tower of the prison complex. When he was within a mere twelve meters of the structure, he scanned the windows: dark, unrevealing recesses, holes actually. Archimedes raised his hands to his face and cupped them around his mouth.

"Santiago Freeyare!" he bellowed, extending each syllable as far as it would go before breaking. *"San-ti-a-go Free-yare!"*

A shot rang.

A puff of dirt flew up from the spot on the ground where the slug hit, far enough away from Archimedes for all to realize it had been only a warning.

Gumbo, at a safer distance, cursed and lunged for the trunk of the Turboboom, flinging it open, digging through the contents like a dog after a bone, upsetting clothes, tools, Archimedes' medical bag. He extracted two weapons and handed a pistol to Wench. "Here."

"What's this for?"

"Whistling Beer Barrel Polka," Gumbo jibed.

Meanwhile, back in harm's proximity, Archimedes stood undaunted. He fished in his pocket and took out the shiny trapezoidal memento of his former link with the suspected occupants of the building. He held the amulet high against the sky, like it was an offering to the gods. In a certain respect, it very well was. Using his left hand as half a megaphone, he called his own name. "Archimedes Freeyare!" He shouted only once.

Anxious minutes trundled by. No gunfire.

Shortly there appeared a figure in an upper window, darting back and forth, leaning out of the window, popping back in, then vanishing altogether. Chances improved immeasurably that the prison was not in the hands of Government law enforcement agents. In fact, it was an increasingly good bet that Reform Freeyares still lived there, although they didn't get regular mail delivery. In the time it took to imagine a man walking down twelve flights of stairs, the conjecture proved certain. An individual stepped from the building, unarmed, un-uniformed, and clearly unaffiliated with the Yaramon Administration. That individual and Archimedes faced each other like chess kings in opposition. They exchanged Freeyare salutations. Then they hugged like old buddies.

"That's got to be Santiago," determined Wench.

"Guess so," said Gumbo, "but I'm still hanging onto this." He brandished a Ubitza light carbine.

Wench stuffed his clip-loaded 9mm automatic down a rear pocket, carefully making sure the safety was in place. "Yeah," he agreed, "I'm getting tired of surprises, too. Come on."

They bounded up the rise toward the prison like a mini-cavalry to the rescue, although Archimedes needed no rescuing.

Santiago greeted them.

Santiago Freeyare, nee Coward Santiago, was hardly a large man; however, it was obvious that he'd spent many hours weightlifting. What was also apparent was that one of his parents must have been Oriental, and the other one Black. His surname suggested a third racial element in the mix. What prompted the given name was anybody's guess, although it likely led to his penchant for bodybuilding. Santiago was bright-eyed, big toothed, and had a wiry mustache that encircled his mouth and arced down into a tiny goatee. His head was closely shaved, Buddhist style, and his own identifying open trapezoid dangled in miniature as an earring from his left lobe. Santiago wore a very clinging white tee-shirt tucked into thin cotton pants. He was barefoot.

So much for the monkish attire Wench had come to associate with Freeyares. So much, too, for their normally submissive nature. Santiago's shirt was emblazoned with the militant slogan: Not Anymore.

Santiago, however, greeted them with a soft-spoken and affable "Gladdameetcha, boys!" He extended a hand. In no way did he object to Wench and Gumbo bearing arms, either, admitting candidly, "we keep a fair to middling defense ourselves, as you may see."

Wench's trepidations lessened.

"I've explained something of your quest to Coward, here," said Archimedes. "He also thinks you're acting foolishly, but -"

"Lemme show you," Santiago offered.

The four of them entered the east wing of the prison. They would soon number five. Their entourage was growing.

Chapter 24

INSIDE, Wench was amazed at how unprisonlike everything appeared. Okie Federal never was one of those austere, iron-barred lockups. Nevertheless, the Freeyares had certainly done wonders to make a hoosegow a home. The floor was cement. The walls were cement. All surfaces were painted a cool aquamarine, a wise color scheme, considering. The double-ganged twin set of main doors (looking like an airlock, functioning as such) opened into a spacious central hall. On Wench's left, as he entered, a reception desk in disarray lay unused. Past the desk, a pair of swinging glass galley doors separated the hallway from a dining room; Wench could see through them a more traditionally dressed Freeyare munching tiredly on a sandwich, a steaming mug by the Freeyare's elbow. Further beyond the cafeteria entrance were two elevators. Both in working order. Wench assumed that the prison had its own generators, and probably a backup solar power plant. Where the Freeyares were getting fuel for the generators was unimportant. Wench turned to his right. On that wall, again, words, brushed on in indelible black, swore openly: Not Anymore. A simple staircase led to the second floor.

"We could use the elevator," said Santiago. "But let's walk." He ushered his guests in the direction of the steps.

On the next level, through a fire door, they found themselves in a narrow passage linking more

233

entranceways and spotted with fire extinguishers hung at eye level, like paintings.

"In here," beckoned Santiago, pushing open a massive steel door marked, informally, LAB. It sure was.

Wench and Gumbo gazed around, craning their necks like gawkers amidst Bigapolis' skyscrapers. Veteran science writers, they had an appreciation of fancy laboratories. The roomy facility held several ranks of gleaming ebony worktables, encrusted with chrome hardware - everything the modern scientist could want or require. Clean glassware of all shapes and sizes stood tantalizingly on shelves. The big stuff, the expensive machinery, was adorned with dials and indicator lights like badges of honor.

Wench asked, "how did you manage all this?"

"The three Bs," Santiago said proudly.

Archimedes explained: "begging, borrowing and bilking."

One of the worktables supported an experiment in progress: a centrifuge was humming beside a rack of partially filled test tubes, and an opened notebook. Gumbo was the first to notice something else, something much less appealing, that seemed out of place, here. In the far corner, atop a low stool, squatted a frighteningly familiar, pot-bellied device. It was the height of a refrigerator. It was shaped like an enormous metalloid gumdrop. It had three fishfin airfoils near the base. It had a distinct, attached nosecone. It had, on the side, spray painted in wide stroked red letters, the phrase: Praise the Lord.

"That's not what I think it is, is it?" inquired Gumbo, pointing to the device.

"Armed and dangerous," a girl's voice concurred.

They spun around to see a strikingly beautiful young woman in lab coat and short skirt come in through a side door, carrying an Erlenmeyer flask. She could have been anywhere from sixteen to twenty-one years of age, but no older. Her skin was the hue and purity of brown crayon. Her straight, inkjet hair, cropped in a '20s flapper style, favorably accented her

Oriental inheritance.

"My daughter," Santiago announced.

"Hiya!" she bid, raising her flask in a toast. "My name's Darling. Call me Dolli. I work here."

"You aren't a Freeyare?" asked Wench.

"No, she's not," Santiago said brusquely.

"Daddy doesn't want me to join the order," she pointed out, "do you, Daddy?"

Daddy remained silent.

Gumbo, on the other hand, anxiously sought to steer the discussion, which was getting off track, back to the atomic bomb that garrisoned the corner like an obscene warder of thermonuclear destruction. "Why?" he demanded to know.

"Why I can't be a Freeyare?"

"Why the damn bomb!"

"Oh, You never can tell when it may come in handy," she said flippantly. Darling Santiago pranced buoyantly across to the central worktable where she'd been brewing chemicals; her skirt flounced in the warm breeze that wafted in from the open windows. She set down the flask and propped herself up on a high chair, knees up, showing her smooth legs, sandaled feet and nail painted toes.

235

She was, perhaps, being more flirtatious in her actions than one might initially assume.

"My daughter's immaturity often gets the better of her, I'm afraid," Santiago apologized.

Archimedes smiled, placed a hand on the shoulder of his former associate and brother of the cloth, and urged, "the *project?*" He gave the last word added weight.

"Yes, certainly, of course," Santiago replied, as if he'd remembered a roast he'd left in the oven.

The breeze smelled hot. Rays of sunlight, reflecting off the curved surface of the atomic device, bent into sardonic grins.

The wiry Freeyare walked over to his daughter, slid open a narrow drawer under her worktable, withdrew a bunch of keys that had been laced together with string. He walked over to a tall, steel storage cabinet, unlocked it with one of the keys, and swung aside its door, revealing six inner shelves. Each shelf contained racks of fat test tubes; the containers were full, to various levels, of an amber gel; some test tubes were securely stoppered, others had cotton wadded in their mouths. Santiago, casually, readjusted a few of the racks that had become crooked.

Wench hoped. "Living virus cultures?"

"Yes. And hardy little buggers they are, too," explained Santiago. "They seem to thrive in this climate. Long as they aren't exposed to direct sunlight for too long. It kills 'em."

Darling Santiago, pen in hand, without diverting her attention from her work, admonished: "don't get high, again, Daddy, please?"

"High?" That struck Wench as odd.

Archimedes, too, was nonplussed. "If I remember correctly, that stuff's as lethal as an Ebola-B cocktail. Don't tell me you managed to take out the sting all by yourself?"

"No, no, no." Santiago shook his head emphatically. "It mutated a third time. Most unstable molecule I've ever seen. But in this form, it seems to be content. Hasn't exhibited any inclination toward altering a single pyrimidine in years. Replicates like a rabbit, and true. Trouble is, it ain't the BLISS antidote we were searching for, way back when; damn germs reverted to stage one!"

"They transmit BLISS?" Archimedes was stunned.

Wench was crestfallen. "You've got gallons of the stuff," he accused.

Gumbo tightened his grip on the rifle.

Santiago placed one hand upon his brow. He waved the other one in a hasty gesture of appeasement. "Wait a mo', boys," he implored, "the material ain't what you think - "

"What Daddy means ... " Darling bounced off her chair like a sprite and strode over to her father, stuffing a pen into her coat pocket. She kissed her father on the cheek and turned to the three agitated visitors. She explained, " ... Daddy's a good scientist, but not the best teacher in the world ... what Daddy means is that 'Baby Virus' - I call this 'Baby' cause the second mutation was 'Auntie' and the original was 'Uncle' - induces a temporary BLISS-like condition. The effect is long-lasting, wholly non-addictive, non-cumulative, and generates no side effects whatsoever."

"How?" asked Archimedes.

"Well, viruses normally infect via cellular invasion, as you know. That takes days. These don't. In fact, these die. Rather immediately. They disintegrate within the system. The capsids unglue, releasing nucleic acid. The acid gets into the bloodstream, producing the euphoria, the quick kick. You can snort these bugs, eat 'em, shoot 'em up. No diff."

"Antibodies?"

"Unnecessary. Ain't it grand?"

"I see."

"Yeah. Thanks kid," Santiago acknowledged.

Darling smiled graciously, virtually curtsying with girlish charm.

"Then you're implying - " Wench interjected.

Darling jerked a thumb at her father, simultaneously including every other Freeyare ensconced in the former prison complex. "The guys like to get stoned on the stuff," she added.

"Ha!" Archimedes couldn't quell a laugh.

Santiago also broke into a grin, grabbed a stoppered test tube out of the cabinet and tossed it to Wench, remarking, with a soupcon of irony, "c'est la virus!"

Wench caught the vial, unconcerned that his purpose was being teased. A notion had been planted into his brain much the same way the very culture within his grasp had been originally sown. It is a facility of the human mind to latch upon information and work it, stir it mentally, deep in the subconscious recesses of the cerebral cortex, adding further data over time until, like a goulash, dinner is ready. The stew often proves unpalatable; sometimes, though, brilliant deductions are cooked.

In this case, Wench couldn't quite put his tongue on a conclusion of tremendous importance.

Gumbo, in the meantime, had his head stuck out the window. No telling what piqued his curiosity. "Hey, Santiago," he called, motioning for the Freeyare to join him, "you people own any wheels?"

"Coupla motorbikes," Santiago responded. "Why?"

"Look!"

Along the margin where the broad wall of sky met the gold roasted ground, swirlings of sand seemed to be carrying a convoy of vehicles directly toward the prison fortress. There was, at the head of the group, a glimmering green tractor-trailer snorting white steam through its silver nostrils. Several vans kept pace, long antennae whipping, insect fashion, to and fro. Enough cars of ordinary shapes and sizes to fill up a drive-in theatre formed the main body of the approaching traffic jam. Even an all-terrain vehicle did its best to stay with the pack. In no time, sound rattled teeth and walls.

Hesitancy followed.

"Separatists?"

"Feds?"

Wench recalled, and none too fondly, his previous encounter with the Government's zealously capable police forces.

"No, wait," Gumbo cautioned.

Too late.

Alarms clanged defiantly.

Gunfire responded from the upper stories.

Battle cries were raised, like pennants.

Coward Santiago reached into another cabinet similar to the one that held the virus cultures, withdrawing a burnished gray submachine gun for his daughter and, of all things, a dieselgun for himself.

"Not again!" Wench shouted.

"Not Anymore!" Santiago corrected.

The girl checked over her weapon and set it for firing with the skill of an infantryman. She shucked her lab coat, revealing the orange halter top she was wearing underneath. Prepared for war, she also cried "Not Anymore!" and charged out of the laboratory; her father followed closely on her heels, hefting the dieselgun as if it weighed no more than a hero sandwich.

"Wait!"

Gumbo had managed to make out, at extreme distance, though the invading forces, so to speak, were encroaching upon them at such an astonishing speed that details forthwith became clear to the most myopic of individuals, a flag. The banner featured a five-pointed star against a vertical swath of blue, on the left, butting two horizontal bands of white and red, on the right.

"They're just Texans!" announced Gumbo.

Wench, his automatic at chest height and aimed innocuously at the ceiling, turned. "Texans?"

Chapter 25

TEXANS. In a mad rush. In spite of the lack of a proper Zoomway, returning home. Texans, with only one thought on their minds, who would certainly not give the supposedly deserted Okie Federal Penitentiary a second glance. Texans who, even if they did stop to venture into the facility, to get out of the sun or stretch their legs, could simply be sent on their way again by a man in a lab coat pretending to be a Zoomway technician. Texans, nonetheless, who should not be provoked.

"Texans, as in deep in the heart of." Gumbo thrust a finger at Archimedes. "Your yahoo pals have incited a riot with the wrong army!"

As time hung around, not wanting to go anywhere, this was the situation:

A ragtag conglomeration of fiercely determined settlers, some of them drinking, in a nationalistic frenzy, were being, they perceived, attacked. Mistaken or not, offense was profoundly taken. Offense was given aplenty, as well. Militant Freeyares, driven by a religious fanaticism the links of which historical precedent is infinite, plunged blindly into the fray. Chance and unbridled pugnacity had ganged up to place our three adventurers in the teapot of the tempest. They set to bickering first, sought shelter later.

"He wanted to come here!"

"You could have said they were trigger-happy!"

"We shouldn't have left Alabama!" "And gotten BLISSed out, eventually?" "Better than wiped out

241

chasing wild geese!" "Some wild geese!" Hostilities swelled, then crested around them. They must have spent forty minutes under cover in the laboratory before the maelstrom subsided, incessant thundering giving way to an occasional pop and crack, victory yelps of departing Texans floating in like the jetsam of noisy neighbors.

They unanimously decided it was safe enough to steal out of hiding: Wench from under a stone worktable; Gumbo out of a corner, partially obscured by a storage cabinet; Archimedes flat off the ground, facing the main door. The three had barricaded the side door, which only accessed a closet; they barricaded it, anyway. Wench and Gumbo gripped their weapons tightly. Archimedes abhorred firearms, refused to have anything to do with them.

When they determined it was practical to attempt a getaway, they moved as gradually as a ballet adagio without the music. They edged toward the door, keeping low, wide and out of sight. Wench held his pistol, with both hands, up and away from his chin. He led the way. He heard a noise. He whispered, "what's that?"

"Freeyares!"

A concussion. The main door blew open.

A volley of revolver bullets sang past, like accelerated bees.

An old man, a wrinkled geezer with no meat on his bones, with unshaven face, a tumorous nose and a lower jaw that was larger than the rest of his face, in hunting cap, silk shirt open around the neck, Levis and boots, holding his six-shooters at his waist, jumped in between Wench and the doorway like the wrath of doom. Without thinking, Wench let four rounds go. He had no choice. His aim, at this range, was astonishingly good. In an unholy sign of the cross, boils of blackish red burst from the old man's forehead, chest and shoulders. Crimson flowers began to blossom, the aged attacker collapsed.

Enough silence to fill a cemetery tumbled after.

"God ... dammit!"

They heard Gumbo's choked squeal.

Wench pirouetted. Archimedes was already there.

On the ground, jerking violently in pain, Gumbo, clutching at his lower right calf with one hand, was spasmodically making and unmaking a fist with his other hand. His head lolled in agony. His leg was soaked in blood. Gumbo had been shot.

Archimedes, in the process of ripping off his own shirt to apply a makeshift tourniquet, did not hide the seriousness of the injury, or his diagnosis. He vocalized the worst. "Trauma." He labored to stem the loss of blood. "Mars'll go into shock if I can't stabilize him. Hell! My medical bag is in the car. I can't risk moving him like this. We're stuck in a useless chem lab and I ... feel like a horse's ass!" Archimedes punctuated his impotence by throwing the nearest solid object he could find (a trivet) across the room. It ricocheted smartly off the far wall and landed, spinning, on a worktable, shattering a piece of glassware as it did so.

Gumbo kept on howling and thrashing.

"Dammit, Mars, calm down," the doctor begged.

Wench jolted. "That's it!"

"What?"

Wench was looting the storehouse of honey-colored virus cultures in a quantum leap. Withdrawing a full vial, he handed it to Archimedes as if doing the final scene of a television commercial.

"You're joking - "

"BLISS him out."

"I can't."

"Hell you can't."

"It hasn't been tested."

"You'd rather watch Mars die?"

Years of scientific method and medical conservatism evaporated from Archimedes in the time it took him to snatch the vial out of Wench's hand. The man had a point. The doctor popped the tube and allowed some of the syrup to ooze onto Gumbo's lips. "Take it," he urged. Wench willed a miracle. Gumbo, still alert enough to lick his lips, gagged. "It ain't marmalade," said Archimedes, weakly attempting to ease the tension.

There wasn't much else they could do but wait on the edge of the precipice and hold their balance. Really, only Gumbo was in danger of slipping over; however, they cradled him like a babe, as if their own dear lives depended upon it.

It took two minutes, 120 seconds. Try counting out 120 seconds with a needle stuck in your finger or hanging up-side-down by one leg. It's quite a long time, isn't it? In 120 seconds a mountain can be dynamited away, and battles can be won or lost. At the end of two minutes, Archimedes, greatly relieved, tears moistening the sides of his nose, said, "his pulse is normal."

"It works?"

"It does."

"He's going to make it?"

"In spades."

Wench slapped the doctor on the back, yelped in joy, and scrambled to the cabinet of biologicals. He reorganized one rack of test tubes in particular, stocking it with the fullest vials he could find, the way a shopper might fix an egg carton with the largest, freshest eggs. He removed the rack, tucked it under his arm. He searched around for something more.

"What are you doing?" asked Archimedes. "We've got to get out of here."

"Looking for notes. Ah!" Wench grabbed up a spiral-bound, paperback composition pad and some obsolete computer diskettes. "Found them!"

With his prizes, Wench assisted Archimedes in carrying Gumbo from the lab. They carried him unglamourously, granted; it was necessary. Archimedes hoisted Gumbo's feet while Wench supported the serenely semiconscious man (becoming more "relaxed" every minute) under the shoulders. The notebook, disks, virus cultures, and Gumbo's carbine rode conveniently on Gumbo's roomy belly. It was the most practical way for them to travel, after all.

Down the stairwell they passed two battle-scarred, full of resolve Freeyares going up. One of the sectaries thought he recognized the doctor; for good measure, and thinking quickly, the doctor barked a lesser used Freeyare salutation. The ploy was effective and the three were not challenged. Wench overheard the Freeyares exchanging

245

comments: "Deliverance is at hand, brother"; "Praise the Lord." When they were in the main lobby and heading for the front door, Wench told Archimedes, "we'd better floor the Turboboom, dirt roads or not." This proved to be entirely wise advice.

The fighting hadn't ended; they realized this once they were in the great out of doors and lumbering toward the waiting Turboboom. It had simply lulled. The Texans, sports fans to the man (or woman) and lovers of physical activity, grouped in the West. Wench and Archimedes noticed them reorganizing for a second charge. Fortunately, Wench, Archimedes, and Gumbo who was now caterwauling Jesus Jones' first big hit song, "Love Is a Pudding," at the top of his lungs like an intoxicated partygoer, were headed East.

"Women and children first," Wench quipped.

They threw everything into the back seat of the car, including Gumbo. Wench drove. The doctor tended his patient from the front seat. Later, he asked Wench: "what are you going to do with the cultures?"

Wench shifted the Turboboom into cruise control. He loosened his grip on the steering wheel and, with a confident expression, replied. "You know, there's a line from Schiller's *Ode to Joy*, the poem upon which Beethoven based a symphony, which reads, roughly translated, something like even a worm can know contentment. But a worm can't think, create, raise its worm's voice in song, scrawl graffiti on the side of a wall, communicate ideas. This isn't the worm's fault. To a worm, its

246

uniquely annelidan biology is all there is; in that, it can be absolutely content."

"The point?" Archimedes solicited.

"Man is not a worm."

The doctor would have welcomed more time to deliberate Wench's cryptic remark. He may have gotten the pith of it. A blinding flash of light from behind, however, erased preoccupation with philosophy.

Wench, Archimedes looked back.

The horizon jiggled. For an instant it made a double exposure of itself, then focused. At the point on the curved horizon where Okie Federal lay out of view, a false sunrise, whiter and larger than the actual sun, occurred. It ballooned out, quickly, lightning streaking its outer skin, and deflated as rapidly as a punctured gum bubble. In its place, a wispy black smoke trail curled into the sky, resembling not so much a mushroom as a string bean with a button cap. Then came the sound: a shocking whump like god's fist slamming into the earth.

When it passed, Wench and Archimedes responded.

"Damn!"

"They used it."

"I guess it came in handy."

They drove home. Not to Alabama. Wench captained the Turboboom to Bigapolis, knowing full well that his vow had become a certainty.

Chapter 26

HOMECOMING. Wench paused outside the offices of the *Daily Parade* and reached into an unzippered pocket of the gray polyester windbreaker he was wearing. The drop curtain had fallen, but the play was not over. That is to say, night had enveloped downtown, swiftly, which it usually did this time of year. It was eight-thirty; other sections of Bigapolis would be electric with activity; not here. The albino facades of the buildings, particularly pallid in moonlight, resembled stage props: white against black, nothing moving, not even the intimidation of a breeze. Wench always considered the long, lean *Daily Parade* tower, with its bulbous, art deco, combination observatory & restaurant crown, to symbolize an arm angrily shaking its fist at the inequities of the universe. In its present guise, the skyscraper more appropriately resembled a phallus, screwing the cosmos. Here, the headquarters of the Moralist Broadcasting Agency (MBA) occupied two entire floors and a walk-in closet. Wench extracted a plastic six-pack of coughers, raised it to his mouth and pulled out one with his lips.

Wench was not a smoker. However, tonight he desperately needed the benefits of a mild narcotic. He puffed, tentatively. The ghostly fumes ascended directly into the evening like a fakir's magic rope.

In twenty-five minutes or so, he would begin. Nine o'clock was the targeted hour. By nine-thirty he would know. The decision would be made.

248

Wench recalled Archimedes' admonishment that a choice, right or wrong, is the province of the chooser; a forced choice, right or wrong, can never be condoned. Archimedes was correct, as he was about many things.

Archimedes had the measure of it, Wench concluded, as he inhaled, waiting. The Government is not a dictatorship. BLISS, per se, represents no villainy. The relative pros and cons of self-centered indulgence are, for practical purposes, mere argument fodder, subjects for classroom discussion. Popular choice had unquestionably made the entire issue moot, by a majority of 70 percent.

Archimedes wisely realized, and Wench agreed, that the same popular choice may well be the force to bring the country back into balance. It seemed so obvious, but solutions always seem obvious in hindsight. Free enterprise. Open competition. The pat phrases had glided off Archimedes' tongue. Build a better mousetrap. Wench smiled to himself. Build a better mousetrap, he thought, to trap a better mouse - Angus Barlow Yaramon.

Deep in the cushion of night, Wench heard a couple, likely a couple, of BLISS revelers, distant. Perhaps they were coming from a movie. Perhaps they were going to a movie. Maybe one of Wench's own movies: that was the crux.

The present Government had defeated itself.

The Administration had committed such a basic error, though an understandable gaffe, to be sure. In essence, it had strangled itself with its own intricately woven cat's cradle. The Government had put together an elaborate arabesque of dominoes, then offered Wench the option of protecting those tiles or setting them to topple. They tossed Wench the keys to their house of cards. They gambled, to their credit; they lost, though. In a way, Wench felt sorry for them. Wench also thought, silly of them, silly and sophomoric.

Gumbo had charged him: "we still live in a democracy. More so than the old days, what with every living room cabled, televideo-wise, into the General Elector. And you're the front runner, now. Use that against them. Hit them during prime time. Hit 'em hard. They can't stop you."

In all honesty, Wench had to admit, there was no real reason for the Government to stop him. The Administration wasn't stupid; they knew there was no anti-BLISS. Furthermore, the public openly rejected existing "curative" treatments; they craved their frequent jags of contentment. Besides, hadn't Yaramon risen to power by giving the people what they sought: religion, answers, BLISS? Wench wasn't going to get anywhere by handing the people what they certainly didn't want. The irony of it was - the Government had no notion that Wench was about to do precisely the opposite.

Blame it on an insufferable complacency.

Wench took a long drag on the cougher, getting the hang of it. Again, he remembered another of Archimedes' postulations: must blame be fixed? Were events simply the machinations of an inflexible continuum trying to balance itself? Let's not get overcome with existentialism, Wench chided inwardly. Do what you must.

Fifteen minutes before nine.

Wench supposed that there was a chance that he could get killed. He didn't want to think about it; the likelihood seemed as plausible as myth. Anyhow, by his death, the Government would only succeed in extending its lease on political dominance for a very short time. Hardly worth the effort. Besides, Wench maintained that he'd been executed once before. Double jeopardy, you know. This gave Wench a charmed life. He could probably walk through walls!

Wench, Gumbo and Archimedes certainly had no difficulty getting from Okie Federal back into Bigapolis. Even the Zoomway proved no barrier to them, perhaps because Government bureaucracy moved significantly slower than the Turboboom. Fact is, all Wench had to do was tell the spick-and-span minion of the toll booth who he was, adding, "li'l BLISShed out ... sorta forgot my askie code," with a feigned slur, and they were ushered into the ultrahighway without so much as a wrinkled brow. Wench imagined that the Transport Office Automotive Division (TOAD) probably had not been notified of his "defection."

If that's the case in administration, what must the situation be like among the huddled masses? They're no doubt content in the assumption that Astin W. Wench, the media guru, a name to conjure with, is on a confounded sabbatical! The former staunch opponent of BLISS who ultimately saw the light and, after said revelation, rapidly rose to the position of Secretary of Entertainment, will assuredly return. And what inspirational, thrilling, breath-taking spectacle will he offer the amusement-starved populace when he does?

251

Wait and see, reflected Wench.

His right arm exhibited every indication of cramping up from his grip on the monstrous dieselgun at his side. He wished he could rid himself of the unwieldy weapon, but Gumbo was correct in insisting that he carry some persuasive firepower with him (over Archimedes' disapproval of guns). Wench hoped he wouldn't need persuasion.

Archimedes had cautioned him.

They'd arrived at Wench's suburban estate directly from Okie Federal shortly after midnight, 27 hours after leaving the prison, one week ago. Wench, obviously, had no idea where he lived during the last nine years: Archimedes had to give him directions. The house, a triple story, Tudor style structure painted white with brown trim, was easy to locate. A carved wood shingle swinging freely from the wrought iron main gate declared: The Copper Birches. The place was kilometers out of town, at the end of a quiet stretch of the road, with nothing contiguous to the property but pasture and a private duck pond. Certainly there was nobody around to witness a growling Turboboom pull into the gravelly driveway and discharge its three road weary passengers. Fate was being more than kind.

Archimedes earlier had cautioned Wench about the unpleasant side effects that can result from bringing a person out of BLISS. Nonetheless, he insisted upon being reunited with Lowia the way he remembered her. She had no choice. The comparison was as with sweet to sour.

"Honey, you're home," Lowia chirped gaily, wrapped up in a pink terrycloth bathrobe. She presented Wench with a slurpy kiss. She was, in spite of the hour, wide awake and even a touch amorous. "You really ought to have telephoned first. Who are your friends?"

Wench smiled crookedly in response to the almost comical lack of perturbation in Lowia's BLISS infused personality. Did she believe he had gone out for a beer with the boys? Worked late?

"This is Titus ... and Mars. You remember Mars, don't you?" Gumbo was slung between Wench and Archimedes like a hammock, bearing a Cheshire cat mien that could have been framed and hung in a museum. Archimedes stood bare-chested. The three were disheveled, smelling pungently of sweat, blood and thousands of dusty kilometers. "Mars got hurt, but he'll be okay."

"Oh. Can I punch you up some coffee?" she asked.

"Anything would be nice."

They tucked Gumbo into a bed of two fluffy blankets and a hypoallergenic pillow. After Archimedes dosed their fallen comrade with antibiotics and more of the Freeyare virus culture ("bottled serenity," Archimedes called it), he and Wench and Lowia slipped into the kitchen, sipped coffee, snacked on some strawberry cheesecake and listened to the very late news. They heard exciting progress reports about the new Zoomway annex, movie reviews, rousing Separatist-baiting, but not a spoken word concerning Astin W. Wench. Lowia's daughter, by the way, was out, staying with friends; she frequently stayed with friends; she led a very independent life, at eleven years old. That made it easier to drug Lowia.

Dawn had almost cleared the sky of night when Archimedes, holding Lowia's slender wrist, announced to Wench, "she's coming around now." What happened was indelible.

"No more BLISS?"

"She'll be her own woman, so to speak," explained the doctor.

"My woman. My Lowia," Wench stressed.

"Except she will also remember everything. She won't respond as you did. She wasn't under Deep BLISS. Expect some depression, and be very patient with her, please."

Three minutes to nine. Wench plucked the unfinished cougher from his mouth and threw it to the ground. In anger, he crushed the butt underfoot; the anger derived from the caustic memory of the morning Lowia, his Lowia, emerged from BLISS. He had barely time to go over it in his mind again; he did; it gave him the resolve that, coupled with the stimulation from the cougher, made him ready no matter what.

Lowia had screamed. She screamed not in pain. She inflicted a mortal wail of agony upon them that was as a person dying. She was, if not dying, drowning in a flood of memories no longer dammed back by BLISS. Her face contorted, stretched, bled tears, tears and spittle together. Her thrashing body pummeled against the bed. Wench and Archimedes had to forcibly restrain the woman. She was strong, strong as an adrenalin-powered victim fighting for survival. She raked her nails along Archimedes' arm, leaving welts like tattoos and drawing blood. She subsided from that initial reaction. The screaming, which began so incessantly it appeared she might asphyxiate herself, eventually broke into intermittent high-pitched yells, and then into a pattern of low moans corresponding to each of her rapid exhalations. She was breathing, after all; Wench, especially Wench, and Archimedes could take heart in that. Several excruciating minutes later, Lowia, with both hand, gulped from a glass of water that Archimedes had carefully given her. She sighed: it was like the deep gasp a child makes to straighten out chaotic emotions following a temper tantrum. Archimedes placed the partially emptied glass of water on the night table. Wench, meanwhile, seated at the foot of the bed, watched her with apprehension, love, and more than a little guilt. He wanted to apologize to her for forcing her through the experience. He started to reach out. Seeing him, she pulled back perceptibly and widened her eyes, revealing a feral expression. "I hate you!"

This was BLISS withdrawal at work. Like exhibition baseball, sample questions prefacing an exam, or demonic possession, it didn't count. It was scary, yet it was a grossly inaccurate distortion of Lowia's true feelings.

The following afternoon, Lowia, more firmly in control of herself, although still subject to waxing and waning depression, tried to reason.

"You went away," she asserted.

"I came back."

"We've never been apart before."

"We've been together a long time," Wench added.

"A long time," Lowia agreed.

"Some of it hasn't been too easy."

"It was comfortable."

"You can't want out?" Wench asked.

"Of course not ... only - "

"This BLISS thing?"

"Don't make it sound like a thing."

"How should I make it sound?"

"Not like a disease ... or a lover."

"It gets in the way like a disease or a lover."

"It doesn't," she insisted. "We were happy. We were a family. We had a home. We watched our daughter grow up in that home. We were like everybody else. Not like before. We were regular people. Oh, honey, do you have any idea what it meant to me ... to be normal ... to be happy?"

"Under BLISS? Brainwashed?"

"I wasn't brainwashed. I was better."

"Better?"

"Yes. Better than drugs. Better than running off to a damn shrink every week. It was ... what's so damn terrible about being happy, anyway?" She began to sob again. Her eyes leaked.

Wench had no right to answer. Only wrong questions. He took her in his arms, to hold her, to prove to her that it didn't matter what had happened, to show her that he wanted her, unvarnished with BLISS. He felt her tears through his thin shirt. Then she pulled away, crying loudly. She ran into her bedroom and toppled like a fallen tree upon the unmade bed, continuing to sob deeply into the pillow.

Chapter 27

HIS watch peeped the ninth hour, nudging him from reverie and returning him to his purpose. It was nine o'clock. It was time.

Wench's destination, the twenty-third floor, the transmission facilities of MBA, were operated by computers. A technical crew came in every day before lunch to place their imprimatur on the electronics, but they'd departed hours ago. Wench would have to breech those computers, not possessing the proper passcard. Doing so would touch off a snake pit of alarms. But by the time any security forces arrived on the scene, the vote would be cast. Wench would have succeeded, or there would be no reason for the Government to worry about him ever again.

With a soft grunt, Wench lifted the dieselgun and carried it into the building. The street level doors sighed apart and, after he'd passed through, clapped shut. Of course the place would be open - it was a news office, after all, even if by definition and nothing more. So far so good. The coast was clear.

The bank of elevators waited open-mouthed in front of him, at attention, like the palace guard: express cars on the right, locals on the left. At this hour, they would all ascend non-stop to the twenty-third floor. Wench dragged the dead weighted dieselgun laboriously into the nearest elevator, joking to himself, "come on, there's always room for one more," and smacked the designated plastic square 23 on the service panel with the palm of his hand. In ten seconds, the elevator door rumbled closed.

"The next stop of this elevator will be the twenty-third floor," a feminine pre-recording announced. "No smoking, please." The car shuttled upward, exerting a subtle g-force that Wench could feel against the soles of his boots. The equivalent of one orbit on a Ferris wheel passed. The elevator braked, opened up and stated, "this is the twenty-third floor, thank you."

Wench clambered out, fighting the brattish reluctance of his cast-iron and steel, japan lacquered sidekick that was beginning to leak oil and smell like a gas station. Wench had the weapon's muzzle pointed in a rough proximation of the right direction and his hand not too far from the ignition switch.

"Anybody home?"

There wasn't supposed to be anybody on this floor. And fortunately, there wasn't. With a breath of relief, he let the dieselgun fall. It was no longer required. Piece of cake.

Scintillating and counting down to innumerable predetermined functions, behind glass, before Wench, the computer banks of MBA held their ground, but vulnerable, like so many unprotected chicks in the path of the fox. Wench hadn't come to destroy. That was all the difference.

The weak crystalline partition gave way with a twinkle. Somewhere a klaxon wailed its song of violation. Wench penetrated his arm, jiggled a knob, and he was inside. The machinery shuddered, was raped.

He worked rapidly, assuredly. He shed his windbreaker, at the same time withdrawing from its protected inner pocket a three-cm videocard that he and Gumbo had prepared some days previously. Gumbo was well-recovered by then, limping around with a cane that he would need for the rest of his life, deemed Archimedes. They recorded the card on Wench's home equipment; the quality was surprisingly good. Meanwhile, Archimedes placed a batch of telephone calls, primarily to other scientists. Wench's phones were secure, and visual (the Government having given him everything, bless them). Eventually, Archimedes enlisted a parish of Conservative Freeyares to assist them. This was not inconceivable, after all; if cloistered monks can become renowned for their preparation of varied comestibles, why can't Freeyares engage in pharmacy? Lowia - Wench loosed a sigh - Lowia stayed out of his way, most of the time, speaking to him at meals, sleeping alone. If this worked, Wench would make it up to her. He would more than make it up to her.

Wench confronted the ordered ranks of digitized and RAM booted electronic gear, the reflected flashes and modulations of rainbow hued lights painting his face in psychedelic moires. The equipment, literally, stared back. It may have ended in a stalemate, except that Wench knew what to do. He knew the launch codes.

He punched PROGRAM INTERRUPT after taking the main feed from AUTO and shunting it into a STANDBY mode. He ran a MONITOR signal into the STUDIO3 terminal, directly above him, so he could check his progress. He made certain the TRANSMIT flasher was operational. No point in going on if he couldn't detect outside jamming or signal interference, not that there was the ghost of such a possibility with all the overrides and protective junctures at his disposal. Okay. He tapped in SCHED on the keyboard, and the proper date, bringing an itemized TV menu onto the main screen. Damn! It was the fifteen minute format. Quickly, Wench ordered MIN2MIN, hoping that they hadn't altered the syntax. They hadn't. There it was. Scrolling up against the high resolution, non-glare VDT, Wench read that at 9:20 and 9:21, two :30 COMMLs would be followed by a full minute BLISS spot. Now here's vindication for you, Wench thought exultantly. He steered the white cursor over to the 9:20 line and, with delight, fingered DELETE. The line winked away. Wench did the same thing with the 9:21 listing. He put the cursor back on 9:20, smacked ENTER, smacked VTR2 (the three-cm unit). Because his card was pre-timed at two minutes, he would not have to program a fill for the 9:21 slot and wouldn't risk sending dead air, which was illegal and could trigger a failsafe jump that might pre-empt the very card he wished to broadcast! Now a pencil thin band of bright red was demanding INSERT MEDIA, INSERT MEDIA, INSERT MEDIA ... Wench checked to make certain the card was properly oriented and placed it onto the player's extruded metal tongue. The machine immediately swallowed the card; the flashing light died. The computer indicated READY. Wench had time, so he requested a PREVIEW on STUDIO4, keeping STUDIO3 open, of course. PREVIEW WHAT? asked the computer.

Wench typed in 9:20. Instantly (as the particular function was programmed this way), he saw the fadeout from this week's episode of the highest rated TV show into a commercial announcement. The segue into his own card was clean as a whistle. That was enough. Wench killed PREVIEW. He brought the whole system back into AUTO and punched BRDCAST with finality. In real time, it was 9:15:42. Wench flopped into the chief engineer's cushiony swivel chair like a shagged fly ball into a fielder's mitt, inclined, interlocked his fingers against his stomach, and waited for the show.

It was not long before Wench's homespun commercial made its nationwide debut. In millions upon millions of homes, television monitors wiped in on Astin W. Wench wearing, as the critics would later report, a tasteful light sport jacket, cotton slacks, and an appropriately butter-colored tie. He sat cross-legged on a plain, white plastic stool. The background was beige. Wench, charismatic to the teeth, looked squarely into the camera, thus, at the home viewing audience. He spoke:

"Hello. You're probably wondering who I am. You know my name. You've seen my movies. You've read my novelizations of those movies. Give up? I directed *Return to Blondland*. That's right. I'm Astin W. Wench. And you're probably asking yourself, 'how can he produce so much popular entertainment and remain as happy as he is, relaxed, and free from everyday concerns?' Well, I'll tell you. I take this." (He holds up the little golden box.) "Seren. Government formulated, doctor tested Seren. The better alternative to BLISS. Each no

261

calorie ultracap of Seren gives you eight hours of contentment, without harsh withdrawal. The product works gently in the system for fast, fast well-being and is non-habit forming. Unlike BLISS that is available only by Government dispensing truck, Seren can be carried with you at all times in its convenient golden package. You take it when you want it, any time you want it. Seren enhances all your pleasures. With Seren, movie going or TV watching can become a religious experience. Even the joys of a single sunset turn into celebration. And when you have work to do, or, as in my case, a book to write," (he smiles), "Seren leaves you clear minded and refreshed. Seren comes with a money back guarantee. It will soon be widely available in drugstores and supermarkets. If you would like Seren, please vote YES on your video selectors when the question appears on your screen. A YES for Seren does not mean NO to BLISS. Select YES and you are selecting a choice. But if you had the choice, wouldn't you choose ... " (zoom in on package) "Seren? I do."

Hail, free enterprise.

Chapter 28

ASTIN W. Wench had been working on his personal memoirs, a project that occupied him exclusively over the past six months, no more than two or three hours this evening when it occurred to him that he really hadn't anything else to say. From the confines of his study, he saw snowfall dusting the purple evening outside, the small window in imitation of a television screen. He could hear Lowia moving about downstairs, humming contentedly to herself. The new, matte-finish, brown, alphanumeric keyboard she had given him on his birthday responded firmly and efficiently to the ministrations of his fingers these last months. It now hummed confidently, awaiting his next command. Hanging on the wall to his left was one of Wench's favorite photos, taken last year: a PantsOn®-color glossy of Gumbo's inaugural, picturing Wench and Lowia standing proudly behind the new President. Other painful, sorrowful memories flushed through Wench like an injection of summer. He shivered, nonetheless. He could not continue. He read again what he'd written:

The unparalleled popular acceptance that Seren enjoyed in the ensuing months laid the groundwork for the unraveling of the Yaramon Administration. Sources within Washington often pointed out that Reverend Yaramon himself was wearing his welcome thin in the public sector, much like the guest who stays too late. Infirmities of age coupled with an intransigent party policy contributed to the former President's decision to step down from office gracefully. However, the impact of Seren upon the national temperament cannot be interpreted too lightly.

One need only examine the resurgence of variety and vitality in the media and culture, certainly a direct outgrowth of the competition Seren brought against BLISS, to see that the Government's "bread and circuses" hold upon the population had irreparably weakened. In essence, the monopoly had been fragmented. What's more, the common man, having embraced unadorned contentment as a virtual way of life for so long, could now enjoy the sort of existence once offered exclusively by BLISS as well as Seren's more involved awareness. The choice was now the province of the individual. Having such a choice heralded the unceremonious finale to the Yaramon years.

Parenthetically, the unfortunate BLISS riots that occurred during the latter "yellow glad days" must be said to have had marginal, if any, impact on the Government's deteriorating strength. True, many lives were lost; even a BLISSed out electorate found it difficult to easily forgive those who had allowed the terrible incidents to arise in the first place, but the rioters had only their foolish paranoia to blame. Furthermore, recognizing that among the effects of BLISS over the years was the significant diminution of protest, restlessness and the like, it is apparent that the authorities were not prepared to deal with confrontation on a massive scale, or forgotten how.

The Chattanooga Easter Rising is a perfect example of this. With Seren grabbing an increasing share of the marketplace, rumors quickly began to circulate that the BLISS Company, in an effort to diversify and stave off potentially devastating economic losses, would be closing down less profitable formulating facilities. Somehow, it was perceived that the Chattanooga, Tennessee, plant would be the first to get the axe. This was not the case. Nonetheless, on that April 27, BlisCo employees and BLISS fanatics amassed outside the Chattanooga labs, carrying placards and shouting slogans. What transpired next was textbook in its predictability: an indignant crowd quickly transformed into an unruly mob, somebody threw a rock, the facility was ransacked and several people were killed.

Ironically, these BLISS riots, coming during the concluding term of the Yaramon Administration, seemed to analogize the Separatist clashes that underscored Yaramon's earlier tenure; although fostered by divergent causes, BLISS figured in them all.

It may also have been severe, poetic justice that Vice President Thackery Cinder, an eager antagonist at many of those Separatist actions, would meet his untimely death under the wheels of a runaway garbage truck at a BLISS riot. By the time Cinder was killed, though, the Government had become hopelessly ineffective and a change of political feeling was already heavily in the air.

Backed by the powerful forces of Seren, Incorporated, and the United Separatist Action (U.S.A.) which believed its own interests and the

265

interests of the State of Alabama would be protected, Marshall Sebastian Gumbo was swept into office by a resounding mandate of 70 percent in favor, 16 percent opposed and 14 percent undecided. Gumbo, by no means a newcomer to politics, having served for a time as Governor of Independent Alabama, was chiefly foreseen as the man who could bring the nation together again. At his inaugural, President Gumbo, a standout in any crowd with his widely imitated beard and characteristic hobble, pledged to the country a brand new beginning, "TV that we will be able to confidently show our grandchildren, and wholly effortless weight loss programs."

The influences of Reverend Yaramon, who quietly retired from politics altogether to take up his post as Chairman and CEO of BlisCo, rapidly faded like a retinal afterimage.

Wench had reached the end of his narrative. The terminal's cursor blinked at him, eye to eye, insisting that he continue. Wench was a professional. He resumed:

One final, sad epilogue must be appended to this important chapter in our nation's history. We must recognize, and never forget, Titus Archimedes; his achievements shall always endure. It was, after all, Archimedes who devoted much of his life to synthesizing the virus that is the source of Seren. It was Archimedes who enabled Astin W. Wench, among others, to reawaken public consciousness, in turn bringing the country out of mediocre complacency and into a fresh era of creative freedom. It was Archimedes who, in the final analysis, predicted our future.

266

Barely six months into the Gumbo Administration, Titus Archimedes died, of stroke, at the age of 52. Born in Eureka, California, to working-class parents, Archimedes always strove for excellence. He attended Moneoye University and was graduated in an unprecedented eight years with doctoral degrees in both medicine and biochemistry. Although he chose to pursue a vocation in research, Archimedes remained a highly competent physician throughout his life, often submitting papers to such prestigious organizations as the Internal Microbiology Association and the Annals of Proper Eating.

Archimedes always remained something of a loner, however, and skeptical of society as a whole. It was his doubting and, some would add, existentialist nature, that drove him, during the BLISS years, to espouse Reform Freeyareism. Though never actually in favor of the ascetic principles held by orthodox members of the sect, Archimedes contended that most human endeavor was transitory and, in the long run, history took care of itself. There could, after all, be a great deal of truth in what Archimedes believed.

Certainly Titus Archimedes would find it fitting and proper that, after weaving his own minor threads into the tapestry of the universe, he should bow out. The man would have appreciated the economic structure. He lived long enough to see the fruits of his labors, though, which is reassuring to know. He lived, in his own words, to figuratively witness "the wobbly globe that we stand on correct itself and re-enter an unwavering orbit around the mother sun." This was enough for Archimedes.

267

Posthumously, he was awarded the Medal of Freedom by President Gumbo. A postage stamp was issued in his likeness, and ambitious plans were made to base a movie musical on his life, as well as drafting the novelization.

Wench stopped. The memories weakened him. He scanned those last few paragraphs he had written, now displayed impassively on the laser optic terminal of his comm interface. The typescript letters, like little stings of the past, pricked hurtfully into his mind. He thought about tomorrow.

Lowia was not certain she preferred Seren over BLISS. There was Alabama, and the Separatist question, to answer. The world hadn't changed too much; it wasn't perfect; it was getting better. Wench would recover, as well. The cathartic process of putting it all down in electronic bits had already begun its healing.

Lowia asked him, from the doorway, "have you finished?"

"For now." Wench, with tremendous satisfaction, struck five keys and shut down the terminal.

About the Author

SAM Bellotto Jr. began life as a magazine editor in New York City. For 20 years, he waxed poetic about mopeds, garbage collection, and musical instruments. Tiring of the rat race, he relocated to Western New York and morphed into a successful word puzzle author and computer game developer. He has written nearly a dozen puzzle books and his computer games are sold all over the world. He lives in Rochester, NY, with his dog, a coffee brewer, and a widescreen TV.

www.ingramcontent.com/pod-product-compliance
Lightning Source LLC
Chambersburg PA
CBHW010832250626
47157CB00010B/3253